# SIGNIFYING NOTHING

# SIGNIFYING NOTHING

*a novel by*
## CLIFFORD THOMPSON

iUniverse, Inc.
New York   Bloomington

iUniverse books may be ordered through booksellers or by contacting:

iUniverse
1663 Liberty Drive
Bloomington, IN 47403
www.iuniverse.com
1-800-Authors (1-800-288-4677)

Because of the dynamic nature of the Internet, any Web addresses or links contained in
this book may have changed since publication and may no longer be valid. The views
expressed in this work are solely those of the author and do not necessarily reflect the
views of the publisher, and the publisher hereby disclaims any responsibility for them.

ISBN: 978-1-4401-3269-8 (sc)
ISBN: 978-1-4401-3270-4 (ebook)

Printed in the United States of America

iUniverse rev. date: 03/30/2009

# ACKNOWLEDGMENTS

For their support, advice, and encouragement during and after the writing of this book, I am indebted to my wife, Amy Peck; the Thompson and Famutimi clan; Tom Rayfiel; Anne Rumsey; Amadou Diallo (the photographer — not the slain immigrant); Andy Cavin; Kevin Harris; Tracy Brower; Ruth Bruun; Charles Hawley; Eileen Kelly; Clarence Haynes; Mondella Jones; Norris Smith; and the management of the H. W. Wilson Company, my employer of long standing.

I also owe a debt to Oliver Sacks's article "Speed," published in the August 23, 2004 issue of *The New Yorker*, and to Amy for showing it to me.

*For A, M, and E,*
*chambers of my heart*
*— and —*
*For Ma and Grandma, always with me*

# SIGNIFYING NOTHING

# PART ONE

# THE WEEKEND

# —ONE—

On a spring evening in 1979, in the house where he had lived all of his nineteen years, Lester Hobbs did what no one had ever heard him do: he spoke. One moment he was galumphing across the living room in his undershirt and jeans, skinny arms swinging, hands trembling slightly as they sometimes did; the next, he stopped, arms going stiff at his sides, neck craning forward, a fierce expression taking over his normally placid, baby-smooth brown face. His words were not spoken in the soft, halting way that a thirteen-month-old says "Momma" for the first time; they were full-throated, even loud, like the words of a man accustomed to speaking authoritatively, a drill sergeant or film director. Even more surprisingly, they not only made sense — they were delivered with rhyme and rhythm. In short, the boy was rapping:

> *Momma Daddy Sister Brother on the FLOOR next to me*
> *We were sittin' in a circle looking AT the TV*
> *Momma went into the kitchen when comMERcials came on*
> *Gettin' drinks for everybody and-a MAKin' popcorn*

The suddenness, the loudness, the seeming impossibility of this outburst had an effect on Lester's parents that was — under the circumstances — understandable, even predictable. His mother, who was fortunately seated and unfortunately holding a nearly full mug of English Breakfast tea, fainted dead away, the tea making a large stain on the cushion of the not-yet-paid-for sofa that was never to come out completely. Ten feet away, Lester's father, who had been reading an editorial in the *Washington Post*, did not so much lose consciousness as enter another form of it; mouth open, he stared unblinkingly at his son, though he was later unable to recall what he had seen. Seconds later, having finished his rap, Lester glanced repeatedly from his mother to his father and back again, the intense facial expression of a few moments earlier replaced by mild curiosity, as if he had not caused this scene but merely walked in on it.

This was what awaited Lester's older brother, Greg, when he walked in the door that evening.

Greg Hobbs, on a Metrobus on his way home from Howard University, was in a good mood. Walking out of the school library, after a good stretch — for him — of plowing through macroeconomics, he had spotted the short, adorable Gina, a senior, and had called to her, as he'd done several times over the past couple of weeks. The first time he did that, stumbling through his small talk, she seemed confused, as if he must be mixing her up with someone else, since she certainly didn't know him (ah, but he had noticed *her*); but he had slowly worked his way past that, so that today, his shtick of flattery and mild teasing drew from her a smile and a "See you later, crazy boy." Crazy boy! In his experience, that was girl-speak for *Just don't act too stupid, and you can get in my pants.*

It hadn't been easy, but he had gotten her attention. That was how it usually went for him, he thought, settling back into his seat in the middle of the bus; he always traveled the hard road to what he wanted, when it came to girls and everything else in his life. But he felt good about that. He knew he wasn't quite handsome (he *did* once overhear someone call him "cute"), but he used what he had — his sense of humor, and brown hair that needed neither straightening comb nor stocking cap to be wavy. In junior high and high school, despite a chubby build and an initial fear of fighting, he had turned into someone who could handle himself. Part of it had been necessity, the need to defend himself in scraps that began with insults about his brother. He had taken karate and boxing lessons, spent time working out, and watched in amazement as his triceps grew into hard, separate entities and his chest transformed from sagging near-breasts to twin expanses of muscle; he had seen the amazement in the eyes of other boys as Greg Hobbs, former punk, wore their asses out. Less because of stupidity than laziness, his grades had been mediocre in high school and downright abysmal in his first freshman year (there were two) of college. (Greg, who should've been a junior, was a sophomore.) But now he was applying himself and doing okay.

So it was a contented Greg Hobbs, philosophical about the past, guardedly optimistic about the future, who went home that evening to his parents' house — where he was knocked silly by the present.

Something was very wrong. The first person he saw was his father, who seemed to have gotten stuck in the act of rising from his chair. His eyes were terrified behind the black frames of his reading glasses; he gripped the armrest with his right hand, while his left held the newspaper, which rattled with the trembling of his body. "Dad! What —?" Getting no answer, Greg looked left, toward his mother, whose head was thrown back on the sofa, eyes showing slits of white, hand clutching a tea mug, its contents all over the sofa. "What's goin' on?!" Only now did he notice Lester, the one person doing what he normally did: standing in the middle of the floor, digging in his ear with the pinkie of his right hand, his left hand trembling.

*Okay. Think.* Whatever happened seemed to have hit his mother the hardest. Throwing Lester a look that contained all he usually felt about his brother — bafflement, tenderness, exasperation — Greg went to his mother. "Ma," he said, bending over her, gently taking her by her narrow shoulders. "Ma, wake up. It's me, Greg. Ma, what —"

"Oh. Greg. I'm okay," she said, opening her eyes, sounding short of breath. "It's just — your brother —"

That was when he heard it.

Lester's words made Greg look back over his shoulder, but it was Lester's appearance that etched itself into his memory. There was his brother's face, as he never dreamed he would see it. Gone was the expression of one who doesn't understand what you're saying and is only vaguely curious about what it might be. No — the drawn-together eyebrows, wrinkled-up nose, and bulging eyes now formed a look that said, *What the hell's wrong with you?* Greg was too startled at first to comprehend what was happening, and so the first words he ever heard his brother say are lost to history. In Greg's memory, they started with:

> *...Brother Brother fightin' bullies on my BE-HALF*
> *Hangin' with me more than others, makin' ME LAUGH*
> *Sister Sister where my sister? She just LEFT HERE*
> *Left her parents left her brothers left me IN TEARS*

Slowly, Greg turned to face his brother, whose rhyming seemed to be over, whose face was returning to normal. "Oh, shit," Greg whispered. He walked around Lester, giving him a wide berth, not taking his eyes from his brother until he was out of the room. At the wall telephone in the kitchen, he pushed the numbers on the keypad with a trembling hand.

"Hello?"

"Sherrie."

"Ye — *Greg?*"

"Yeah. Listen. You got to come home. I mean, like, *now*."

\* \* \* \*

Sheridan Hobbs — Sherrie to her family, and few other people, if any — felt her breathing become shallow. For Greg to call her at all meant that something unusual was going on, and for this brother of hers, who never took anything seriously enough, to tell her she had to come home *now* ... "What's going on?"

"It's Lester. He's — he's *talking*. I just heard him. He's not just talkin', he's like *rhyming*. No joke."

Sherrie sat on her sofa, leaned forward, closed her eyes, put her fingertips to her forehead. She took a deep, silent breath, and her voice became a study in deliberation. "Tell me exactly what happened."

She knew from the deep silence at the other end what was coming. It was the story of their relationship: the things Greg said and did caused her to treat him like the younger brother he was, and when she did, he got angry. "I just *told* you what happened!"

"I mean, start from the beginning."

Letting out an angry, bewildered sigh, he did as she said. With every word he spoke, Sherrie felt the foundation beneath her becoming less certain — as if she had one foot on a dock and the other on a ship that was heading out to sea. When she had heard the whole story, she said the only thing she could be sure of: "I'd better come home."

"That's what I'm saying."

"Okay. I'll be there tonight."

She hung up the phone, set it next to her on the sofa, and said, "Oh. My. God." Her thoughts ran in a dozen different directions at once. She had to act; thinking of what she had to do required the concentration of a tightrope walker, but she made herself concentrate. First, she had to cancel her evening plans.

"Oscar, hello, it's Sheridan."

"Heyyyy." She could picture him breaking into the boyish, crooked grin that unsettled his square wire-framed glasses. "I was just on my way to pick you up."

"Listen, I'm sorry, something just happened. I have to go see my family tonight."

"Oh. Everybody all right?"

"Well, I think so, but — I can't go into it right now. I'll call you when I come back, okay? Tomorrow or Sunday."

"How you gettin' there? Train? Your car's in the shop, right? Let me take you to the station, at least."

She didn't know if she wanted this, but there was no gracious way out of it. "Okay, sure. Thanks. I'll be ready when you get here." After hanging up she went straight to pack her overnight bag.

Sheridan Hobbs, twenty-three years old, lived in a one-bedroom apartment in a Baltimore neighborhood that had caused her father — when he'd helped her move in, eight months earlier — to look around at the street, at the abandoned house on the corner and the broken glass on the sidewalk, as if looking at an ill-dressed wedding guest whom he wanted to ask, *You're not wearing* that, *are you?* What he had actually said to her, after the last box had been brought in and he was about to go home, was, "Watch yourself around here, okay, honey?" She had assured him that she would, and she had — mostly by being *in* this neighborhood of working-class-to-poor black folks without really being *of* it. She went back and forth to Johns Hopkins, where she earned a modest stipend as a graduate student in chemistry; she went to places — museums, restaurants — in other neighborhoods in Baltimore; and when she was in her own neighborhood, aside from buying groceries, she was in her apartment, which felt to her at times like a submarine, so different was its interior from its surroundings. There were *books* in her apartment, for one thing, on shelves that took up most of the wall that faced you as you walked in — *Roots*; *Black Macho and the Myth of the Superwoman*; *Up from Slavery* by Booker T. Washington; *Why We Can't Wait* by Martin Luther King Jr.; all of Jane Austen; and many others, including her undergraduate chemistry textbooks and, of course, the Bible.

The wall that was covered by books divided Sheridan's living room from her bedroom. On the other side of the wall, she was laying the next two days' clothes on her bed, while thinking of her car in the shop. She would have admitted to no one that she was glad it was in the shop on the night she had to travel the forty-five miles back home; otherwise, in order to justify to herself the fact that she owned a car, she would've had to drive it to D.C. tonight, and she was afraid, absolutely terrified, of driving in the dark. On the other hand, it meant that Oscar was driving her to the train station, and she wasn't sure how she felt about that, mainly because she wasn't sure how she felt about him. Was it right to let him do these things, or was it just leading him on? Should she simply relax and accept it as a gesture arising from their friendship, though she knew, of course, that he wanted more than that? Did *she* want more than that?

Focus, she told herself. You've got to get home.

*　　*　　*　　*

Meanwhile, her parents had come back to life. Mr. Hobbs — Patrick — had finally made it out of his chair, and Mrs. Hobbs, Madelyn, was off the sofa. Both stood in front of the now vacant-looking Lester in attitudes of gentleness and awe, as if their youngest child were a newly arrived, seemingly benign visitor from another galaxy. Madelyn placed a tentative hand on her son's upper arm and half-whispered, "My goodness," while Patrick was saying, just as quietly, "All these years. Lester. All these years. Just listening to people, storing up words. Was that it, son?"

Greg watched the scene from across the room, arms folded, listening to his parents trade mostly incomplete sentences: "I never would've believed ..." "A miracle. That's what it is. ..." "Like he was touched by God ..." "Couldn't be anything else." "All these years." "Just a miracle." With every one of these hymns of praise, Greg felt something in him getting fuller, until finally, slapping his thighs, he heard himself say, "I'm going out. I'll be back."

His parents looked at him as if he had started laughing during a eulogy. "Don't you care that your brother is talking after nineteen years?" his mother asked.

"Yeah, I care. It's not much I can do about it, though. He's the one talking. Sherrie said she'd be here later. I'll be back then."

There were two things that led him to walk out of the house. One was the need to get away from the scene he had just witnessed, in order to digest it. The other was jealousy. He knew he was wrong to feel the second thing, but he couldn't help himself. As far back as he could remember, and no doubt before that, nothing he did — even if it was truly outstanding — received the level of attention that Lester got by managing, however poorly, to perform a normal, everyday act. You got a B+ on your report card? Nice going, son — say, did you know your brother fed himself this morning? Oh yes, you got your blue belt in karate — *and*, your brother tied his own shoes! Greg loved Lester, but sometimes ...

Without thinking about it, he walked three blocks in the fading sunlight, in this black neighborhood of small, well-kept houses, to the home of his friend Clive Tompkins. "Hey, what's up," Clive said when he opened the door.

"Hey. Whatchu doing? Can you step out a while?"

Clive's face clouded over as he watched Greg's. "Yeah, let's go. What's going on?"

"Some strange shit, that's what."

Hands in pockets, Greg and his darker, thinner friend took off down the sidewalk. Greg had known Clive well enough to speak to since they were little boys, and they had become friends as high school sophomores, despite what had happened between them as that year began. Greg, who had recently completed his transformation from punching bag to Nobody To Mess With, was sometimes unable to resist having fun with easy targets, of whom the meek, skinny Clive was the easiest. Never really intending to hurt or anger him — never, in truth, thinking about the other boy's feelings at all — Greg sent the occasional punch Clive's way, until the day Clive got his fill of them. They were in the school library. Greg was laughing about the punch he had just thrown, but he stopped laughing when Clive came rushing at him like a bull, caught him off balance, and sent him stumbling into a bookcase, where a shower of hardcover novels fell on his head and shoulders. The students who were nearby began to laugh. The librarian, a fiftyish, matronly woman, who had witnessed the episode and knew how things stood between Greg and Clive generally, could not bring herself to discipline Clive — could barely, in fact, suppress a smile. Clive was as surprised as anyone over what he had caused to happen, but he stood his ground, angry-faced, ready for whatever was coming. As for Greg: the instant the first book hit his head, he understood two things — how angry he had made Clive, and how shamefully he, Greg, had behaved, particularly since he had been on the receiving end of bullying himself and should have known better. Bringing himself up to his full height after the last book had fallen, Greg took in the boys and girls doubled over in laughter, Clive standing there ready to scrap, the librarian watching it all with an unreadable expression — and he did the only thing he could think of: he started laughing himself.

Now, as they walked with no discussion of where they were going, Clive said, "Man, what's *up?*"

Greg stopped walking and told Clive what had happened. Seeing the astonishment on his friend's face, he himself felt the events sink in. He became light in the head, almost dizzy.

They started walking again, in silence. Out of long habit — following their feet — they turned a corner, walked a block, then turned again, this time onto 12th Street, the neighborhood commercial strip. Passing the corner food market and the beauty salon, they went into Kim's.

Kim's was one of those small stores that seem to have been made from pieces of other stores. It wasn't a restaurant, though you could order several kinds of sandwiches and even eat at the one table in back; it couldn't be called a stationery store, though pens and notebooks could be purchased there, nor was it exactly a newsstand, though the *Washington Post*, *Time*, *Newsweek*, *Jet*, *Ebony*, *Sports Illustrated*, and a few comic books were sold. It was not a grocery store, candy store, or tobacco shop, even though it functioned partly as each. It was Kim's. Greg ordered a steak and cheese sandwich from the Korean man who had seen his face a thousand times yet showed no sign of recognizing it; Clive, who had eaten at home, got a Coke to keep Greg company, and they went to the table in back.

For a minute they ate and drank without talking, until Clive began to chuckle.

"What's up?" Greg asked.

"I was just thinking about — Lester's kind of like that frog in the cartoon. The one that sings for that one guy but won't make a sound for anybody else."

The humor in this observation, and the feeling of relief that there was something funny in the whole thing, hit Greg so hard that he had to work to avoid choking on his sandwich. When he had swallowed what was in his mouth, he began to laugh, and Clive joined in.

As they were howling, Greg was dimly aware of a young man entering the store with one of those new "boom boxes." Slowly, the song that it played worked its way into his consciousness, until, all at once, he stopped laughing and looked very serious.

Clive said, "What's wrong?"

Just as suddenly as Greg had gone quiet, a smile broke through the surface of his concerned look. "I don't know. Maybe nothing," he said, listening to the words of the Sugar Hill Gang's *Rapper's Delight*.

# —TWO—

Like many men, Patrick Christopher Hobbs — Pat — had never overcome his wartime experiences, but what Pat carried with him through the rest of his life was not a physical disability or a chip on his shoulder: it was an almost debilitating case of gratitude. When Pat was shipped to Korea, in 1950, he was certain that he would not come back alive; unlike the occasional soldier whose fear of death drove him to a state of temporary or permanent insanity, Pat was actually calm, since fear of death suggested an attachment to life, while Pat — though he loved life — had given it up for lost. On the day near the end of his tour when he was shot in the shoulder, he passed out, not from pain or loss of blood but from relief that the wait for death was over, that his fully expected end had not been worse. When he woke up in the army hospital and found out that he was going home in one piece, with a Purple Heart to boot, he was literally speechless with thankfulness. In his mind, though, he thanked God, and he wondered, as he would for many years, why God had spared him. Since he couldn't know, he promised himself and God two things: that he would never forget how lucky he was, and that he would try to be worthy of his good fortune. Pat rarely talked about these feelings, because talking too much about the evidence of God's grace in one's own life had always seemed to him little better than bragging. But these feelings went to the core of his being.

With the passing of the years, of course, Pat's thankfulness was covered over by the concerns and innumerable details that fill any life, and yet it still lay at the bottom of everything. Especially in the first years after the war, Pat accepted what life offered him, grateful for anything at all. The offerings were benign, luckily — or perhaps not luckily, since they failed to shake up the gratitude that caused him to move through life like a kind of moral zombie. Back in his hometown of Washington, D.C., the GI Bill covered his studies at Howard University; one of his undergraduate professors encouraged him to apply to the university's law school and offered to write a recommendation, so why not? Meanwhile, in his junior year, he had met Maddie. She was crazy about him and seemed to want to marry him; she was nice, and pretty in an innocent sort of way, so why not? After law school, a job opened up for an attorney in the U.S. Postal Service, where he spent the next twenty years and counting. Regular raises, decent salary, steady government work. God had seen fit to send these blessings his way. Why not accept them?

Meanwhile, the children came along: Sheridan in 1956, Gregory in 1958, Lester in 1960. Lester's problems weren't obvious at first. He was slow to crawl and walk, but so were a lot of children, and he got there eventually. He didn't seem to have any emotional problems; it fact, he was the most easy-going of Pat and Maddie's children. By the time he was three, though, this had come to seem too much of a good thing. Not only did he never cry or scream; he wouldn't say so much as "Momma." When it was clear that something was not right, Lester's pediatrician referred his parents to a specialist, a white man at Georgetown University Hospital, who confirmed their fears. After running tests on Lester, this man informed Pat and Maddie that their son had two problems, one of which was not so unusual, the other of which, the doctor admitted, he had never encountered before. The first, he said bluntly, was that Lester was mildly retarded. The second was that his brain seemed to be missing the connection that in other people translated words into thoughts. Lester seemed to respond to language the way most people respond to music: just as those people recognize patterns of notes once they have been repeated often enough, but cannot identify the notes themselves, Lester could understand "Don't chew with your mouth open" if he was told enough times, but the meanings of "with," "your," and "open" would elude him, perhaps forever. That last thing the doctor said — the thing that kept Maddie in tears for weeks — was that it might be easier in the long run to think of Lester not as a son but as an intelligent pet. As for Pat's reaction to all this, he was sober, and sad, but — in the end, at bottom, as was his way — accepting. It must, after all, be for a reason; and he wondered to himself, in his acceptance and gratitude, what the reason was.

Lester attended public school in the buildings adjacent to the schools where his siblings went, the ones reserved for special-education students. Sheridan and Greg walked him there every morning and picked him up every afternoon — an open invitation for taunts from other children, which, as Greg once told Clive, made him feel as if he were walking to and from school naked every day. Lester could never go anywhere — or be left at home — by himself, and up until he was twelve even his bathing had to be supervised. On the other hand, he was never in a bad mood, and he would smile, if a tad vacantly, at *anything* you gave him; the simplest jigsaw puzzle kept him engaged for hours. He never complained. How could he? He didn't *talk*. Until …

*     *     *     *

Sheridan felt both relieved and annoyed when she arrived at her parents' house that Friday night: relieved because the hysterical scene for which she had been girding herself did not materialize, and annoyed because, given the way she had inconvenienced herself to get here so quickly, part of her *wanted* the hysteria, rather than the smiles — nervous as they were — with which her parents greeted her.

The two of them answered the door together, taking her coat, spouting one-liners in such similar singsongs that after a while it was hard to tell who was saying what:

"Sherrie, thank God you're here. It's like a miracle."

"Nobody's going to believe it. But we've heard it."

"This will be a day we'll always remember."

"Always!"

"It's so good you're here."

Sheridan went into the living room. Lester, sitting on the sofa with a child's jigsaw puzzle on his lap, turned toward her — not with any sign of a new personality, but with the wide, dull-eyed grin she had seen innumerable times before. As fond of this grin as she was inwardly, as relieved as she was to see it, she was unable to give way to affection until she had gotten rid of her annoyance, and she looked for a way to do so, settling finally on this: "And where is *Greg*?!"

"He went out a little while ago. He said he'd be back before long."

Sheridan sat beside her brother, placing a hand on top of his, which stopped its mild trembling. He continued working the puzzle with his other hand, a smile of complete contentment on his face. Sheridan said to her parents, "So tell me what happened."

They were doing so when Greg walked in. "Oh, you're here," he said to his sister.

"You always did have a firm grasp of the obvious."

"Good to see you, too."

"So where did you go, after telling me I had to come home, 'like, now'?"

"I went *out*, awright? None of your damn business anyway."

"Gregory! Don't talk to your sister like that."

"If she's my sister, why's she sound like my mother?"

"If I *were* your mother—"

"—I'd abort myself!"

"EVERYBODY! ENOUGH!"

This shout, which brought the other shouting to an abrupt halt, had come from Pat — but it was delivered on behalf of Maddie. Everyone knew what family squabbles cost her emotionally, and it had always been Pat's job to remind them. Sheridan and Greg looked down, their expressions nearly identical mixes of annoyance and regret. Maddie glanced back and forth, anxiously, between her two older children. Only Lester's face was unreadable.

That soon changed. Pat was two words into a sentence — two words now erased from all memory — when Lester, suddenly standing, shouted:

*Sister Sister readin' to me from a BOOK that I like*

> *It's the one about the boy who wants a SHINY new bike*
> *Momma called us to the table — "Dinner's READY!" she said*
> *So we got up from the sofa — Sister FONDLED my head*
> *"I can read it to you later," Sister SAID with a smile*
> *Then I sat down at the table and I WAITED a while*
> *Daddy at the record player choosing JAZZ for the meal*
> *Momma bringin' in the dinner — mashed poTAtoes and veal*

As Lester's face changed, for the moment, back to its old self, Greg turned to Sheridan. She was sitting, gazing up at her younger brother, seeming about to either scream or throw up.

Wearing a broad grin, Greg said to her, "Welcome home, Sis."

*         *         *         *

It was in the late 1960s, when she was in her late thirties, that Maddie Hobbs (nee Bell) came to understand that life is an ever-changing thing. Her understanding was brought on not by the war in Vietnam, the birth of the Black Power movement, the assassinations of Martin Luther King and Robert Kennedy, the moon landing, or any of the other historic events of the era — instead, it had to do with Saturday mornings. As Maddie settled into her life as a wife, mother, and part-time arts and crafts teacher in the public schools, Saturday mornings became her favorite times. Their focus was the Hobbses' dining room, where the children, aged nine, seven, and five, sat around the table in their pajamas, eating whatever breakfast cereal they had seen advertised on TV that week, while their parents, in bathrobes, drank coffee and read the newspaper — what they could read of it, anyway, given how much they listened to and commented on all the talk from Sherrie and Greg. Oh, the talk. It would have been hard to say what it was about, because it could have involved one or many things, from a classmate's remark to the turning point in the Civil War, from long division to the merits of the movie playing at the theater down the street. Maddie had by then begun to accept Lester's condition, and while he colored contentedly in a book or on a napkin, the rest of them bantered, argued, laughed, reminisced … Saturday mornings were better than dinner times because of their unhurried nature — no homework and few dishes to be done afterward, just a slow, relaxing progression toward cartoons on TV and play. Sitting amidst all this talk and noise, all this *life*, Maddie felt for the first time ever that she had reached a plateau, the place where she was supposed to be; and a part of her believed — if not consciously — that it would go on forever.

Then Sherrie and Greg turned ten and twelve, and suddenly, as if responding to secret instructions, they seemed to become different people. (It was about the time that ... no, she didn't want to think about that.) They got up late on Saturday mornings; they barely talked to each other as they wolfed down breakfast, and the few words they did exchange amounted not to playful banter but to verbal eye-clawing of the kind they continued to engage in as adults. After breakfast, they no longer headed into the living room with Lester to watch cartoons, their little shoulders and the backs of their heads so still and adorable as they sat cross-legged on the floor together, transfixed; no, they went off to see their different sets of friends, while Lester stayed behind, looking as if something was wrong but he couldn't quite figure out what. This deterioration saddened Pat, but to Maddie it felt like a death. Worse, it evoked thoughts of her own childhood, which she had spent her adult life alternately compensating for and trying to forget.

But Madelyn Bell Hobbs was nothing if not an optimist. And on this Saturday morning, a decade after the deterioration had begun, a day after Lester had spoken — shouted! — his first words, Maddie rejoiced inwardly to see the members of her family make their way to the dining table. She and Pat, both early risers, were sitting there reading the *Post*; one of Pat's hundreds of jazz records was playing in the living room; she had made coffee, and one by one the children, in pajamas, took their places. It took all of Maddie's restraint to keep from saying, "Well! We're a family again."

She wanted to say this in spite of her new, uncertain feeling toward Lester, who was the first of the children to come to the table. Normally, she would have fondled his hair and ears as she buzzed about, getting coffee and napkins; but now, despite all her talk about the miracle and the blessedness of his sudden speech, she felt a little ... well, *afraid* was too strong a word, but she had to admit, if only to herself, that this new development made her a little nervous. Who could tell what set off these rhyming bursts, which, underneath it all, she found unsettling, despite the wonderful things they might mean for her son? Would her hand on his hair or ears make him do something else he'd never done before, something … violent?

And she wanted to be upbeat, despite the quiet that settled over the family when all were assembled. The night before, Sherrie, the last one to experience Lester's new abilities, had been too rattled afterward to discuss anything; there had been an unspoken agreement that that would happen the next day, and this morning's gathering had the nervous feel of a meeting at which important things would be said, though no one knew what.

So the Hobbses just sat there, gazing down at the polished surface of the table or past each other's shoulders; Maddie's own gaze wandered to the corner of the ceiling, just above the white molding, where there were fine cracks in the yellow paint. The only sounds were of spoons in coffee cups, quiet sips, the smack of Lester's lips as he ate cereal, and jazz playing quietly in the living room. And then Sherrie, glancing at her mother before letting her gaze settle on her father, said, "Well, I think there are two things we have to address."

Greg, coming out of a daydream, said, "'Address'? What is this, Congress?"

Sherrie's eyes darted quickly in Greg's direction, then back toward her father again. "First, we need to have Lester examined." Lester looked up from his cereal at the mention of his name, then back down when he didn't hear it again. "We don't know why he's suddenly started talking, or what's setting it off, or what might set off something *else* in him. And the second thing is, we've got to be very careful who we tell about this, at least at first. I mean — here's a boy who never said a word for almost twenty years, and now he's not just talking but *rhyming*? Nine out of ten people hearing that would think we're crazy, and the tenth would call the *Post*, and then it'd be a circus around here."

"You got a point there," her father said. "Okay. Mum's the word, for now. Now where do we take him to be examined?"

"I think Hopkins is the best place," Sherrie said. "They've got the facilities and the specialists. I'll start asking people."

Her father nodded. At that point Maddie could no longer restrain herself. "I knew this family would know what to do if we put our heads together," she said. In response, her husband, in that way of his that infuriated her, looked down — as if to spare her the only possible answer to what she had said. Sherrie and Greg glanced toward her with a mix of impatience and pity. Well, Maddie thought. Maybe I should have kept that to myself.

*    *    *    *

Later, taking a bath, Sherrie was so lost in thought that she kept forgetting to wash herself. Part of the cause, of course, was having heard her brother shout rhymes after nineteen years of silence, but after the shock of that — the first wave of it, anyway — had subsided, she marveled over something else. What, she tried to remember, had she been expecting as she made the trip from Baltimore? Hearing Greg say that Lester was talking in rhymes, what did she think was really going on? She had been surprised — no, shocked — by the news, but between hearing it and seeing for herself, clearly some skepticism had set in. Why? Didn't she trust her brother not to lie about something like this, aggravating though he was about other things? Were there other true things she had simply refused to believe, for reasons that evaporated when she tried to think of them?

She thought of Oscar. They had been out together several times now, and he was nice-looking, perfectly polite, smart enough; but she had been keeping her distance, limiting their physical contact to brief kisses at the door, not putting too much of her lips into it — and she could feel his impatience with that, as gentlemanly as he was. Did she just not trust him? If not, she couldn't say why not. And she had been more intimate with men less nice than Oscar. It wasn't like she was a virgin.

She had met Oscar at the bus stop near Johns Hopkins, before she had bought her car; at the time he was riding the bus to and from the school where he taught third grade, his own car having gone in the shop. A couple of times since then, Oscar had remarked on how unlikely it was that they had met at all, given that they both rode the bus for such a short time. Sherrie thought, but didn't say, that what made it more unlikely still was Oscar's being almost too shy to talk to her. Six times (she had counted) they had stood near each other, just the two of them, waiting for the bus — Oscar saying nothing, looking at the ground, at the sky, at his watch, anywhere but at her, except when he thought she wouldn't notice. One good consequence was that Sherrie had plenty of time to study him before he said a word, and as he slowly — oh so slowly — worked up his nerve to speak, his looks grew on her: the long, skinny but broad-shouldered body swimming around in those tweed jackets, the nearly handsome face hiding behind those square wire-framed glasses. And so, during their seventh wait together, when he ventured to say, "Excuse me, I've got twenty after two, do you know if that's right?", she was ready to forgive him for taking a week to come up with such a pathetic approach — especially given how nice and deep his voice turned out to be.

The first time they went out together, Oscar paid for dinner in a restaurant that, Sherrie came to realize later, was well beyond his means. When they got there, Oscar seemed like a man who had witnessed gentlemanly behavior all his life and who, finally getting to practice it himself, ended up performing a spoof of it — helping Sherrie out of his car (which had come back from the shop), holding her arm as she stepped over a puddle, and almost literally tripping over himself, stumbling over his long, narrow feet, on his way to hold the door for her. Just when Sherrie had begun to wonder if they would both survive the evening, let alone enjoy it, Oscar began to relax. At the table he asked her questions about her work, which she answered perfunctorily; just as perfunctorily, she asked him if he liked teaching third grade. His answer surprised her. "It's not so much that I enjoy it — although I do," he said. "It's more like … it's where I'm supposed to be. It feels *right*. When I have a good day, which is not every day, I feel close to my kids, and I have the sense that they feel close to me. I enjoy having the sense that I'm really helping them, and they're definitely helping me, because they make me feel like I'm doing something important. Everybody wants to feel like that, I guess." Here he smiled, his glasses tilting slightly on his face. "It's funny: sometimes after being with my kids, when I'm around adults, they just seem like bigger versions of the kids. They have the same emotions as my third-graders — jealousy, boredom, laziness.

Sometimes they hide it a little better, and sometimes they don't. I feel like the kids make me a little more sympathetic to the adults." He smiled again, looking like one of the kids he was describing — except for the broad shoulders under that tweed jacket. (She had never seen such shoulders on such a slender man!)

Hearing him describe his feelings about his own work, she felt moved to talk about hers again, in a way she hadn't in quite a while. "When I was little," she said, "I was always asking my parents — or any adult — how the things around me worked. What made the car run, what made the sky blue, why hubcaps seemed to spin backwards. And sometimes they could answer me, but the less they were able to, the more persistent I became, and the more annoyed they got."

Oscar smiled. "No adult likes looking stupid to a kid."

"No," Sherrie said. "But I couldn't help myself. So, with chemistry, I feel like that same little girl I was — just like you were saying. Only, as a chemistry student, I'm *supposed* to ask questions. I'm *supposed* to want to know how things work. And it never ends. Everything you find out leads to ten more things to find out. You know, like — the Karles, this husband-and-wife team, came up with mathematical formulas for figuring out crystal structures, and then it became a matter of figuring out how to demonstrate it. So then they figured *that* out — with X-rays. Once they did *that*, they opened up a whole array of structures that could be analyzed, all sorts of peptides — sorry, this is probably boring. I get carried away." He smiled at her, and she smiled, too, realizing she had gotten carried away because she felt so comfortable.

He drove her home and walked her to the front door of her building. As he stood with her there, saying he had had a good time, she could feel him about to kiss her, and she was ready. But then, suddenly, he was slinking back to his car, having lost his nerve. He didn't try it on their second date, either, or their third. It was only at the end of their fourth dinner together, when the mood had passed in her and she had concluded that they were better off as friends, that he ventured to put his lips on hers. She returned the pressure, in a friendly but not passionate way, and then went inside — setting the tone of the relationship they had had ever since.

That was Oscar: slow, steady, close to her, and somehow unable to get any closer.

These were the thoughts she had as she bathed in her parents' tub, the sunlight pouring through the window onto the mountains of white suds from the bubble bath.

\*    \*    \*    \*

Pat and Lester, meanwhile, went out to the car. As usual, Lester followed his father down the brick front steps and the short walkway, while Pat began the monologue he kept up intermittently whenever he was alone with his younger son. "Let's see what your Momma put on the list *today* I won't be able to find. It's always *one* thing. ... Know some'm, Lester, it's *warm* out here. Guess it is May, though. ..." Pat saw, across the street, a man who looked to be in his twenties, and he noticed the young fellow's flared pants; he looked down at his own straight-legged pants, which he realized hadn't been the style for some time. He also noticed, though, the young man's short hair — men's hair did seem to be getting short again, which meant that the times had gotten back around to Pat on that front at least, even if his hairline had fallen back like a defeated army. Well, he thought, I'm forty-eight — can't expect a man to keep up with fashion his *whole* life. Really, he was grateful to have that excuse. ... In the car, he unzipped his navy blue Peters jacket, pulling the large zipper by the worn leather tassle, letting his paunch expand and relax inside his rayon button-down shirt; he reached over to help Lester with his seat belt — Lester could do it by himself, but sometimes it took a while. Soon they were off to the grocery store.

"Look at this lady, Les. She calls that driving? Stop your Sunday driving, lady, it's only Saturday! Ha, ha ... I guess she — Oh!" Pat had remembered the new development with his son. Lester could now talk back to him. Or could he? He hadn't actually engaged in a conversation yet. Would he ever? Would he just continue shouting rhymes from time to time? Or was he finished with that? Pat sneaked a glance at him. "You've got us guessing, Les, that's for sure," he said, while his son aimed his usual trancelike stare at the road.

Lester walked behind his father into the cool air of the Giant. Pat pulled the grocery list from his pocket and read his wife's schoolteacher-neat script: "Sweet potatoes. Ten ears of corn. Apples ..."They were already in the produce aisle, so Pat began filling the cart. This was his favorite part of the market — the yellows of the grapefruit, squash and bananas, the greens of the limes and peppers, the reds of the tomatoes and apples forming areas of brightness, as in an Impressionist painting. He would wonder later if this sight, all its colors, had begun a process in Lester's head; they had left the produce aisle for the frozen meat section when Pat heard:

> *I was little, sittin' backwards, in a GRO-cer-y cart*
> *Feet were danglin,' arms were shakin,' folded OVER my heart*
> *Momma droppin' food behind me in the CART while I shook*
> *Then she turned and saw me shakin,' and she GOT a sad look ...*

There were moments in Pat's life — the war had been full of such times — when he felt at a remove from what was right in front of him, so impossible did it seem. Here was one such moment, as his nineteen-year-old son, mute until yesterday, stood next to the pork chops, shouting as if to someone a block away about a trip to the store he had taken as a toddler — while the other shoppers stood like figures in a museum, staring, tentative smiles on their faces, wanting to laugh but not sure it was safe. This was true of all but two people nearby: a boy and a girl, maybe eight and ten, who danced to the beat of Lester's rhyme:

> *"Little Lester, are you chilly? Oh my POOR little one!*
> *Oh my sweetie, let me warm you" — and she PUT my coat on*
> *I was happy, she was happy, like HYENAS we grinned*
> *Then she went to get the rice and it was CALLED Uncle Ben's ...*

As in those times when one is between sleeping and waking, and opening one's eyes requires a supreme effort of the will, so Pat had to peel himself apart from the crowd of dazed spectators. No, he told himself, with a rapid shake of his head; this won't do. He approached Lester, who had taken on the expression, the bearing, and the sound (if you ignored the words) of a Confederate general rousing his hungry, filthy troops. Gently but firmly he took his son by his suddenly rock-hard upper arm. Guiding Lester with one hand, the grocery cart with the other, he made his way to the checkout aisle, trying to ignore the stares and the now-exploding laughter as Lester roared in his ear:

> *... left the cleaners and went home — she got me SOMEthing to eat It was white and hot and lumpy — it was CALLED Cream of Wheat ...*

Mercifully, there was an empty aisle. The young cashier rang up the items quickly, considering her inability to take her eyes off the still-shouting Lester. Pat, meanwhile, took out more money than the groceries could possibly cost, threw the bills toward the cashier, grabbed the bag, and, without waiting for change, jogged toward the door, pulling Lester behind him. In the car, he wondered: What was I thinking? Why didn't I think Lester would do that in public? Did I somehow *want* that to happen?

He was just lucky they hadn't seen anyone they knew. Yes, Pat was grateful for that.

# —THREE—

Greg, at that moment, was heading out the door to Clive's house. He had an idea. It went against the plan his family had just come up with, but fuck the plan. The whole thing was just Sherrie talking anyway, and his parents going along with her, like they always did; in that house it was Matthew, Mark, Luke, John, and Sheridan.

Clive's mother answered the door, wearing a yellow-and-white plaid apron, a sweet smile on her wide, dark face. "Come on in, Greg. You can go right upstairs. He's in his room."

"Okay, thanks."

"How's your family?"

"They're doing fine."

"I heard your sister's in town."

No secrets in *this* neighborhood, Greg thought. "Yeah, she's just visiting for the weekend."

"Well, tell 'em I said hello."

"I will," he said, disappearing upstairs before he had to say any more.

Clive was stretched out on the bed that took up most of his room, propped up on his elbows and reading *Hamlet* for his English class.

"Hey," Greg said, sitting on the chair at Clive's desk.

"Hey."

"How's the play?"

"'S all right. 'Bout a young dude that doesn't know what the fuck he's doing. Kind of like us, 'cept it's Denmark and it's, like, 1300."

"Better you than me. I had to read *Macbeth* in tenth grade. Shit was painful."

"I was there, remember?"

"Oh yeah. You ready?"

The two of them took a bus farther into the northeast section of the city. The previous evening, in Kim's, when Greg had laughed with Clive about Lester and then heard *Rapper's Delight*, he had what felt like an awakening. Rapping seemed to be the new big thing; his brother was doing it, after nineteen years of saying nothing; Greg and his family could be sitting on a gold mine. He said as much to Clive, who reminded him that his cousin, Edward Harper, sometimes filled in as a deejay on WHUR, Howard University's radio station. Maybe Edward would have advice. Greg had heard Edward on the air himself; from the man's warm, resonant bass voice, Greg had formed a mental image of a tall, handsome, broad-chested, narrow-waisted man, with a moustache but no beard, living in an apartment where two or three beautiful, half-dressed women could be found on any given night.

Now, on the bus, they passed block after block of row houses, somewhat smaller than the free-standing homes in the Hobbses' neighborhood; here and there were commercial strips or housing projects. Half a block from where they got off, they walked up narrow, cracked cement steps to a house built on a small grassy mound. "Cliiiive," sang the woman who answered the door — a kind of genetic variation on Clive's mother, Greg thought, like a Mrs. Potato Head put together by a different kid. Clive introduced Greg to his aunt, who went off to find Edward while Clive and Greg settled on the clear-plastic-covered sofa in the living room. Greg glanced around the room, at the spotless, forest-green wall-to-wall carpeting and polished wood furniture, until he found what he was looking for.

"There they are," he said, laughing, pointing to the china cabinet.

"What?"

"The two plates up there. Martin Luther King on one, John F. Kennedy on the other. Can't be a real black family without—"

He cut himself off, as Clive's aunt had come back in. "He's in the basement. You can go down."

It was only as he and Clive approached the door to the basement, the sound of an old record getting louder with every step, that Greg realized his mental image of Edward had taken on water. For one thing, this was not an expensive apartment, but Edward's mother's house. And then there was Edward himself.

Three things increased as Greg followed Clive down the basement steps: the number of records, 33s and 45s, Greg could see, stacked on shelves, on the floor, against the walls; the volume of the record now playing — "La La (Means I Love You)," a Delfonics hit from eleven years earlier; and Greg's desire to laugh. It wasn't so much that Edward, standing in the middle of the floor amid still more records, was funny-looking — it was that he looked nothing whatsoever like Greg had imagined. Not only wasn't his waist narrow: it was the widest part of him, as if a normal-sized man had tossed aside his belt in favor of a Hula Hoop. Edward's body tapered off in both directions starting from his waist, ending in noticeably small brown loafers at one end and a rather bullet-shaped head at the other. The lenses of his wire-frame glasses were so thick that his eyes looked like black peas, but those peas, following Clive and Greg down the steps, gave the impression of missing very little.

"Hey, Edward," Clive shouted above the record, "how you doing, this is my friend Greg I told you about." Edward extended a pudgy hand — which was soft — for a handshake, which was softer. Greg was unsettled by that, but more so by being introduced as "my friend Greg I told you about." Now that he was in a position to reject Sherrie's advice about keeping Lester's new ability a secret, he felt funny about doing it. He decided to say as little as possible until he had found out how much Edward already knew. This resulted in a moment of awkwardness, which Edward broke by smiling and saying in that bass Greg recognized, "Clive said you wanted some advice about rap, or some'm?"

Greg felt some tension go out of him. "Yeah. I know somebody who — can we turn the music down a minute?"

"Sure." Edward stepped around a stack of LPs and stopped in a tight space between a turntable and more stacks of records, under which, Greg noticed after a moment, was a mattress. With the precision of a surgeon, the love and care of a grandmother, he lifted the needle from the record. The sudden silence seemed as loud as the Delfonics.

"Thanks," Greg said. "Yeah, I got a friend" — here he shot a quick sideways glance at Clive — "that I think could be good at, you know, rap."

A small, knowing smile was on Edward's face. "A friend, you say?"

Greg understood. "It's not me. It's — my brother."

"So what're you, his agent?"

"Well, he's kinda — shy. Quiet." Another glance at Clive, who looked very serious, as he usually did when holding in a laugh. "When he starts rapping, though, it's a different story. I was wondering if you had some advice for him, if he wants to do it like, you know, on a record or something."

"What's he rap about? I assume he writes his own stuff."

"Yeah. Um. It's mostly — stuff he's been through."

"Okay. Now here's the thing." Edward's eyes, which were made to seem small and far away by his lenses, and the rumble of his voice, like thunder from a distant storm, gave his words the air of authority sometimes produced by remoteness. "Basically, in any genre of popular music you want to talk about, you've got two kinds of songs that make it big and strike a chord. One is songs about love — I'm no good since my baby left me, I'm so glad my baby's back, Girl tell me what to do to win your love, etc. Then you've got your social commentary. With soul music, you've got Smokey doing 'Ooh Baby Baby,' but also you've got Marvin Gaye doing 'What's Goin' On.' With rock, rock and roll, there's everything from 'Heartbreak Hotel' to that Barry Manilow shit on the love side, but you got protest songs there, too — 'Abraham, Martin and John,' 'Blowin' in the Wind.' Blues, same thing: Ma Rainey doing 'Cold in Hand Blues,' Billie Holiday singing 'Strange Fruit.'

"No reason why anything should be different in rap music. Now, *Rapper's Delight* is big right now, and it's basically about — nothing.

Dude goes over his friend's house and doesn't like the food. But that's the kind of thing you can only do so many times. Eventually, rap's going to get like everything else — a lot of love songs on one side, a few social commentary songs on the other."

Greg said, "Social commentary — you mean what's happening out on the street …?"

"I mean what's *behind* what goes on out there on the street. The *reasons* for it. Poverty, etc. Nobody's gonna want to hear about thugs and guns and gangs and all that. …"

*     *     *     *

Sherrie and her mother were talking in the living room when Pat and Lester walked in. Maddie said, "How was the store?"

Pat stood before his wife and daughter, nodding slowly, as if having given much thought to a complex issue. Lester, quiet again, stood beside him, wearing his occasional look of thinking about something from long ago. "It was good," Pat said. "Educational."

"Educational?"

"Oh yes." He explained why, watching the color drain from his wife's face as he talked. When he'd finished, he joined Maddie and Sherrie in sitting down; while Lester wandered to another part of the house, the three of them stared grimly into the middle distance.

Sherrie spoke first. "Well, I guess we should've seen that coming."

"That's what I was thinking," Pat said. "And it means we'll have to be *very* careful about taking Les out of the house."

"*Yes*," Sherrie said.

"*Oh*," Maddie said, shaking her head, seeming to consider the ramifications of all this. "*Oh*."

More silence followed this. Just when it was starting to become unbearable, to suggest that no one was talking because no one had any ideas about a solution, Pat surprised his wife and daughter by smiling and saying, "You know, it was really kind of funny."

Together, Maddie and Sherrie said, "It *was?*" Sherrie added, "How?" — her tone meaning, *I can't possibly see how.*

"Well," Pat said, still grinning, "one second, he was just Lester, same as he's been all this time, and the next, there he was, shouting about riding in a grocery cart and eating Cream of Wheat." He saw the two women's faces, on which not a trace of humor could be found, and he felt his smile falter, like a high-flying kite when the wind suddenly stops. He laughed again, a little desperately this time. "All those people just looking at him, frozen, like ..." Here the kite crashed to the ground. He stood up. "Well, I didn't exactly finish the shopping. Think I'll go to a different store this time." Heading for the door, he added, "By myself."

He went out into the sun again, making his way from habit toward the car and thinking about where to drive. Then he decided he would just walk to the store on 12th Street; the produce there wasn't the best, and neither was the selection, which was why he usually drove to the Giant, but then he didn't need very much today, and it was a nice afternoon for a walk. Might clear his head. He thought of his failed attempt to make light of the food-shopping episode and realized who might've helped matters: Greg. Pat's older son sometimes laughed when he shouldn't, but on the positive side, he recognized when something was really funny. Sherrie was grown up and on her own now, and it was time, Pat thought, to admit that she didn't have the world's most highly developed sense of humor.

He thought of one Christmas a few years back. It was about 1971, when Sherrie and Greg were around fifteen and thirteen. As part of the tradition the family had formed over the years, they bought their tree on the Saturday that was closest to being a week before Christmas Day. It was the same every year: the children sat in the back of the car, Lester in the middle, and Pat drove, with Maddie on the passenger's side, to the asphalt lot on Minnesota Avenue. There, big men with lumberjack coats or pea jackets, knit hats, worn-out work gloves, and expressions of profound disinterest held trees up for viewing at the family's request. The Hobbses then debated among themselves, pronouncing one tree too short, the next too tall, the one after that too bare on one side at the bottom, and so on, until the winner was placed — to the extent possible — in the trunk, secured with twine, and driven home with extreme caution by Pat, who could see only the trunk hatch in his rear-view mirror. At home, hot chocolate was poured, the family's favorite Christmas albums were put on the turntable by the window (Nat King Cole, the King Family, Bing Crosby), and everyone sipped and sang while decorating the tree — everyone except Lester, who watched from the sofa, next to the cardboard boxes of light and bulbs, which had been brought up from the basement before the purchase of the tree.

On this particular Christmas, everything went as usual, until they took the tree into the house. Maddie had laid a white sheet, the same one as every year, on the floor in the corner of the living room where the tree would go; Pat and Greg laid the tree horizontally on the sheet, and Pat placed on its trunk the red metal stand with the four green prongs, its bottom sporting numerous round dents from years of being hammered into place. Several hands tightened the four screws, and then Pat rose to stand the tree up. That was when the trouble started. The tree simply would not stay up on its own. The moment his hands left it, the thing would fall back toward him, like a drunken man being taken home from the corner bar by his young son. This scene repeated itself three, four, five times, until Greg took over from his father, with the same results.

The tree was made to stand several hours later, through a makeshift method that involved an enormous planter borrowed from a neighbor, several very large rocks, and — in an event unique to that Christmas — the scrapping of the old red and green stand. Prior to that triumph, which everyone felt too frustrated to enjoy (in part because the end result was ugly as sin), several other attempts had failed. While the forgotten Bing Crosby album spun silently on the turntable, while half-inches of hot chocolate grew cold in mugs around the room, the Hobbses sawed the trunk, readjusted the stand, sawed the trunk some more, readjusted the stand again, debated, argued. The lowest point came when Pat, feeling cautiously optimistic after having hammered the bottom of the stand until (a) it seemed flush with the trunk and (b) his ears were ringing, stood the tree up, let go, and took a step back. Then came two seconds of perfect quiet, during which the tree stood absolutely straight. Pat had opened his mouth to say, "I think we finally did it," when the tree, as if pushed from behind, came crashing to the floor.

More distressing than that were the reactions of the children, which were what made Pat remember the whole episode on a May afternoon several years later. Sherrie, too frustrated to speak, tears nearly squirting from her eyes, half-walked and half-ran up the stairs. Greg, meanwhile, erupted into violent, bug-eyed laughter, laughter that tore itself from him in jerks, as if escaping from too small a space. Pat and Maddie merely looked at each other, seeming to wish the same thing: that they could each become two people, one to go after Sherrie and say, "Come on, it's only a Christmas tree," and the other to tell Greg, "Have some consideration!" Not knowing how to respond to his two older children, Pat ended up imitating his youngest: for a time, he said nothing at all.

*    *    *    *

After Pat left the house, Maddie and Sherrie sat quietly, taking occasional sips from their second cups of coffee. The quiet took the place of talk about Lester, of whom neither woman knew quite what to say; the quiet itself came to feel like a form of talking about their son and brother, valid in its own way, and when it seemed to have lasted long enough, Maddie felt free to change the subject.

"You know who I saw on the bus last weekend? I knew there was something I'd been meaning to tell you."

The closed-mouth, faintly mischievous smile on her mother's lips made Sherrie apprehensive, but there was only one thing to say: "Who?"

"Calvin Thomas."

"Oh." Sherrie sipped her coffee. "Him."

"We were both going downtown. He was the same. Just as sweet, and smiling, and—"

"Nervous?"

"I always did like him more than you did. He was crazy about you, though. I can still see him the way he was in high school, carrying your things and holding doors for you, so busy beaming at you he could barely see where he was going."

"He could never come *out* with anything, though. I never saw anybody so scared to say what he was thinking. He'd just talk, talk, talk, and never come to it."

"Oh, anybody could *see* what he was thinking. Anyway, he asked about you, of course. *He's* in *law* school now. About to finish his first year."

Sherrie's eyebrows rose.

Her mother said, "Anyway, he was a lot nicer than" — she spat out the next two words, as if they were something strange that had turned up in her food — "Benjamin Giles."

"You mean to say," Sherrie asked, her voice dripping with sarcasm, "you didn't like Benjamin?"

"What was there to like, besides his perfect teeth and light-colored eyes? Never saw anybody so arrogant. And still a teenager! I never will forget the time—"

"Oh, here we go."

Sherrie had recently described to someone — it must have been Oscar; who else did she go out with? — her parents' tendency to talk about events, over and over, years, even decades after they occurred, as if they had happened this morning. True to form, her mother was now describing the time Benjamin took Sherrie to the senior prom, as if it had taken place five hours and not five years earlier, and as if Sherrie herself had not been there: "—opened the front door and said, 'Hello, Benjamin, don't you look handsome in your tuxedo.' Think he said so much as 'Thank you'? Oh, no. Just stands there like he's Prince Philip, not even a smile, and says, 'Good evening. Is Sheridan ready?' So I invite him in to talk while you're getting ready upstairs, and all I can get out of him are one-word answers, while he's sittin' on the couch stiff as a stick, like he'd catch some germs if he sat back —"

"Momma, that was *five years* ago."

"I know. All I'm saying is, I never knew why you'd choose somebody like him over Calvin."

"Momma — it's over, okay? I've barely seen either one of them since then. I started and finished college since all that was going on."

"Yes, I suppose so. ... Well what about now? Are you still seeing that fellow — what's his name — Oscar?"

Sherrie never ceased to marvel at how good — annoyingly good — her mother's memory was for details like this. She said, "I still see him from —"

At that moment, to her intense relief, the doorbell rang. Her feeling of relief was not to last long.

# —FOUR—

To explain why the ringing doorbell was a sign of trouble, it is necessary to say a few words about Washington, D.C.

The nation's capital, home to the Hobbs family, is a geographical curiosity — a southern town in the eyes of some, a northern city to others, just south of the Mason Dixon Line and yet one of the destinations in the twentieth century's great northward migration of blacks. Washington, overwhelmingly black, might best be described as a northern city full of southerners.

In segregated southern towns in the early and middle years of the twentieth century, places with a limited number of distractions, a favorite pastime of the residents was talking — to each other and about each other. In a word: gossiping. These mostly churchgoing people did not consider gossip a low-level sin or a guilty pleasure; they did not consider it at all, at least not enough to give it a name — they merely engaged in it, as one sleeps or eats, in order to meet a basic need. Many such people, on moving north, settled near each other and to a large extent re-created the gossip networks they had known in their former homes.

Two such people were the sisters Celestine Johnson and Floretta Childs, septuagenarians both, who had known Madelyn Hobbs's parents in Virginia. Celestine, two years younger than her sister, had moved to Washington some fifty years earlier, where she met her husband and settled down; following that gentleman's death, in the mid-1960s, Floretta — herself a widow by then, still living in the town of her birth — moved to Washington, both to take care of, and come under the care of, her sister. In their northeast Washington environs, two short blocks from the Hobbs family, Celestine and Floretta connected (i.e., gossiped) with other former residents of their hometown and with transplants from similar towns in North Carolina, Tennessee, and Arkansas. Maybe once a month, one or both of them paid the Hobbses an unannounced visit, to "check up on my peoples," as they said — and, once in a while, for other reasons.

It was the wrinkled, light brown finger of Celestine Johnson, with its cheap but ornate ring and bright red, severely chipped nail polish, that rang the Hobbses' doorbell that Saturday afternoon. Then the sisters waited silently on the porch. Celestine wore a floral patterned pants suit and a curly wig whose deep brown — the hair color of a woman in her early thirties — contrasted sharply with her sagging jowls; Floretta, always the more conservative, wore subdued tones and had her lead-gray hair tied back in a bun.

For Madelyn Hobbs, the sight of the sisters, as she opened her door, set the usual pattern in motion: outward cheer ("Well, hello, Celestine! Hello, Floretta!") and an inward mix of sighs and affection. Today, though, confusion was added to the mix, since the two ladies had visited only six days earlier. In Madelyn's smile and "Come on in" were a hesitance that only her husband or one of her children would have been able to detect.

"Well, look who's here!" Celestine crowed, stepping briskly though somewhat unsteadily to the middle of the living room. That was where Sherrie stood, wearing a smile reserved for such occasions — so practiced it was almost real. Celestine planted a sloppy kiss on Sherrie's cheek. "You home for the weekend?"

"Yes, Aunt Celestine."

Floretta: "Nice to have your children around you, isn't it?"

Madelyn: "It certainly is."

Celestine: "So how's school?"

Sherrie: "Well, it's — I'm —"

Celestine: "Oh, that's *good*. *Whew*, I declare, I got to sit down. Old lady like me should know better'n to do so much walkin'."

Everyone sat.

Madelyn: "Where've you been walking to, Celestine?"

Celestine: "Oh, child, just walking."

Madelyn: "Nothing wrong with that. Want something to drink? How about you, Floretta? Some lemonade?"

Both women said that lemonade would be mighty nice. Madelyn went to get it.

Celestine: "Where's your daddy?"

Sherrie: "Oh, he just went down to 12th Street to get some groceries. He should be back soon."

Floretta: "But didn't he go over to the Giant —"

Celestine (loudly): "It is a nice day for a walk, 'less you a old lady like me, heh heh. So how's Greg? And *Lester*?"

Sherrie (with a dawning sense of unease, looking from one sister to the other): "They're … fine —"

Madeyln (in a singsong, returning with lemonade): "*Heeere* we are."

Celestine: "Oh, thank you, child. I was just asking about your boys. What are they up to today? How're they doing?"

Madelyn (her smile faltering): "Oh — well, Greg is, um, out with his friend Clive. I think Lester went upstairs."

Celestine took a long drink of lemonade, lowering the glass with a loud "Aahhh!" and leaving a bright red lip-print near the rim, perfect down to the creases. "Whew, I needed that. You say Lester's upstairs? Is he by hisself?"

"Yes," Madelyn said. Her eyes met Sherrie's.

Floretta said, "He's always been good at occupying himself, hasn't he? Bless his heart. What's he doing upstairs?"

Madelyn said, "That's a good question. Sherrie, you want to go see?"

"Sure." Sherrie leapt from her seat as if she had just sat on a tack, then went up the steps. She slowed down about halfway to the top. On the one hand, she was happy to escape the living room, because by now it was abundantly clear what was going on: Lester's performance in the Giant had been witnessed by either Celestine,

Floretta, or another member of their gossip circle, a network to rival the KGB's, and the sisters had come over to find out — as surreptitiously as possible, of course — what was what. Another minute in their company and Sherrie was in danger of either spilling the beans or giving those biddies an unpleasant piece of her mind.

On the other hand: she knew her mother wanted her upstairs to make sure Lester didn't erupt into ear-splitting rhymes while the sisters were downstairs, but Sherrie didn't know how to do that; for all she knew, the sight of her might *provoke* something in Lester. And so, after nearly running upstairs, she made her way slowly down the hall to her brother's small room, putting one crepe sole very quietly in front of the other.

His door was open, as usual; except for when he closed it to get dressed, which he had finally learned to do by himself, the idea of privacy had never occurred to Lester. He lay on his back on his single bed, hands behind his head, looking into space, the picture of innocence and serenity. The sight of him made Sherrie relax, in spite of everything. When she sat at the foot of his bed, affectionately squeezing the toe of his tennis shoe, he smiled at her in that sweet way of his, looking into her eyes and yet giving the feeling that it was only partly her he was seeing. That look had spooked her sometimes when she was younger, but she had come to recognize it as being the most affection that Lester could give, and now she was grateful for it.

"Hey, buddy," she said, smiling back at him. "You're causing quite a stir downstairs, you know it? You're gonna have the whole neighborhood talking soon, if it isn't already. I'm supposed to be up here checking on you, but I don't know how, exactly. Seems to me you're just gonna do what you're gonna do. You look pretty calm right now, though." She looked around the little room. The pale yellow walls were decorated with posters of cartoon characters, which their mother had put up years ago — whether to draw out Lester's personality or give the sense that he had one wasn't clear. These pictures of Mighty Mouse and Under Dog had accomplished neither, but since no one knew why they had failed, or what might work in their place, they continued to hang there, forgotten. On the bare wood floors were Lester's shoes and stacks of simple puzzles.

"What goes on in that head of yours, Lester? You know ... I work with a chemist who thinks she's found the structure of an opiate in the brain. Big deal — something that helps you go to sleep at night. But what makes you do what *you're* doing? You've got us guessing, little brother." She sighed. "Well, Mr. Lester Hobbs, I better get back downstairs, before the Nosey Sisters think something's fishy. Which it is." She felt reassured, though she couldn't have said why, as she went back down the hall. She was close to the bottom of the stairs when the feeling was obliterated by the first of the shouts.

\*     \*     \*     \*

At that moment Greg and Clive were on a Metrobus, returning home from Clive's cousin Edward's house. They had spent the first part of the ride discussing Edward's advice and how to apply it, and had arrived at a plan, the first phase of which was scheduled for later that day. Then they were quiet for a while.

Greg broke the silence. "Whatchu doin' the rest of the day?"

"Readin' *Hamlet* for that paper I gotta write."

"Yeah, that's right. My condolences."

"Tell you the truth, it's not that bad. I kinda like it."

Greg turned in his seat to look at his friend. "You always did have a nerdy streak. I see it's gettin' wider."

"Yep. Tragic. What are you doing?"

"Econ."

"Think I'll stick with Shakespeare."

"After that, though, I'ma call up Gina. See if me and her can get together later."

Clive's eyebrows rose. "You got her number? After she was lookin' at you like, 'Who the fuck is this?'"

"Damn straight I got her number. That's what perseverance'll do. Gals like to see a nigger keep tryin' — showin' that *con*fidence." Greg enjoyed talking this way, less because it made him sound worldly than because it was his way of affirming for himself the wisdom he had gained, the progress he had made in his life; he got out of this what others got out of writing down the titles of books they had read, or counting their sex partners. He asked Clive, "What about that girl you were talkin' to? What's her name — Robin?"

"Still talkin' to her."

"Better do some'm 'sides talk, bro. Gals get bored after while."

"You should have your own newspaper column," Clive said. "Advice to the Lovelorn from a Motherfuckin' Third-Year Sophomore with No Girlfriend."

Greg said, "Fuck you," then joined in his friend's laughter.

The bus got to their stop. At the corner, Greg said, "Hey, I see my dad." He turned to Clive. "So — later."

"Later," Clive said, with a sly smile.

Pat Hobbs was indeed, just then, walking home from 12th Street with two bags of groceries. He was lost in thought. Remembering the Christmas tree episode had set his mind upon a string of other memories, connected one to the next by the smallest of tangents, fragments of his life that he had retained for reasons that were beyond him. He had settled, for the moment, on one memory from eleven years earlier — preserved as arbitrarily as the others, except, perhaps, for what it had revealed to him at the time about his children, about how little control he had over what happened to them. He remembered it, he supposed, for that reason — and because it had shamed him.

The time was an August night in the late 1960s, when Sherrie was around twelve, Greg ten, and Lester eight. Pat and Maddie and the kids had gone to the drive-in. The five of them were not in the car, but on it: Pat and Maddie sat on the hood, leaning back against the windshield; Lester lay sideways, nestled among his parents' knees and ankles; and Sherrie and Greg were side-by-side on the roof, on their stomachs, chins resting on stacked fists. The show was a triple feature, a grade-B horror picture followed by an equally low-budget science-fiction movie followed by an even lower-budget attempt at film noir. The third movie started just after midnight; what with the lateness of the hour, the cheesiness of the third movie's script and acting, and his having already watched two other movies, Pat found himself a little bored — but not unpleasantly so. Except for the movie, the night was quiet, cool, black as pitch; peaceful. Pat was surrounded by his wife and children. He was content.

And then he heard it.

"Damn, school starts in 'bout two weeks," Greg said in a low voice.

"Ten days," Sherrie answered. They were apparently no more engrossed in the third movie than Pat was.

Greg said to his sister, "How far you walkin' wit' us?" Sherrie, who up until then had gone to elementary school with her brothers, was about to start junior high school.

"I'll be with you till Otis. Then you're on your own. Why? You don't think it'll make a difference, do you?"

"I don't know," Greg said. "Prob'ly not."

"Why don't you get one of your friends to walk with you? Like Clint or Darnell?"

"Them punks wouldn't be no help. They can't fight. Or else they'd run."

"Sounds like you need some new friends."

"Shit, if they could fight, they'd just be messin' wit' me and Lester like everybody else."

In trying to follow the conversation, Pat had been confused — until now. The words "messin' wit' me and Lester" not only made everything clear; they brought several years of Pat's blissful unawareness to an end. He had known Greg to get in a few fights over the years, but so did every boy. It was an unpleasant part of growing up. But Greg had never told him what this conversation suggested, which was that Greg and Sherrie, walking their retarded brother to school, were a daily attraction for neighborhood bullies. Why hadn't they ever said anything? Maybe they didn't think their parents could do anything about it, and, indeed, Pat didn't know the answer. But not to have even mentioned it? Pat felt hurt to the core — hurt, and judged; this overheard conversation between his children was like a charge that he was ineffective as a father, and every second it went on was like a lash.

"Well, there's safety in numbers," Sherrie said.

"Not if you numberin' punks."

Had they told their mother, but not him? No — Maddie (who seemed to be sleeping now) would have mentioned it. So this was as much a judgment on her as on him; except that *he*, Pat, was the father, the protector.

Greg said, "Clint and Darnell —"

But he was cut off, as Pat heard himself whisper menacingly, "Some of us are trying to watch the movie!"

The words did the job: Sherrie and Greg were quiet for the rest of the movie, which Pat now had to stay around for, having so harshly declared his interest in it. The silence continued during the drive home, and though this was due mainly to the late hour, Pat felt that the silence, too, was a judgment, this time on his ridiculous behavior. In the days that followed, he tried to make up for it, asking Greg and Sherrie, in humble tones, direct and indirect questions about what he'd overheard; but all he got was evasion. He felt he had failed his children, failed to do right by the second life he had been given back in the war, and he didn't know how to atone. At first he didn't, anyway. Then he came up with a way to atone, to protect his children, a way that turned out to be woefully inadequate. There was that one time … but he didn't want to think about that.

Walking home from the grocery store on 12th Street, Pat shook his head to dismiss that horrible memory. That was when Greg caught up to him. "Hey, Dad."

Pat, who had been thinking of the ten-year-old Greg, was startled to find his grown-up son beside him. "Oh. Hey. Where're you coming from?"

"Just hangin' out downtown with Clive. Let me take one of the bags."

"Thanks. Listen — everything okay with you, son? I mean, aside from what's happened with Lester?"

Greg seemed mildly confused for a moment, then answered, "Yeah. Why?"

"I just want to know. Your studies coming okay?"

"Yeah. I'm gettin' ready to do some studying now."

"Good, good. Just — let me know if I can do anything for you, okay?"

"Yeah, um — okay."

They walked quietly after that, Pat trying to think of another helpful thing to say, Greg puzzling over what his father had already said. Then they got to the house, where their thoughts quickly took on a different character.

*       *       *       *

Father and son, standing in the doorway with a view of the living room, said together, "Uh-oh."

The scene reminded Greg of the one he had come home to the evening before, after Lester's first outburst, though with a couple of differences. For one, instead of both of his parents and his brother, today's cast was his mother, Sherrie, and — bad news — Aunt Floretta and Aunt Celestine. (Greg's father, to the disapproval of his mother, liked to call the younger of the old ladies "Telestine.") For another, all were standing, rather than seated in an un- or semi-conscious state. All did, however, look awe-struck.

What had happened was this:

When Madelyn, sitting on the sofa, heard Lester shouting from the second floor, she looked toward the stairway. Her gaze met that of Sherrie, who was halfway down the steps. For a moment their eyes had the same frightened look; then Madelyn saw her daughter's become narrow and hard. Sherrie said to Floretta and Celestine, "Is this what you came to hear? Come hear it, then." She went back upstairs, and Madelyn, Floretta, and Celestine, after trading nervous glances, followed her. Crowding into the short, narrow upstairs hallway, they saw Lester standing in the doorway to his room.

He held himself like a Wild West gunfighter about to draw both pistols. The skin around his eyebrows was puckered in his fury, and he shouted at the top of his newly discovered but powerful lungs:

> *... Bottom feeling wet and sticky, diaper weighing five pounds*
> *I was walking cross the floor and it was fallin' on down*
> *Brother laughing, sister screaming, Momma running to me*
> *Daddy sittin', head a-shakin', I continued to pee*
> *"Lordy Lordy, how much longer do we have to do this?"*
> *(That was Momma talkin' bout me while she wiped shit and piss) —*
> *"Five years old and wearing diapers" — then she didn't say more*
> *Daddy Sister Brother smelled it, and they went out the door*
> *Then I started wearin' undies, Momma so proud of me*
> *I just walked up to the bathroom, when the time came to pee*
> *Then I learned to dress myself and eat my food with a fork*
> *Sister Brother went to school and Momma Daddy to work*

*Sister Brother took me with 'em, bullies pickin' on us*
*Tauntin' Sister, hittin' Brother, raisin' all kinda fuss*
*Brother Brother hittin' back, but they were too much for him*
*Smacked his head and punched his nose and kicked him right in the shin*

Almost as jarring as Lester's rap itself, for the four women who stood stiff and silent listening to it, was its abrupt end. With the word "shin," Lester's face and body relaxed. Then, like someone who goes to his window after hearing a noise outside and satisfies himself that it is nothing important, he turned and went calmly back to his bed.

Sherrie started back downstairs, followed by the two elderly sisters. Madelyn, for a moment, appeared unable to move or speak; then she rushed toward Lester, sitting beside him on the bed, where he had lain on his back again, and put her hands to his cheeks. "Oh, Lester, I'm sorry. …" She looked in his eyes, and he gazed back the only way he could, and as only he could: seeming to see both more and less than what was in front of him, seeming to recognize her and yet not recognize her. It was that, finally, that drew tears from Madelyn's eyes and sent her back downstairs with the others.

That was when Pat and Greg walked in.

Pat: "Do I have to ask?"

Sherrie: "Sadly, no."

Celestine: "Bless me, it's a miracle."

Floretta: "It most surely is."

Celestine: "I always said there was some'm goin' on inside that boy's head, even if he wasn't sayin' nothin'."

Greg: "What did he say *this* time?"

Sherrie: "Stuff about when he was little. Wearing diapers, going to school."

Greg (after raising his eyebrows and filling his cheeks with air): "Daaaaaamn …"

The only one who had not spoken so far was Madelyn. She stood with her moist eyes on her husband, as if he were the only other person in the room; finally, silencing the others, she said, "Oh, Pat — he remembers *everything!* But he's — still — I don't know if I should be — happy, or, or —"

Pat dropped the groceries and hurried to his wife, who sobbed in his arms. The other four stood quietly, hands at their sides, looking away from Pat and Madelyn — and each other. Until Sherrie said to the sisters, not unkindly, "Maybe you should let us be alone."

\* \* \* \*

Floretta and Celestine, during the walk back to their house:

"Well, I wouldn'ta believed it if I hadn't seen it."

"That's two of us."

"Good gracious me, that musta made 'em think they was dreamin'. The boy don't say a word his whole life, and then up and starts to shoutin' like a preacher."

"And *rhyming*, Sister, don't forget."

"Rhyming like somebody on the T-V! And look to me like his momma and daddy's just as shocked as we is. Lord, have mercy. I reckon we best pray for 'em."

"You ain't said nothin' wrong there, Sister."

If no malice toward the Hobbs family is evident in that exchange, it is because the sisters felt none; and if some might liken their visit to the descent of a pair of vultures, that was not the sisters' view of things. They might have said, if asked, that their desire to know what was going on was not blameworthy but merely natural, a result of the curiosity in every human being. If anything, in their view, they were providing a service. Should the man who writes for the *Post* be criticized for finding out the facts himself, instead of filling his article with hearsay? Floretta and Celestine, though employed by no news agency, felt a duty to find things out — felt it so strongly that they did not even think about it. Having fulfilled that duty, they now headed home to attend to another, which involved extensive use of the telephone. (Here again: should we point our fingers at the television news anchor for telling us what he knows?)

The sisters' afternoon of telephone calls might also be compared to the physical act of love. It felt good to all involved, and the consequences appeared, for a time, to end there. But, as sometimes happens ...

# —FIVE—

Meanwhile, for Greg, zero hour was approaching.

After standing around for a few moments, feeling useless, while his father comforted his mother and Sheridan the Wise delivered sage observations in low tones, Greg eased away from the scene and headed toward the basement. He thought, going down the steps, how spare his living space seemed, compared with the basement where Clive's cousin Edward lived; Greg had records, but they were in modest metal racks next to one wall, beside his turntable, not occupying nearly every available inch of floor space, like Edward's. The other signs of Greg's musical sensibility were the posters that flanked his bed — one of Bootsy Collins, with his star-shaped guitar and glasses and knee-high gold boots with nine-inch heels, and the other of the many members of Earth, Wind & Fire, sporting Afros, standing calmly and smiling like the welcoming committee of some black planet. Between the posters, above the headboard of his bed, was a small picture of Bruce Lee torn from a magazine. Apart from these things, the basement was very much a basement: fake-wood tile floors, expanses of white stucco wall, two naked lightbulbs on the ceiling, two shelves of various family members' books forming a right angle in one corner, cardboard boxes of various family members' old clothes filling another corner, a third corner taken up by Greg's mother's abandoned exercise bike, and a door leading to the laundry room and second bathroom. Competing with all this, Greg's own touches in this room — the records, the posters, a couple of dumbbells, a small TV set, the turntable, his dresser and metal wardrobe closet — amounted to an only partially successful attempt at self-expression, a rabbit stuck halfway out of the hat.

He sat on his bed with his curved red telephone and dialed Gina's number; the man who answered told Greg in an ocean-deep voice that she was out and would be back later. Greg then began studying economics. At exactly three o'clock, when he had been studying for two hours, he tried Gina again. The same man answered, and Greg hung up without speaking.

It was time. He phoned Clive and exchanged several words. Then he found his small cassette recorder, put in a blank tape he had bought the evening before, and went upstairs. His mother, sister, and brother were all sitting in the living room; Greg said, in as casual a voice as he could manage, "Ma, I'm going for a ride with Clive. How 'bout if I take Lester with me? We'll be in the car, mostly."

"Okay, sure," his mother said. She added, after a sigh, "I don't guess it matters much now if he's in the house, out of the house, in the car, out of the car — seems like we can't keep people from finding out."

"Yeah," Greg said. "Come on, Lester, we're going for a ride, bro. Let's go wait on the porch." Lester, like a dog responding to the sound of his name spoken in a certain way, quickly fell in behind his brother. The two were heading for the door when Sherrie asked Greg, "What's that in your hand?"

With a great effort of will, whose only sign was the small, tight smile that disfigured his face, Greg said, "My tape recorder. I wanted Clive to hear something. Why?"

He and Sherrie looked each other in the eye for a quiet moment — the sort of moment that, occurring between rough men on the street, can be followed by either the quelling of tension or a bloody fight. Sherrie's gaze asked, *What are you up to?* while Greg's said, *What's the problem?* This time, Sherrie backed down, looking away, and the brothers stepped out to the porch.

They sat on the metal glider, moving back and forth slowly, the houses and small lawns of their quiet neighborhood laid before them like figures on a bright painting on that sunny May afternoon. "Ain't family life some'm else, Lester?" Greg said. "Everybody all in your business, 'cept when you want 'em to be, and then —"

At that point Clive drove up in his father's car, and Greg and Lester got in.

*　　*　　*　　*

It has been said that a poor man works for his money, while a rich man's money works for him. If that is true, then the population of Washington, D.C., in the late 1970s — at least the city's black majority — existed at various levels of poverty. At the more comfortable end of that spectrum were such people as Patrick Hobbs, whose salary as a government lawyer had allowed him to raise three children in a relatively small but perfectly comfortable house. (Blacks with *real* money crossed the Maryland state line to live in the suburbs.) At the other end were those who lived nowhere, dressed in rags, spent nights on benches and days muttering angrily to themselves and frightening small children. There were many people in between, some of whom lived in government-subsidized housing — the projects.

It was to the projects that Greg, Lester, and Clive were headed. Having given serious thought to Edward's discourse on pop music's two themes — love and social injustice — Greg had decided to try a less-crowded field by recording Lester as he rapped about lower-class life. In order for Lester to do so, he would first have to observe it, which was the goal of this trip.

So it was that Clive eased his father's car to a stop on Brooks Street, in the northeast section of the city, about a twenty-five minute drive from the Hobbs home. Greg stepped out of the car and looked around, perplexed, at the modest but freestanding houses, not significantly different from those in his own neighborhood. "These don't look like no projects."

"Patience, my boy," Clive told him. "We gotta walk a little bit. I don't want to leave my dad's car where we're going." The three of them went half a block to the corner. Across the street was the entrance to an alley that plunged downward; to the right of the alley were the backyards of private houses, while to the left was a grass-covered hill. At the top of the hill was a large red-brick building.

"See that?" Clive said, pointing to the large building. "We were out here to see my aunt one time, and I said, 'What's that building?' And she said, 'Projects.' Lincoln Heights, or some'm. As they say around here, that be's our destination."

They crossed the street and started down the white, rough-surfaced alley. Greg felt an unpleasant tingling in a deep corner of his intestines, familiar to many who have faced the reality to which their fantasies — hatched in comfort — have brought them. Where the alley became level, they stepped onto the hill, climbing up through tall grass, approaching the large building. At the top of the hill, facing windows with black iron bars, Greg stopped. He looked behind him, down toward the alley and the backyards on the other side of it, bordered with wood or wire fences, dotted with trees. Then he faced forward again. To his left, around the corner of the building, was — what? A gang fight in progress? A drug deal, which could turn violent with a shift in the wind, or the appearance of three strangers? Where was he about to go, with his best friend and his helpless little brother? Greg traded a glance with Clive, who seemed just as nervous; looked at Lester, whose expression showed nothing; and gripped the cassette recorder as if it were a weapon. And then, without a word, the three of them turned the corner, where they found —

Children. There were two sets of them: about half a dozen boys and girls, between eight and ten years old, played softball with a plastic bat in a fenced-off plot of dirt; adjacent to them, on a concrete surface, a group of older boys played basketball — the "basket" being a bottomless blue milk crate attached with wire clothes hangers to the top of a slide. Greg, Lester, and Clive walked along the edge of the falling-down fence, past the softball players, stopping at the area where the basketball game was taking place. Most of the boys ignored them; a couple glanced their way but kept playing. On the other side of the basketball game was a narrow street, on whose sidewalk a middle-aged woman strolled leisurely, in no apparent fear for her safety.

Greg felt relief, followed in short order by other things. We occasionally have moments of sudden clarity, when ideas that made sense to us as little as a minute ago strike us, all at once, as ludicrous — so much so that we wonder why they didn't before. Greg was in the grip of such a moment now, as the doubts that had been blocked by his high hopes came flooding into the front of his mind. These were the colorful, dangerous projects, where Lester would give spontaneous, rhymed, play-by-play commentary, which Greg would capture on tape? Why had Greg ever thought Lester would do that, when up until now he had rapped only about the past — and when the timing of his raps was unpredictable anyway? Greg was too embarrassed to meet Clive's eyes, or to say anything. Instead he watched the boys play basketball, observing the concentration in their faces, the surprising skill of some, the touching clumsiness of others. He watched their shots as they bounced off the milk crate or — less often — went in; with no rim, the ball could not swirl before it sank. These boys had no room for error.

Rousing himself, Greg turned to Clive and was about to speak — when he noticed something funny about Lester's face. His brother had the look of a man smelling something unpleasant. When Greg realized what was actually going on, he said what he had intended to say to Clive, only more forcefully: "Let's get outta here!" It was, of course, too late.

> Sister born in fifty-six — they put her IN the big room
> Brother came in fifty-eight and got the LITtle room soon
> I was born and then my brother took the BIG room with me
> Sister got the little room and we three SLEPT hap-pi-ly ...

The boys and girls, seemingly controlled by one mechanism, swung their heads simultaneously in Lester's direction. The younger kids ran toward him, stopping at the edge of the falling-down fence, eyes wide; the older boys, looking cool, as if seeing just another stranger shouting autobiographical rhymes at the top of his lungs, approached more slowly. Greg wanted, more than he had wanted anything in recent memory, to go back to the car. Two things were stopping him. One was that Lester, as Greg discovered when he tugged at the inside of his brother's elbow, had gone stiff as a pole, his feet planted wide apart, his arms in the gunslinger position; pulling him harder, Greg suspected, would cause him not to walk but to topple over sideways, like a statue. The other problem was Clive, who seemed to have entered a trance, in which he could do nothing but stare with his mouth open at Lester. "Clive!" Greg shouted to no effect, before he realized that this was the first time his friend had actually heard Lester's rhyming; until now, he had only heard *about* it. In his anxiety, Greg gripped the cassette recorder more tightly, inadvertently pressing the "record" button with his thumb.

On the other side of the fence, four feet away, one of the younger boys said, "What's he talkin''bout?"

"He one a them rappers," a girl said.

"What's he *rappin'*'bout, then?"

"I don't know. He look mad as shit, though."

As the kids talked among themselves, as Greg's usually articulate friend failed to make a sound, his formerly silent brother rapped on:

> *Twelve years later Sister said, "This room is TOO small for me."*
> *Daddy said, "Move to the basement." Sister SAID, "But you see,*
> *Basement's dusty musty smelly, it's no PLACE for a girl."*
> *Brother said, "Then I'll move down there. It will BE my New World."*

One of the younger boys asked Greg, "Is he on a record?"

Another, older boy answered for him: "How he gon be on a record, talkin''bout that stupid shit?"

Greg had had enough. He shouted: *"CLIVE!"*

Except that his eyes were already open, Clive looked like a man awakened suddenly from a sound sleep. "Yeah!" he said.

"Come on! Let's get outta here!" Greg tugged at Lester's elbow again; if anything, he had gotten stiffer.

"He's not walking. We gotta carry him!"

"WHAT?"

"Can you hear? He's not *walking!* Pick up his legs!"

Greg plunged the recorder in the pocket of his jeans and grabbed his brother, who was still shouting rhymes, under the arms. Soon he was moving backward, followed by Clive, who strained with his skinny arms to hold up Lester's legs, as if he were transporting cannonballs by wheelbarrow. From the corner of his eye, Greg could see the younger kids following them, dancing to Lester's rhymes:

*Sister moved into the big room, to the SMALL room I went*

*Then the big room was the guest room, where my SISter was sent*
*When she came home for a visit, after SHE moved away*
*Brother moved down to the basement, on a COLD winter day*
Clive said, "Whadda y'all been feedin' this boy, rocks?"
"Just keep moving!"
They made it back around the corner, to the top of the grass hill, before Clive's arms gave out. "Man, I can't do it no more."
Between heavy breaths, shouting to be heard above his brother, Greg said, "Okay. Go get the car. I'll get him to the bottom of the hill. Meet us down there."
"How you gon do *that?*"
"Just go!"
Clive shot Greg a doubtful glance, then took off at a jog down through tall grass. Greg heard a girl say "Where they come from?" as he bent low in front of his still-rapping brother, hooked an elbow around each thigh, and put him over his right shoulder. In this way, the two descended the hill. They were about halfway down when Lester's rap stopped abruptly. At the same time, his body relaxed, all at once, like that of a boxer floored by a single punch. The sudden redistribution of weight upset Greg's balance, and he fell backward, Lester landing on top of him.
"God fuckin' damn!" Drenched by now in perspiration, feeling the itch of dry grass against his wet skin, afraid of what he might be lying on, Greg pushed upward with all his strength, bringing the two of them to their feet. Arms around each other's waists, they continued down the hill, Greg's heart exploding at regular intervals. Near the bottom Greg saw, felt, something move in a gray blur over the tops of his sneakers; it was gone by the time he figured out what it was and hollered "Aaaaahhhh!" Just then he saw Clive driving toward them. He grabbed Lester's wrist and ran for the white car as if it were Noah's ark, heading out into the rising water without them.

*   *   *   *

Five minutes later, with the car stopped at a light, Clive was the first to speak. "Well, this is one afternoon I won't forget."
"That's at least two of us," Greg said from the back, where he sat

next to Lester. His heartbeat had returned to normal, and the breeze from the open driver's-side front window had dried the perspiration covering his upper body; he felt human again. His disappointment and embarrassment had gone, too, driven away — at least for the time being — by his relief at having escaped something worse, though he wasn't sure what.

Clive said, "Did you record anything?"

"Nah." The question, though, reminded him of the cassette recorder bulging in the pocket of his jeans, and more to occupy his hands than anything else, the same way he might pick at a callus on his palm or crack his knuckles, he pulled out the recorder. To his surprise, the small red light was on, and the tape was rolling. "Hey, I *did* record something! I don't even remember pressing the button!"

"You musta done it in all the excitement and forgot about it. Or else you didn't know you were doin' it. Play it back and see what's on it."

"I gotta rewind it. It'll take a minute."

"Yeah … man, all this running around the projects got me hungry. Let's go to Kim's."

At Kim's Greg and Clive bought steak and cheese sandwiches and Cokes, and the three of them sat in the back at the single table, where Greg passed some of his food to his brother. "All right. Ready to hear the hit song by the new rap sensation?"

"Hit it."

Greg pressed "play." With surprising clearness came the words:

> *Twelve years later Sister said, "This room is TOO small for me."*
> *Daddy said, "Move to the basement." Sister SAID, "But you see,*
> *Basement's dusty musty smelly, it's no PLACE for a girl."*
> *Brother said, "Then I'll move down there. It will BE my New World."*

Greg watched Lester as Lester's voice blared from the little device; except for the motions of his jaws as he chewed, his face was motionless — he might have been hearing a radio weather report. After the word "world" came a sound like that of a heavy object being dragged over rocks (actually the sound of Greg stuffing the recorder into his pants pocket), followed by silence.

As Greg turned off the recorder, Clive shook his head slowly.

"Man, I swear, if I hadn't been there myself, I wouldn't have believed it. Nineteen years he doesn't say a word, and then —" He shot a nervous glance at Lester, then turned back to Greg and laughed nervously. "*Damn*, I'm so used to talking in front of Lester like he can't hear, but ..."

"Something else just hit me," Greg said. "What he said about all of us changing rooms — I had forgot most of that stuff, but he's exactly right. *Exactly*. Plus — that thing about me saying the basement was my 'new world?' When I first moved down there I kept saying I was like Columbus going to the New World —"

"I kind of remember that," Clive said. "Right when we were first hanging out."

"—Well, *I* had forgot all *about* it. Till now." Greg turned to his brother again. "Damn, Lester. You're like a *human* tape recorder."

"A griot," Clive said.

They ate for a minute in silence. Then Greg heard *Rapper's Delight* playing near the front of the store. He looked up to see a young man with a boom box.

"I'm having some bad déjà vu. That's that same dude that was in here yesterday."

"Uh-oh," Clive said. "What's he gonna inspire you to do this time?"

"Not a damn thing. I learned my lesson."

"Well, hey — Edward said you could try socially conscious rap, or love rap. You still got love to try."

While Clive laughed, Greg seemed to have been struck by an idea. "Love," he said. He added, smiling now, "L-O-V-E."

# —SIX—

As Saturday night fell on the Hobbs household, its members were scattered among the various rooms. From his bed, Lester watched *The Love Boat* on his small black-and-white television; on *his* bed, Pat read a *Post* editorial while his wife, next to him, worked the *TV Guide* crossword puzzle; in the basement, Greg's eyes wandered from his economics textbook; and on the living room sofa, Sherrie read *Atlas Shrugged*.

The telephone rang. A few seconds later, to Sherrie's surprise, her father shouted, "Sherrie, it's for you." She went to the kitchen phone.

"Sheridan."

"Yes, this is — *Oscar?*"

"Yeah. How you doing?"

"Fine. How'd you get the number here?"

"The operator. I remembered your father's name. Hope you don't mind me calling."

"…"

In the basement, for the third time that day, Greg called Gina on his private phone. He expected the deep-voiced man to answer again, and was surprised when a soft female voice said, "Hello?"

"Hello, can I speak to Gina?"

"This is she."

"Oh — hey. This is Greg."

"Who? — *Oh.* Hi."

"That's more *like* it."

Laughter. "I'm sorry. I didn't recognize your voice on the telephone."

"We'll have to do something about that."

"Did you call before?"

"Yeah. This afternoon."

"Oh, okay. My father said somebody called."

"So that was your father. That's a relief."

"Why? Who'd you think it was?"

"You know — boyfriend. Husband."

"I don't have a husband."

"How 'bout a boyfriend?"

"Well ... not to speak of."

"'Not to speak of?'" Chuckle. "What's that mean — some poor guy's out there thinking he's your boyfriend, not knowing he's 'not to speak of'?"

"You want to plead his case for him? You're a good sport."

"Not *that* good. I was thinking about pleading *my* case for *me.*"

"And what's your case?"

"Well ... I'd like to see you, sometime when we're not rushing to class or the library."

"What did you have in mind?"

"How 'bout if I take you to dinner? Maybe a movie? What are you doing tomorrow night?"

"I was going to study for finals. Don't you have to?"

"Yeah. I like to mix a little pleasure in with my work, though. To reward myself."

"Can I let you know tomorrow?"

"Yeah, okay." Chuckle. "Gotta check in with Mr. Not to Speak Of?"

"No, I don't."

"So how come he's not to speak of? I want to know so I can avoid the same thing."

A pause, followed by: "If you really want to know, he's charming. Handsome. Smart. Funny —"

"No wonder he's in the doghouse."

Laughter. "All that kind of blinded me for a while to the fact that he's really selfish. I blame it on him being an only child."

"Hmmm … what are you? How many brothers and sisters you got?"

"I have two sisters. I'm the oldest."

"*Really.*"

"You sound surprised."

"Nah, you just — don't seem like an older sister."

"Why? What's an older sister seem like?"

"You know … thinks she's right all the time. Serious all the time. No sense of humor. Like *my* sister."

"Maybe there are things about your sister you don't know. Maybe other people see her differently."

———————————

"Maybe I shouldn't have called. I know you said you'd be back tomorrow. I just got worried. You seemed pretty grim when you left."

"Oh, that's … sweet," Sherrie said. "No, it's okay. Everything's fine — well, mostly."

"You don't have to tell me about it right now — I mean, you don't have to tell me. I'm happy to listen, of course."

"I can tell you about it … I'll be back, um, tomorrow night."

"Maybe I can come by."

"Yeah …"

A pause, followed by Sherrie's asking: "So, how are you? Anything going on there?"

"Nothing much. Graded a lot of homework today. Saw my brother this afternoon. You know I told you we're supposed to be planning this party for my parents' anniversary. Well, my brother was supposed to do all this calling and finding out about prices, but he can't hold up his end of anything. I had to kind of tell him about himself."

"How did he take it?"

"About like I expected: he got all defensive. That's him, though. Won't take anything seriously, then when you call him on it, he gets serious and then some."

"Sounds like a pain."

"Yeah."

"Sounds like Greg. It's frustrating, because he'll joke around and shift all the responsibility for being serious onto me, like with what happened this weekend — and when I *do* take on the role he's forced me into, he accuses me of acting like his mother."

"What're you gonna do. You pick your friends, not your relatives."

"So true."

Silence.

"Well … I'll let you go. I'll talk to you tomorrow evening."

"Okay."

"I miss you."

" … "

––––––––––––––

"I don't know how other people see her. Whenever *I* see her, she acts like she knows everything. She'd jump off the Washington Monument before she'd admit she didn't know what to do. Till this weekend, anyway. This one thing happened that freaked the whole family out, but it was almost worth it to see the look on her face. That was some funny shit — excuse me. Anyway, I won't go into that. …"

"Well, I'll let you know about tomorrow, okay?"

"Solid."

––––––––––––––

"Pat," Madelyn said, putting down her *TV Guide*.

"Humph … ?"

"Do you ever feel like you love one of the children more than the others?"

Following a long pause: "Why?"

"Don't you have an answer?"

"A good lawyer never asks a question without already knowing the answer, or answers one without knowing why he's being asked."

"Pat, I'm serious."

"Can't you tell me why you want to know?"

Following a long pause: "Do you remember when we went to see those first doctors about Lester?"

"Seems to me I do."

"Pat."

"I'm sorry."

"When they told us Lester would never be normal, I was so devastated. But I adjusted to it, and after a long time it occurred to me: in a way, this is what every mother wants, in a corner of her heart. A baby who won't stop being a baby. I already had two normal, healthy children, and now, if I could just see how lucky I was, I had a special gift. A child who wouldn't stop needing me. And now he's gone too. Now that he's started talking. I feel like I lost him twice."

"He still needs you. We just don't know how, yet. But we have to figure it out. That's what I've been thinking: all this is for a reason. We just have to figure out what it is."

— — — — — — — — — — — —

A sigh from Oscar.

"Oscar—"

"No, I'm — it's —"

"I haven't had a *chance* to miss you, okay? There's been a lot going on here."

"I know. Well, actually, I don't know, since you haven't told me what."

"*Oscar.* I don't … I don't always want to feel pressure to say things, okay? That kind of relationship makes me uncomfortable."

"Well, I'm feeling kind of uncomfortable myself. I don't know where I stand with you. We talk, and it's nice, but some things you just won't say anything about. You let me kiss you, but that's all, and I better not get carried away even with *that*. What is our relationship, Sheridan? Are we friends? Am I your boyfriend?"

"Oscar, it takes time to — build up — trust, and comfort, okay?"

"*Time?* How much time? I've *put in* my time —"
"*Put in your time?* You make it sound like —"
"That's not what I meant. But you know what I mean."

– – – – – – – – – – –

In the moments following his conversation with Gina, full of energy that had no focus, full of happiness that had no explanation he could name, Greg paced the basement, his thick fingers interlocked behind his head. Gina had a boyfriend, but wasn't happy with him — maybe Greg could be her boyfriend, too soon to tell — might see her tomorrow night, might not — ohhhh …

As he calmed down, he came to a stop in front of one of the bookshelves in the corner, where his eye fell on *Macbeth*. Remembering that Clive was reading another Shakespeare play, Greg idly fished the paperback, which he had last touched in high school, from the crowded shelf. He opened it to a page whose corner had been turned down, and read:

> *Tomorrow, and tomorrow, and tomorrow*
> *Creeps in this petty pace from day to day*
> *To the last syllable of recorded time,*
> *And all our yesterdays have lighted fools*
> *The way to dusty death. Out, out, brief candle!*
> *Life's but a walking shadow, a poor player*
> *That struts and frets his hour upon the stage*
> *And then is heard no more. It is a tale*
> *Told by an idiot, full of sound and fury,*
> *Signifying nothing.*

As he read the passage, Greg had two sensations, the first surprising to him, the other unsettling. When he was in tenth grade, each of Shakespeare's words had seemed to him like a large, bitter, throat-clogging pill he was being forced to swallow; but now, unless he was crazy, they made sense, just a little, and what was more, they had a kind of … sad beauty to them. What unsettled him, though, was remembering Clive's comment about *Hamlet* earlier in the day: "Kind of like us, 'cept it was hundreds of years ago," or whatever he said. That comment brought to Greg's mind the image of Shakespeare, sitting down in the year sixteen-whatever to put words on paper — words Greg was standing here reading in 1979. For just a moment, this journey of words across time and space seemed as miraculous as Kirk and Spock's visits to other centuries on *Star Trek*. That moment was enough to make Greg feel light-headed. He had felt the same way once when, during an idle teenage afternoon, he repeated to himself his seldom-thought-of middle name — Christopher — until it, and all other words, seemed to him alien and meaningless, like the random sounds they once were. He closed the copy of *Macbeth* and put it back on the shelf.

He pronounced study time to be over for the night and turned on the small, black-and-white TV at the foot of his bed. There was a movie on Channel Five; Greg knew it was old, since the actor now speaking, who was very famous and up in age, if not dead, was a thin, fresh-faced young man on the screen. His character, whose suit jacket looked a size too large, whose shirt was unbuttoned at the collar, whose tie was loosened and hair mussed, seemed to be delivering a filibuster in Congress: "... Because that's what this amounts to. By gosh, it's the same as if you lined 'em up and shot 'em all. And I'm talking about the kind of people all of us know, or ought to know. Decent, hardworking, ordinary Americans, like the kind who raised you and me, Mr. Speaker. People like my Aunt Meg, who darned socks for my brother and sister and me and put hot food on the table, and — by gosh, told us when we were out of line! People like my Uncle Fred, who worked the land until his hands were callused and his back was bent and his hair was gray, growing the food that kept us and the people around us fed and healthy, and all for — for — *what?* So they can die without a penny to their names, those farmers, so their families can't afford to bury them, so they have to choose between giving a dear old man a proper funeral and eating for the next six months? Because that's what we're talking about here, Mr. Speaker. And to take away people's ability to make an honest living, and put away a little something for the day when they're too old and sick and tired to work anymore, to take away people's dreams, Mr. Speaker, why — it's un-American. Because dreams are the stuff of America. Life, liberty, and the pursuit of happiness — the chance for happiness — the dream of happiness, it's as American as —"

"Damn, *stop*," Greg said, leaning forward to change the channel. He landed on a UHF station, Channel Twenty. In spite of the snowy picture, he could make out three gunslingers standing in the middle of an unpaved street in the Old West. One of them yelled, "You in there!" The camera cut to the swing doors of a saloon; the *chink ... chink* of someone crossing a wood floor in spurs began faintly and grew louder. Then the doors were slowly pushed open by The Man Called Nothing. This was a character in a series of movies, a man of few words played by an actor of few more. The Man Called Nothing was tall and lean, with squinty eyes, square jaws covered by permanent three-day growth, a hat with a flat crown and wide, wide brim, and a thin, half-smoked cigar that seemed to be attached to the corner of his mouth. He walked with painful slowness to the middle of the street and faced the three men.

He broke the quiet with, "What?"

One of the men said: "Draw."

The movie's orchestral score, led by piercing trumpets, started in and grew gradually more insistent in volume and tempo; meanwhile, the camera cut back and forth among the three antagonists — whose hands twitched beside their holstered pistols — and The Man Called Nothing, whose arms hung naturally at his sides. The camera began to shift more quickly, the men appearing closer with each jump, until the screen was a blur of eyes and foreheads, all but one showing beads of perspiration. When the jump cuts were fastest, when the music was loudest, there was a sudden silence — and then three men, one at a time, each drew a pistol, while a fourth man, seen only from the elbows down, drew two. He fired them simultaneously, at positions of eleven and one o'clock, and two men fell dead. The two pistols moved into alignment, the left above the right, and again were fired together. A third man fell. The Man Called Nothing slowly returned his guns to his holster.

He broke the quiet with: "*Now* what?"

Greg — lying stomach-down on his bed — laughed, pounded his fist on the mattress, rolled over, and laughed some more, in a fit of ecstasy for which he had, and needed, no words.

# PART TWO

## THE FORTNIGHT

# —SEVEN—

Another participant in the great black northward migration was Dr.
George Greer's father, John. In the early 1930s John Greer hopped
a train in Mississippi, where he had been born the third of nine
children, and got off — more or less at random — in Baltimore.
There, the strapping, very dark-skinned nineteen-year-old fairly
radiated determination to make something of himself. In a time
when racial segregation dictated most people's actions like a giant
puppeteer, John Greer marched into a small, white-owned carpentry
shop, and, by acting as if he already had it, walked out with a job
as an apprentice. Two years later, having learned all he could, he set
up his own shop on the black side of town, turning it into a great
success. He then embarked on the second part of his life's plan:
raising children — preferably sons — who would, like Alexander
the Great, take up where the old man had left off in conquering the
world. For that, he would need a woman who was nice, pretty, smart
without forgetting a woman's place, and as close to white as you could
get without being the real thing. He found all of these qualities in
the eighteen-year-old Sally George, who, unlike John, had graduated
from high school.

As if nature herself could no more stand in John Greer's way than
the white carpenter or segregation could, John and Sally's marriage
did indeed produce two sons: John Jr., born in 1940, and George,

born in 1942. John Jr. and George, like their father, were tall, with coarse, kinky hair (though theirs was reddish brown); unlike him, they had light skin and delicate, almost classical features. Through his words John Greer taught his sons three things: to conduct themselves like gentlemen, to excel at whatever they put their hands to, and to pursue what they wanted to the ends of the earth. From his deeds John Jr. and George picked up a fourth lesson, which was that when the first and third came into conflict, the first could be quietly shelved.

Both boys were good athletes. While his older brother went into business, George displayed a talent for science and medicine. Their light coloring proved to be an asset in both black and white society; as for the white racism they did face, by treating it as an irritating inconvenience — equal in importance to a cloud of gnats at a picnic — rather than a crippling disability, they achieved success in their respective fields with a single-mindedness that made it look inevitable. Both brothers started families. George had been determined to find a wife as beautiful as his mother, and the woman he married, the mother of his son and daughter, nearly was. John Jr.'s wife, too, turned a few heads in her day. For many men all this would have been plenty, and indeed, for John Jr., the more morally grounded of the two brothers, it was. But George — who was, if anything, better-looking than his brother — was noticed by women of all races wherever he went, a fact that was not lost on him, and of which he was not above taking advantage. Adhering to a code that exists among some men, which counts any missed chance for a sexual conquest as a sin against the god of maleness, he followed such opportunities wherever they led, so long as his marriage and professional career were not jeopardized; even these considerations left room for quite a lot. Because it was often so easy for him, he was fascinated by any woman who seemed as if she might present a challenge.

And so, sitting one morning in his office in the Department of Neurology at Johns Hopkins University, where he was happy in his work; feeling pleased, at age thirty-seven, with such outward signs of success as his large house, good pay, prestigious title, beautiful wife, adorable children, and daily drive in a luxury car to the castle-like red-brick building where he taught; yet ready, as always, for an adventure, he was intrigued by the young black woman who appeared in his doorway. She was pretty, slender but well-built, with shoulder-length pressed hair. She showed enough deference to knock on his open door, but once he had said "Come in," she crossed the red carpeting with a confident stride — and yet with a careful, reserved look in her long, narrow eyes. This was not, Greer could see immediately, one of those timid creatures who would stand still and wide-eyed, trembling with excitement and fear, as they awaited the kill; this one would run, maybe even fight. His mind was made up even before this young lady's full lips parted to say, "Excuse me, professor, I was hoping I could ask you for advice. I'm a grad student in chemistry — my name's Sheridan Hobbs."

When she tapped on his door and Professor Greer looked up from his papers and met her gaze, Sherrie could feel an already complicated period in her life take on a new dimension. It was amazing, she would think later, how much she came to understand in that one instant, about others and herself. The reason she liked Oscar, for example, and yet doubted whether they could make it together, was her inability to imagine in his eyes the look that animated those of the man before her. Despite his smile of greeting, those deep-set eyes focused on her with a combination of ruthlessness and glee that Oscar couldn't summon in three lifetimes; something in Sherrie responded to, maybe even craved, this look and what it signaled. She had talked to Oscar about the need to build up trust, and she had wondered to herself why she didn't seem to trust him. But it was more likely herself, her attraction to Oscar, she didn't trust. By contrast, she now felt she was in the presence of a virtual force of attractiveness, one she could resist but couldn't conquer.

"Please, sit down," Dr. Greer said in his baritone, indicating the two leather chairs in front of his desk.

"Thank you. ..." She began to talk about Lester, his history, and what he had begun doing recently. As Dr. Greer listened, he leaned back in his chair with his elbows on the armrests, and his eyes narrowed slightly with professional detachment. He placed his fingertips together — showing his long, tan fingers and perfect, lozenge-shaped nails with their half-moons. When Sherrie had finished, he stared at his desktop, apparently in contemplation of what she had told him; after several moments had passed, and it began to seem that he was contemplating something else entirely, he all of a sudden looked straight at her. "How old did you say your brother is?"

"Nineteen."

"He was about four or five, you say, when he was labeled as retarded?"

"Yes."

"So that would've been in the early 1960s … and where was that done?"

"Georgetown Hospital."

He nodded slowly, again looking away from her — and then, again, shooting his eyes toward her. "That must have been strange for you. You were pretty small yourself."

"Well, I was — seven or so. I don't really remember when it first happened. Later, of course, it got a little …"

"Hard?"

"Yes. Mostly because of other people's reactions." And my parents', she thought.

"Sure. We unfortunately don't live in a society that accepts difference very well, despite what our political leaders tell us. And, of course, having to suffer through that probably made you resent your brother a little, even if you didn't want to."

A long, quiet sigh escaped from Sherrie, and with it more tension than she knew she had been feeling. "You seem to know a lot about it," she said; indeed, the warm, low, reassuring tone of his voice was making her feel as if she had come to him not about Lester but about herself.

"You observe a lot about people in this line of work," he said.

"To be honest, I thought you'd be more surprised by what I told you," Sherrie said. "Although it's a relief to find somebody who's not shocked."

"Well, Miss — Hobbs? — the brain is an amazing thing when it functions more or less normally, and when it doesn't, sometimes it's even more amazing. I know about a woman who could look at a photograph for five seconds, then tell you everything about it, down to the relative sizes of the books on the shelf behind the person in the foreground. That same woman couldn't recognize the man who showed her different photographs day after day for a month. I know," he said, smiling, "because the man was me. So — I tell you what. I'd like to examine your brother myself. In the meantime I'd like to hear more about his home environment, family life. I'm booked up today, except for lunch — maybe if you're free …"

*       *       *       *

Earlier that same Monday morning, Madelyn Hobbs sat at her dining room table with Lester across from her and an uneasy feeling deep in her stomach. With the weekend over, Sherrie back in Baltimore, Greg off at school, and Pat gone to the office, the moment was approaching when she would have to do what she'd been dreading since Friday night. It was 8:45 now, and at 9:00 Mrs. Bennett — Alma — would arrive. The seventyish Mrs. Bennett, who lived down the block, had earned pocket money for years by staying in the house with Lester at those times when no family member could. Since Lester had turned eighteen and finished with public Special Education (having earned "a degree in sitting around the house," as Greg so meanly put it once), Mrs. Bennett came on a more regular basis, so that Madelyn could keep on teaching art at various public schools. More than a neighbor; more even than an employee, since she lived only a few houses away and spent so much time in the Hobbs house; yet less than a friend or family member, Mrs. Bennett occupied a nebulous category in Madelyn's universe, one whose limits had never been tested — before now. Madelyn had given herself a number of excuses for not telephoning Mrs. Bennett over the weekend to tell her about Lester's new development, reasoning that it would be easier to explain in person, that she should let Mrs. Bennett have her weekend time to herself, etc. All the while, though, she knew the real explanation: that if Mrs. Bennett heard before Monday morning what was going on, she might not show up, and Madelyn would have to face the fact that her own life had changed, maybe temporarily, maybe for good.

Of course, the chances were fair to good that Mrs. Bennett had heard at least something already, given the visit by Floretta and Celestine and its aftermath. Not once but twice following that fiasco, the Hobbses had had visits from older neighbors, card-carrying members of the gossip network, who had obviously gotten the sisters' report either first- or second-hand. Pat and Madelyn had skipped church in order to avoid more of these people. The first visitor was at least forthright about why she had come; Madelyn politely and truthfully answered her questions about Lester, without elaborating on any points, until, after what seemed like weeks, the woman left. The second visitor got a different reception. There was something about her manner, her way of perching on the edge of the Hobbses' sofa in her Sunday finery (she had come straight from church) as she posed indirect, carefully phrased questions about Lester in her Georgia singsong, that Madelyn found infuriating. She was as short with the woman as she'd ever been in her life with anyone — anyone, that is, she hadn't married or given birth to. (Madelyn reflected afterward that she acted as Sherrie would have. Had she been influenced by her daughter's visit, or did that aspect of Sherrie come from a hidden pocket in Maddie's nature? She wondered.)

So maybe it was a good sign that Mrs. Bennett had not called Madelyn herself over the weekend; maybe she had heard about Lester's new ability but was not fazed by it. Madelyn was thinking this, draining the last, cold drops of coffee from her cup, when the doorbell rang.

It was, however, clear, from the moment Maddie opened the door and saw the usual sunny expression on her neighbor's face, that Mrs. Bennett knew nothing of what was going on. "Hello, how was your weekend?"

"Just fine," Maddie said, feeling sick. "And yours?"

"Very nice." She walked into the living room, smiled in that way that made her look five years old, and waved at Lester. "Hiiiii! How's my boy?"

"Listen, Alma, before I go …" Soon the two women were sitting on the sofa, where Maddie brought Mrs. Bennett up to date, watching her expression change from one of happiness and friendliness to one of confusion, anxiety, and dread. "… But don't worry. He hasn't been doing anything else unusual. And I'll call and check in. …" As she rose from the sofa and gathered her art materials, preparing to leave, Maddie thought she knew what an assassin or armed robber must feel right after the act: an overpowering drive to grab what you need, get away, and leave the mess, and any feelings of regret, for somebody else.

She rode the bus to Davis Elementary School. When she walked into the first-grade classroom, the teacher was in a far corner, where seven or eight boys and girls, sitting in chairs and holding books, formed a half-circle around her; the rest of the class worked at their desks. The teacher smiled at her, then went back to listening as one of the boys in the half-circle read aloud. Madelyn took art supplies from her denim handbag as the reading group finished up and carried their wooden chairs back to their desks. Sneaking glances at the children, at their gap-toothed grins or new, disproportionately large permanent teeth, at the close-cut, nubby hair of these little black boys and the brightly colored plastic barrettes in the girls' hair, Maddie remembered how she had felt on returning to work after Lester had started school: she was shocked to suddenly be around boys and girls, no bigger than Lester, who could talk, sing, and tell silly jokes; it was as if she had gone to a land where dogs could do all those things.

She stood now before a roomful of such amazing creatures, as the teacher — who was probably half Maddie's age — said, "Class, Mrs. Hobbs is here to do art with you. Remember we talked about co-op-er-a-tion? I want you to cooperate with Mrs. Hobbs." The teacher then retreated to her desk, and Maddie said, "Good morning, boys and girls. Who can tell me what *season* we're in now? Yes? … Very good. *Spring*. Today we're going to do paintings that show something about spring. Now what do you think of when you think of spring? Yes? …" Soon the children were painting pictures about their ideas of spring, while Maddie walked from desk to desk, giving praise and gentle suggestions. Of the twenty-eight or so students, probably twenty-two of them painted flowers, but some were more creative — one picture showing a boy wearing a T-shirt and a big smile as he ran with outstretched arms, another showing a man in an overcoat with big drops of perspiration leaping from his face, still another depicting a girl on a swing as a snowman melted a short distance away. Even some of the flowers were surprisingly good, but whether they were or not, Maddie loved to watch the little hands gripping the brushes, the serious looks on the faces of the boys and girls as they concentrated the way that perhaps only children can. When her teaching went well, as it often did, Maddie couldn't imagine a better way to spend her time than with these children; they, along with Lester, had allowed her to retain just a little of what it was to be a mother to the young.

It was a little after eleven o'clock, when she was walking out of the school, that Maddie turned her thoughts again to Lester — and realized as if for the first time, with the clear perspective of distance, what she had done that morning. She had left a seventy-year-old woman alone to confront a situation that had caused another person — Maddie herself — to lose consciousness, all so Maddie could spend an hour painting with children. It was true that Mrs. Bennett had been warned, as Maddie had not, about what might happen, and that there was no certainty that Lester would start shouting this morning. Still, given how frequently he had shouted since the first occasion, and the twenty-plus-years' difference between the ages of the two women, the risk seemed the same, if not greater. Poor Mrs. Bennett could be having a heart attack that very moment! There was a pay phone at the corner across the street, in front of a small grocery store; Maddie walked quickly, then ran, toward it. Heart pounding, fingers trembling, she managed to get two dimes in the slot and call her house.

"Hello?"

"Alma! It's Madelyn! Is everything okay?"

"Oh, yeah, everything's — so far, so good. Lester's quiet. I did get kind of worried, after what you told me, so I just called Henry" — her husband — "to come over and stay with me. It might take him a little while to get here, 'cause his arthritis is acting up. ..."

"Listen, Alma, I'll be there shortly. I'm going to cancel my second lesson today. I'll be there soon, okay?"

She hung up, made a second call to say she wouldn't be available for her one o'clock lesson, then walked quickly toward the bus stop. In the midst of her anxiety, her relief that nothing had gone wrong (yet), her determination to get home as quickly as possible — in the midst of all this, she perceived, as through a cloud, that something was being lost. But mercifully, for the time being, she did not have space in her head to think about it.

\* \* \* \*

Greg's Monday had started at six a.m. in the basement, a dark hour in the darkest room in the house. His radio/alarm clock, tuned to WHUR, began playing the soulful strains of Luther Vandross; he rolled over to see the red digits "6:00," surrounded by blackness, as if they were floating in outer space. The only person awake in the house, he fished for his blue bathrobe and trudged to the top floor for a shower. He was testing the water temperature, feeling it turn from cold to warm on his hand, when he remembered that he was seeing Gina tonight, and smiled.

In the shower he laughed, remembering one of Lester's rhymes from the day before. (Greg had laughed while it was happening, too, but neither his parents nor his sister had seen fit to join him.) In the living room, in that gunslinger stance of his, Lester had shouted:

> *I was sitting in the middle in the BACK of the car*
> *Daddy driving, Brother asking, "Is it GONNA be far*
> *Till we get to King's Dominion?" — where they HAD all the rides*
> *Momma said, "It's not too far," and then she ADDED, "Besides,*
> *Here's the family all together, isn't THIS the best part?"*
> *Brother's eyes began a-rollin,' and he LET out a fart*
> *Sister saying, "Oh my God, why do I HAVE to be here?"*
> *Everybody started yelling and I COVERED my ears*

After the shower he sat at the kitchen counter in his bathrobe and ate cold cereal, enjoying the quiet and semi-darkness that lay like a thin gray blanket over the first floor, which was getting its first glimpse of the sun.

Dressed in jeans, a Redskins sweatshirt, and Converse All-Stars, with a backpack slung over one shoulder, he headed for the bus. He had to leave so early because of his on-campus job: serving breakfast in the cafeteria. Hateful as it was, there had been nothing else available at the start of the semester, and the campus job was his only source of spending money. Behind the breakfast counter, in his full-length white apron and matching, disposable hat, he served pancakes or French toast, bacon or sausage, bagels, oatmeal, and sliced melon to on-campus students at their sleepiest and least attractive. To work this job, which he did from seven to nine on Monday, Wednesday, and Friday mornings, was to witness a parade, a showcase of the variety of young black America — at least the segment of it that had managed to get to college and had chosen to do so away from home. Clothes revealed a great deal, even when pulled on over uncombed and un–Afro Sheened hair. There were some, dressed neither particularly well nor especially badly, whom Greg took to be his equivalents — the children of parents who were by no means poor but far from rich. There were those who had to be scholarship students, if their two or three seam-ripped outfits were any indication. Then there was the third set, made up of young men whose jeans were more stylish than others' three-piece suits and women who paid more each year for manicures than Greg spent on shirts; they were the Howard elite, the sons and daughters of doctors and lawyers (not government lawyers, like Greg's father, but corporate attorneys and law-firm partners), who had been told all their lives that they were the princes and princesses of the race, who had been sent to this historically black university to prepare to lead their people. They seemed to like to practice their leadership on Greg, with lines like, "Give me some sausage, and don't be stingy, partner"; "Don't give me one of those *broken* pieces, sweetheart" — things that Greg couldn't imagine even Sherrie at her most stuck-up saying to anyone. Sometimes Greg shot back with "If I'm your partner, can I keep half?" or "Wouldn't dream of it, honeybunch." This morning, though, he felt too good to be bothered by it. He had a date with Gina.

\* \* \* \*

The large window of Pat Hobbs's office, in northwest Washington, gave a view of the muddy Potomac River and, beyond that, National Airport. Sometimes, when he was contemplating a legal point, Pat would turn around in his wooden swivel chair and face the window, hands clasped behind his head, or occasionally holding a Styrofoam cup of black coffee, to watch planes tilt sideways as they approached

National or rise at a steep angle as they departed. This was the part of his work he liked best: when he might have looked to an untrained eye as if he were taking a break or goofing off, but when, in reality, he was performing the meatiest part of his job, debating points with himself, clarifying issues so he could pinpoint the right course of action. In a suit brought by a disgruntled employee, should the Post Office stand firm, or should they recognize that the man had a case, and settle? Such matters were decided largely in these moments, when he was alone.

This Monday morning, though, he would not be alone. Right now, at eleven o'clock in the morning, he had his back to his window, studying the application form on his desk. Ten feet in front of him, his office door was all but closed, as part of a game he sometimes played. Except it wasn't a game.

Only the most distorted view could have made Patrick Hobbs look like a black militant. Ten years earlier, in the late 1960s, he had viewed the emergence of the Black Power movement as unnecessarily racist, as a slap in the face to the whites who had made sacrifices, sometimes of their lives, during the civil rights movement. He understood those militants' anger, of course — he felt it himself — but taking it out on all whites simply wasn't the right thing. When Sherrie, at fifteen, started wearing an Afro instead of subjecting her hair to Maddie's hot comb, Pat worried that his daughter would fall in with a bad crowd. But even in Pat there was a touch of racial rebelliousness, which took a form only he knew about. One of a half-dozen lawyers in his department, and the only black among them, Pat shared with the others the duty of interviewing potential recruits. Most of these were male and straight out of law school, and nearly all of them were white. It was when he knew they were coming to see him that Pat all but closed his door; the departmental secretary, Margie, a young white woman, had to knock before bringing them in, giving Pat time to look up before they entered; and he could then see the young men's faces when they first caught sight of his. Little did these twenty-five-year-olds know that this moment was the first obstacle they had to get over, one that disqualified many a candidate before he so much as opened his mouth. Often one of these boys, before collecting himself, would end his chances with a bug-eyed look that said, *You, a black guy, are my interviewer?* One particularly benighted young man, while shaking Pat's hand, had actually asked him, "Are you a lawyer?"

Now came the knock. Pat cleared his throat and said in his clearest, most official-sounding voice, "Come in."

"Stephen Barnes is here," Margie said, leading in a red-haired, freckled young man. This Barnes fellow made it over the hurdle, though just barely, recovering himself after a quick widening of his green eyes. (Pat could tolerate surprise from these white boys; it was disbelief that caused his blood pressure to rise.) "Hello," Pat said, shaking Barnes's hand as Margie exited quietly, "Patrick Hobbs. Pleasure to meet you. Sit down, sit down. So ..."

Now came the choreographed dance. Pat asked Barnes what interested him about working for the Postal Service, already knowing the answer, which was the same for any applicant: he had been smart enough to make it through law school but had not finished high enough in his class to get a second glance from Covington & Burling, or Kirkland & Ellis, or any of the other top D.C. firms. No one could say this, of course, and so Pat paid attention not to the truthfulness but to the creativity of the answers. Like Madelyn's first-grade painters with their spring flowers, most candidates came up with the same response, and this Barnes was no exception; so Pat listened with one ear as Barnes went on about his desire to serve the country by seeking government work — as if representing the Postal Service in suits brought by employees and wrangling with the Postal Rate Commission over the price of stamps were the acts of a Man of the People, a Martin Luther King for the 1970s. When Barnes had finished, Pat gave his usual description of the projects he might work on if hired as a member of the postal legal team: things related to the Freedom of Information Act, the Private Express Statute, and all the rest. After that he shook the young man's hand, showed him out, and returned to his desk to fill out the post-interview form, on which he neither took Barnes out of the running nor gave him a ringing endorsement. He put the completed form in his "out" box, making this one matter, at least, someone else's problem.

\*     \*     \*     \*

At three-thirty, when his last class was over, Greg headed home. After mumbling hello to his mother, who was alone in the living room, looking glum, he went straight to the basement. There, he put an Earth, Wind & Fire album on his turntable and lay on his back on the bed, mellowing to the sounds. When he was good and relaxed, he got up to get ready, taking a shower, slapping on some cologne, and putting on black pants, his best leather shoes, and his one and only silk shirt. He mumbled "See you later" to his mother and literally had one foot out the door when he heard Lester's rapping begin from upstairs; he paused for the briefest of moments, then kept going.

\*  \*  \*  \*

"... The closest sister to me just started at UDC this year, and my youngest sister's still in high school," Gina was saying, over dinner in a booth at a restaurant on F Street, downtown.

Greg wasn't listening. Because he had spent so much more time thinking about Gina than talking with her in person, her features had taken on an appearance in his mind that didn't correspond to reality. He was now distracted by contemplating the differences between the real Gina and the one who had set up residence in his head. The actual woman's features were softer, less sharply defined than those of her counterpart, more spread out over the reddish-brown skin of her round face; but she was just as short, cute and elfin. When Greg realized he wasn't taking in her words, he paid attention so as not to miss anything he would be faulted later for not knowing. He did it just in time.

" ... So then my mother died —"

"*Oh*. How old were you?"

"Fourteen."

"Wow. Sorry."

"Thanks. So after that, I really had to be the 'responsible' one. I already was, but now the pressure was on. You know, my sisters would fall apart, or just get crazy — once in a while they still do — and I'd have to help my dad pull them back together, but once in a while I'd be like, 'Well, who's pulling *me* back together'? My poor dad — he tried hard. He still does. But sometimes it's just more than he can handle."

Greg laughed. "My dad's tombstone'll probably say that."

"Why do you say that?"

"Well — my younger brother's — retarded. And mute. But ... well, I'll get to that later. Not that you'll believe it. Anyway, my mom, she's mostly cool, but once in a while her feelings about it just get the best of her, but my *dad*, it's like he tries so hard to do and say the right thing that half the time he just won't do or say anything at all. So you've got my mom being hysterical on one side, and my dad not doing a thing on the other."

"He never loses control?"

"My dad? Losing control? I don't even know what that would mean."

"So how many other siblings do you have?"

"One sister. She's two years older than me."

"So do you two bond over all that?"

"Nooooo, not really. You'd think so, but ... we just have two different ways of dealing with things. Me, I gotta laugh at stuff sometimes. Sherrie, she's just serious about everything."

"Yeah, I guess you mentioned that the other night. I have to admit, when I first met you I thought all you *did* was joke. But you're not like that."

"Well ... anyway, I didn't mean to cut you off." He noticed that she smiled when he said that. "How'd your mom die?"

"She had bone cancer."

"Damn, that's rough. Was it quick, or did it take a long time?"

"It was pretty quick."

"Guess that's better in a way, huh? They don't suffer as much. But maybe you didn't feel like you had enough time with her at the end."

Gina shifted her gaze from one of his eyes to the other, then back again. "You're not like I first thought you were at all."

\* \* \* \*

Pat left his office at five o'clock and walked to the L'Enfant Plaza Metro station. Since the previous Friday, his thoughts had fallen into two categories: Lester and non-Lester; and as his body performed the routine motions of waiting for the Blue Line train, boarding, riding two stops to Metro Center, and walking upstairs for the Red Line, his mind, the whole time, was on Lester. What had happened still seemed so unreal to Pat that part of his mind wouldn't accept it; he tried to take it in completely, but without success, as if it were small, far-away print that his aging eyes couldn't quite focus on, despite all his concentration. At the same time, he wondered, with a mix of fascination and unease, what *else* his boy would begin doing. Then there was the effect that all of it was having, and might have, on Maddie. Whenever he thought of that, part of Pat wanted to leave wherever he was, run to his wife, and hold her in his arms; another part wanted to be on one of the planes he could see from his office as it took off from National Airport.

Pat had always, of course, struggled to get his footing where developments with Lester — and his wife's reactions to them — were concerned. His struggle was much like that moment on the dance floor when a person pauses to find the beat so he can move to the music; only for Pat the moment had lasted two decades. The beat kept changing on him. And maybe, he feared, he had no rhythm.

Not that he didn't try. How he had tried, over the years. In the period after Lester was pronounced to be retarded, when Maddie went into her depression — which may have lasted six weeks but was more like two years in his memory — Pat had drawn on reserves he didn't know he had, had become himself *plus* his wife. While Maddie alternated between sitting around crying and just sitting around, looking as if she had died with her eyes open, Pat made sure Greg and Sherrie got ready for school on time, arranged a daytime sitter for Lester and drove him there in the mornings, put in a full day at work, picked Lester up in the evenings, cooked dinner, washed the dishes, put the children to bed, tried not to fall asleep over the work he had brought home, and was so reassuring with his daughter and elder son that sometimes he nearly convinced *himself* that everything would be okay. He even ducked out of work now and then, for school conferences and performances; if his supervisor at the time hadn't been so understanding, Pat might have ended up stocking shelves at the Giant for a living. It was hard. Sometimes at the end of the day he was so tired that he had to persuade himself to remove his clothes before getting into bed.

What got Pat through it all was his love for his wife, love that was like an overflowing river, in which, here and there — like dead dogs or uprooted trees — could be seen spots of real anger at her. But he tried not to feel angry. God had sent him this pretty, loving woman, and it would be wrong to back away from the challenges that came with this gift — mainly, her fragility. Pat had once thought to himself that his wife was like a pond with a thin covering of ice: her surface was bright, reflecting the sun, but put too much weight on it, and … Of course, given the circumstances she had come from, the miracle was that the surface was intact. It was Pat's job, he knew, to keep it that way.

As for Pat's feelings toward Lester during that time, he wasn't aware of having any. His son was like an object whose presence he had to take into account, but to which he gave no other thought — sort of like the net in a tennis game. That was true, anyway, until one Saturday night. Long after he'd put the kids to bed, when he was ready to head there himself, he went to Greg and Lester's doorway to listen for the sound of their breathing. He did this every night, pausing just a moment outside each room to make sure his children were still alive before he went to sleep. This night, though, he lingered in the boys' doorway, leaning against the jamb, staring into the dark room, and thought, with no emotion, as if he were musing about a theoretical figure and not his own son, *It would be so quick, so simple. A pillow, held firmly and quickly over his face, just for a minute or two* … Then he considered what had just gone through his mind, and he knew it was time to have a talk with his wife.

Maybe it was the look on his face as he walked into his and Maddie's bedroom. Maybe it was just a one-in-ten-thousand coincidence that their moods shifted at the exact same time. Whatever the explanation, when he looked toward the bed, expecting to see the same pretty but vacant-eyed woman who had slept and wept next to him for the past few weeks, he found in her place his long-lost wife. "Oh, Pat," she said, reaching up from the bed, cupping his cheek in her warm hand, "You're working so hard. But I'm going to help you now. You've been carrying us all. But you don't have to anymore. Oh, sweet Pat."

And Pat, who had been robbed of the opportunity to act on his resolve, who felt an inexpressible sense of relief — Pat, who had not had sex in recent memory — put his mouth on his wife's. Before he had time for another thought, they were in a clutch, squeezing each other, rolling around together as if moved by a force stronger than the two of them together. In his life, Pat had made love a few times each to a handful of women, and he had made love innumerable times with his wife, but never, with any of them, had he known a session like this — which combined the sheer ardor of their newlywed days with their decade of sexual knowledge of each other. (For years after that night, Pat hoped for a return of that intensity, before concluding that some things in one's life will not be repeated, that one should be grateful that they had happened at all. It was around the time he reached this conclusion that he began thinking of himself as middle-aged.)

In the meantime, though, Maddie became her old self, with new energy and affection. The lion's share of that affection seemed to be directed at Lester; it was like a rain cloud that burst directly over Lester's head, getting the rest of the family damp but drenching her youngest child. Pat was so relieved at the change, so happy to see Maddie being a mother again, that when it came to tending to the children, he himself pulled back — a little too far. The one good result was that the distance allowed him to regain his own affection for Lester: watching the vaguely bewildered look on the boy's face as Maddie suddenly slathered herself on him touched a place in Pat's heart. But turning so much of parenthood over to his wife had other consequences, too.

One memory from that time still made Pat wince. It was evening, and the family was having dinner. As usual, one of Pat's jazz records was playing. Pat, as usual, sat at one end of the table, Maddie at the other; on the sides, to Pat's left and right, respectively, were Sherrie and Greg; at a curve of the oval table, between Maddie and Greg, sat the five-year-old Lester, who was attempting to feed himself spaghetti and meatballs with a fork, while Maddie leaned toward him, offering advice and encouragement like a combination mother and Olympic coach. Between intermittent conversation about school, to which Maddie seemed largely oblivious, nine-year-old Sherrie ate quietly, with her head down; meanwhile, the cooing from Maddie drew looks of disgust from seven-year-old Greg.

What brought things to a head was Maddie's gentle determination to have Lester get a whole forkful of spaghetti, just one, in his mouth — with none staying behind on the fork, falling back to the plate, or decorating Lester's face. Since Lester responded to only a few words, Maddie used her own fork to mime the act of eating as she kept up her patter: "Okay, *that* was pretty good — just a little bit left on your lip — let me dab that for you — now just chew that up, and get some more — not too much — *that's* a good boy — okay, almost. One more time" — all this while stroking Lester's arm, hair, shoulder. Finally, it looked as if Lester was about to get in a whole forkful with no mess. That was when Greg banged Lester's knee with his own. The spaghetti fell back to the plate, with just a little sauce clinging to Lester's lips.

Lester bore this stoically; his mother did not. Her reaction was instantaneous and severe — and seemed to have been inspired by an introductory journalism course. "WHAT is wrong with you? WHY did you do that? HOW would you like it if somebody was mean to you when you were trying your best to learn something? WHO do you think you are? ... WHERE do you get off ... WHEN did you become so..." Pat understood why Greg had kneed his brother, and he could see that the boy regretted the act as soon as he'd done it. A short reprimand, and a call for an apology, would have sufficed. But Maddie seemed unable to rein herself in. Greg looked toward Pat, in a mute appeal for help, and a word from Pat might indeed have brought the tongue-lashing to a stop; but he hesitated. Criticize her mothering, the thin, frayed rope by which she was pulling herself out of the abyss? He didn't dare risk it. And so he kept quiet, fishing around for the newspaper, until Greg ran from the table in tears, Sherrie quietly asked to be excused, and Maddie went back to helping Lester eat.

Now Pat got off the Metro at the Brookland station and walked to the barbershop on 12th Street. As usual, the little three-chair shop was full, and as usual, Jake, the proprietor, waved Pat immediately to his chair, most of the men having come only to talk.

"Whatcha know, Thurgood?" Jake said. The fiftyish, powerful-looking but jovial Jake, who had been cutting Pat's hair for about ten years, had been calling him "Thurgood" for perhaps five, since Pat let slip that he was a lawyer.

"Nothin' worth tellin'," Pat said, climbing into the chair. As Jake's expertly snapped white cloth settled over him, like a parachute reaching the ground, Pat picked up on the conversation among the middle-aged-to-elderly black men:

"That's what's wrong wit' your people, man. How you expect your kids to get somewhere in the world when you give 'em names like that? Saw a gal yesterday walkin' wit' her little boy, and he was walkin' too slow, and the gal said, 'Come on, La King.' What the hell kinda name is that? Show up lookin' for a job and tell the man your name is 'La King,' and see how long it take him to shut the door in your face."

"Shoot, at least 'king' *means* some'm. I see people out here just make up *any*thing and give it to their kids for a name. Heard one the other day — *Rajarria*. Don't even ask me to spell it."

"Well, look here, though — ain't all names made up? And all *words*, too? Why is this called a shoe?"

"Hell yeah, they made up, but they made up wit' a *system*. Why you think some words sound the same in other languages? Like 'one' and 'uno,' and what's the French — uh — *ooooon* ...'"

"Yeah, but *why?* Tell me that."

A man who had not yet spoken said quietly, yet with perfect timing, so that his words came in a brief moment between one near-shout and what would have been another: "They have the same Latin root."

This silenced everyone — until someone else said, "But where'd the *root* come from?" Then the arguing was back on. It was still going strong when Pat, chuckling, left the shop.

From there it was three blocks to his house. The first thing he heard when he opened the door was Lester's shouting from upstairs; the first thing he saw was the face of his wife, who was standing between the living room and the front hall, having gotten up to greet him. Her expression was one Pat had come to know well over the years: a closed-mouth smile, an attempt at good cheer, overwhelmed by her furrowed brow and moist eyes. "Oh, Pat," she said, burying herself in his embrace. Pat drew her closer and thought, briefly, of the plane taking off from National Airport.

*       *       *       *

When Greg had paid for dinner, he and Gina walked two blocks in the fading sunlight to a movie house farther down on F Street. In the darkness of the half-full theater, as they watched *Kramer vs. Kramer*, Greg encountered the hand-holding dilemma; should he take Gina's hand boldly and risk being thought too forward, or should he wait, and risk her losing interest? A tough checkpoint guard, the hand-holding dilemma had turned back many an inexperienced or timid fellow, but Greg, at twenty-one, had experience on his side — a big part of it gained by accident. He had first taken a girl to the movies when he was fifteen, but it was a year, a couple of girls, a great deal of uncertainty, and several half-watched movies later that he made his discovery. His date that fall evening was a moderately pretty, curvaceous girl named Veronica. Before the movie they went to McDonald's, where Greg tried hard but without success to sustain a conversation; he drew so few words out of Veronica, so few changes of expression even, that by the time they were finished eating he had begun to wonder why she had agreed to go out with him. During the movie, which she seemed to find as crushingly dull as she found Greg, she adopted the pose of one so bored that she no longer tries to hide it: she leaned away from him, left elbow on the armrest, head resting sideways in her left palm. Greg, who had by now given up all thoughts of romance, merely wanted to salvage *something*, some human connection, from their evening together. To that end he put his arm around the back of her chair and, with his index finger, tugged at the cuff of her blazer — thinking he would pull the support from under her head and unsettle her just enough to provoke a playful slap, or something. What happened instead surprised him. Veronica's head stayed for a moment more or less where it was, before straightening up; meanwhile, her hand, which Greg had yanked sideways, fell on top of his, and their fingers interlaced. Emboldened, he took her other hand, then tried something else, too — and soon, as who knows what was happening on the screen, she was kissing him as if he had just come home from the war. Later, at her house, he came closer to actual sex than he ever had before. And if he didn't get his first taste of sex that evening, he came away with something more valuable in the long run: the understanding that with girls, what seems to be lack of interest is not always lack of interest, and even when it is, sometimes it can be overcome; and that sometimes a girl is just as willing as a boy is, provided the boy is bold enough to make a move.

And so, five years later, finding himself at the movies with Gina, recalling the lesson taught him by his younger self, Greg made a gentle but unmistakeable motion, taking hold of Gina's small, warm hand. She willingly intertwined her fingers with his, and he felt happiness spread from his core.

Leaving the theater, they talked about the movie while walking hand-in-hand toward the Metro Center stop, where they would go in opposite directions. Following a pause, she said, "So you never told me the big thing that's been happening with your brother. You kind of mentioned it a couple of times, but …"

They had come to the corner of 13th and G Streets, northwest, where a low, square white wall surrounded the top of the escalators leading down to the Metro. It was dark now; few people were on the street. Gina stopped, her back to the low wall, and Greg stood facing her. "No, I guess I didn't," Greg said.

Smiling, Gina said, "Don't trust me, huh?"

"It's not that. I just want you to trust *me*. It's the kind of thing, if you hear it from somebody you don't know too well, you might think they're crazy."

"Well, maybe I have to work on knowing you."

They could see each other's eyes by the light of a streetlamp — a yellow that seemed to break apart at the edges, just beyond where they stood, like the cuff of a favorite old sweater, a dull glow that swelled and brightened now and again with the headlights of a passing car or bus. A passenger on one of the buses would have seen a man and a woman kissing. The man had lost all sense of time; he was aware only of the woman's mouth, its deliciousness. At some point the woman wiggled her tongue, bouncing it like a pinball off the corners of the man's mouth, and in his delight he laughed — and soon they were laughing together for a moment, their lips less than an inch apart. Then they went back to kissing, holding each other tenderly, in that space of light that soon gave way to darkness.

# —EIGHT—

Greg told Gina over dinner that his sister was "serious about everything," which was almost accurate, but not quite. There is nothing, for example, to prevent a person with no sense of rhythm from dancing; that person simply does not dance very well. And while Sherrie, it is true, had a limited sense of humor and tended to avoid situations that called for jokes, she appreciated the *idea* of humor, and on very, very rare occasions she even tried to practice it.

Because Sherrie was uncomfortable making or responding to jokes, her romances tended to be with men who did not value that ability highly — men whose view of jokes was that they were meant for those hours after the important things had been done, hours that always seemed, like the horizon, to be off in the distance. (Such men usually had a take-charge approach to life, which Sherrie liked.) But in many stable relationships humor serves much the same purpose as axle grease, allowing the various parts to work with a minimum of friction and unpleasant noise. When humor was missing, as it frequently was, from Sherrie's relationships, she felt uncomfortable, even more than she realized — especially in the aftermath of serious talks, when she longed for the man to help smooth the transition back to normal interaction. And so there were times when Sherrie, to whom humor was like a foreign language, could relax completely with a man only if he knew how to laugh, and on those occasions she might even try joking herself.

Such a man was the decidedly not-take-charge Oscar. Sherrie had had dinner in a restaurant with him a few nights before Lester's big change. For several minutes over spaghetti and wine she described the usefulness of X-ray crystallography in determining the structures of toxins and opiates, only half-aware that Oscar's eyes were glazing over.

Oscar said at one point, "What's an opiate?"

"It's in your brain. It helps you calm down, rest, go to sleep."

"Oh." He smiled. "Are you an opiate?"

She smiled and slapped his arm. "I know why you became a teacher. So you could spend time with people as silly as you are. I bet that's what your kids call you: the Silly Man. They should make a movie about you called 'The Silly Man.' I bet instead of high school you went to silly school. You should change your name from 'Oscar' to 'Silly.'"

Through most of this Oscar looked at her with a smile frozen on his face, the expression of a person trying to hide the pity he is feeling; but with every sentence out of Sherrie's mouth he felt his smile weakening. Finally, unable to keep it up any longer, he began to laugh at her, managing to say, before he completely lost control: "Are those supposed to be *jokes?*" Sherrie joined in, happy though feeling a touch of embarrassment — just enough to fuel her laughter.

Sometimes when Sherrie wondered whether she and Oscar could possibly make it together, she reflected that the next man she became seriously involved with, if it wasn't Oscar, would have to have a comparable sense of humor. And so, at the very beginning of her interaction with Dr. George Greer, she was attuned to signs of it. She was of two minds about the matter. Part of her hoped that he had a sense of humor, since she was attracted to the rest of him; another part of her hoped he didn't, for the very same reason. Dr. Greer, a take-charge man if ever she had laid eyes on one, might try to take charge of *her* a little too much; and evidence of a lack of humor would help her resist that — and him.

She had had lunch with him, at a diner on the edge of the Johns Hopkins campus, to talk about Lester.

"So you said your brother was labeled retarded," Greer said, spearing salad with a fork as they sat by the window on that bright afternoon. "What's his personality like? Does he have one? I mean, when he's not shouting rhymes?"

Sherrie smiled. "Well … yes, he does. You'd probably have to have lived with him to know it, but he does. I mean, mostly he just sits around, maybe doing a simple jigsaw puzzle or watching TV, but he does respond to things. In subtle ways. Sometimes he chuckles at a cartoon or something silly on TV. If he's in pain, or sick, he cries, quietly — tears just roll down his cheeks, but he doesn't make much noise otherwise. One time — this was sweet — my mother told me that one day after I went away to college, she found Lester just staring at my picture that was on a table in the living room, and just crying to himself."

"Hmm. Does he show any other negative emotion? Ever get frustrated, angry?"

"I have to say he doesn't. The only time I've ever seen him look angry was when he started shouting rhymes."

"And did he attend — what, a school for special students?"

"Yes. Through the D.C. public schools."

"As far as you know, did they have any insights into his personality?"

"I don't think so. They just kind of babysat him, as far as I could tell."

"And so the last professional diagnosis took place when he was four or five?"

"Yes."

He gazed at her, nodding almost imperceptibly, eyes slightly narrowed, as he chewed the last of what was in his mouth. Then he said, "I'd definitely like to examine your brother. Do you think we could set something up for later in the week — or even on the weekend, if that's more convenient?"

"I'll — certainly check with my parents."

"I'll tell you what else. I'd like to see *you* again. How about having dinner with me?"

There had been a subject working its way from the depths of Sherrie's mind to the surface, but it was only with this invitation to dinner that it broke through. Those six words spoken aloud — *How about having dinner with me?* — spurred four others in her head: *He must be married.* A quick glance at his fine, manly hands and the broad gold band on his left ring finger confirmed that he was. This gave her pause. Sherrie was not someone who could enter into — *adultery*, it seemed that was the word — without rousing her conscience. At the same time, the rule against it was, for her, just that — a rule, not a heartfelt conviction; its power came more from her having heard it all her life than from a horror of violating the sanctity of marriage or of hurting another woman, who, after all, might never know. If Dr. Greer's wedding ring had been the first thing Sherrie had seen when she met him, before her attraction to him had formed, things might be different at this moment. But now it would take much, much more effort to backtrack than simply to do what she was about to do. Which was how she came to say, "That sounds nice."

"Are you free tomorrow night?"

"Well — as free as I ever am, with all the work I've got."

"I understand the chemistry comes first. But, uh," he grinned, "maybe we can make a little chemistry of our own."

She smiled at this leaden joke, while sighing inwardly: did this mean he had a sense of humor?

The results of that lunch conversation: Sherrie telephoned her mother, who, unable to teach now, was free to bring Lester to Baltimore on Friday to be examined; and Dr. Greer — "call me George" — was coming to Sherrie's apartment this evening, Tuesday, to take her to dinner. She was standing in front of the mirror in her bedroom, putting in an earring while studying the reflection of her white blouse and just-below-knee-length blue skirt, when her phone rang. With an uneasy feeling she went to the living room to answer it. Her fears were confirmed.

"Hi, Oscar." She had not spoken to him since their telephone argument the previous Saturday.

"Hey. Listen, I felt bad about our last conversation."

"Oh — that's okay. I'm sorry, too. I didn't mean to hurt your feelings."

"No, it's fine. I've just got to learn not to — well, I won't go into it now. I was wondering if I could make it up to you. I know you're working, but how 'bout if I take you out for dessert later? Might make a good study break for you."

"Oh — well — I — I really shouldn't, Oscar. I've got so much to do. Can I take a rain check? For sometime this week, maybe?"

"Okay," Oscar said genially and, Sherrie noticed, quickly — as if he had expected to be turned down. "Well, I'll let you get back to work. I'll talk to you later in the week." When they hung up, Sherrie felt annoyed at both herself and Oscar; she could no longer tell herself that she had absolutely nothing to feel guilty about where he was concerned, having just flat-out lied to him. A minute later George Greer rang her buzzer.

He took her to an expensive seafood restaurant, where they sat by a window with a view of the Chesapeake Bay, from which the light faded as the evening progressed. During the drive there he was inquisitive, asking Sherrie questions about her family, her childhood in Washington, her undergraduate years, pausing between each answer and the next question, seeming to consider thoughtfully all that she said. When they sat down in the restaurant his manner changed. He began talking about himself; Sherrie listened while waiting, unconsciously, for a pause, a chance to comment on what he had said and perhaps add something new of her own — until she realized that no pause was coming, that his questions about her had been, as it were, conversational appetizers, that the evening's main course was his verbal parade of all things Greer. He talked on and on as he fed on salmon, she on cod, as they shared a bottle of white wine (white wine that was better than any she had ever tasted, that made her think she hadn't known before what the stuff was supposed to taste like); he built with his baritone, and seemed to shape in the air with his long fingers, a mountain of words — or rather, a house, one whose frame, it might be said, was his perseverance in life, his belief in himself and its fabulous results. Sherrie heard all about how George and his brother, John Jr., had been inspired by the example of their father, who had minimal education but an unstoppable belief in his own potential. She learned that the two brothers had gone in their separate directions, but that neither of them had let race or anything else stand in the way of achievement. Even as a teenager, playing varsity football, George had seen the power of hard work, discipline, and willingness to take an occasional risk. The results spoke for themselves in his current life, from his position at Johns Hopkins to his two lovely children and even to (here he furrowed his brow) his marriage, despite the strains and difficulties that plague any marriage, the need once in a while for each partner to get some breathing room and take stock. ... Clearly, he was lucky, and yet to a large extent people made their own luck, wasn't that true?

Sherrie had two reactions to all this. She was swept along by the content of this talk, by the force and confidence it showed, but at the same time she was aware that only a monumental ego could produce it. If someone else were saying these things about him, she would want very much to get to know him better, particularly since he was so handsome. ... It was, perhaps, this latter point, together with a healthy quantity of that excellent white wine, that helped make the difference in the end — that led her to say yes when, at the end of the meal, he offered to take her to a very comfortable spot where they could sip some of the finest scotch to be had anywhere in the city.

The spot turned out to be an efficiency apartment near the Hopkins campus, which, Greer told Sherrie, belonged to a friend who was often out of town and asked Greer to look in on it once in a while. (For Greer, who bent the truth frequently but departed from it altogether only when necessary, this was one of the latter occasions. The apartment had belonged to a former graduate assistant of his, who had moved to the West Coast to become an assistant professor; Greer had taken over the lease, unbeknownst to his wife, for evenings just such as this.) The apartment was sparsely furnished, with wood floors and no carpeting, blinds but no curtains. It did have a few essentials: a worn but comfortable sofa and chair, a small, black-and-white television set, a turntable and even a few records and, in one corner, a neatly made double bed. As Sherrie sat on the sofa, Greer put on music that Sherrie recognized as being part of her father's jazz collection, though she couldn't have said what it was; she knew only that she found it pleasant, the leisurely trumpet line backed up quietly by piano and bass. She was on the point of asking who the artist was when Greer said, "Now," went to the kitchen area, returned with two small glasses and a half-full bottle of amber liquid, and sat beside her.

"This is single-malt scotch. Eighteen years old," he said, filling each glass halfway. "There isn't anything better. Some will tell you it tastes best if you put ice in it, let the water blend with it just a little. I prefer to take it as it is, burn and all. It's got a lot to offer, if you let it. It's aged enough to become what it's going to be, to see its potential in full flower." He took a small sip, and Sherrie did the same.

"You have to let it be what it is," he said. "You sip this, you can almost see the barley fields it came from. Same with good wine: it's all about bringing the grapes to life. Letting a thing be what it is, and appreciating it, seeing the beauty and uniqueness in it." With that, Greer, whose attention seemed to have been carried away by his own words, gazed directly and significantly at Sherrie.

Sherrie, meanwhile, swallowed her tiny mouthful of scotch to keep from spitting it out; she barely avoided coughing, as what felt like a flame made its way down her throat and brought moisture to her eyes. Then she met Greer's gaze straight on, and said, "You know, Dr. — George — I really appreciate … everything. Your taking me to dinner, and telling me about yourself, and sharing this" — she held up her glass — "with me. I feel like I know something about you now. But you don't know much about me. We seem to be … you seem to see me as a potential friend, but if I'm going to be your friend, you need to know what I'm thinking too, okay? I don't mean this minute, but in general."

Greer smiled. "Of course. Forgive me. I guess I'm so taken with what I know about you already that I wanted to prove myself to you. The old peacock-showing-his-feathers thing. Maybe there's just a little insecurity mixed in with everything else."

Later, when she woke up in the dark, it took Sherrie a moment to recall where she was. When she remembered, she draped her arm around the waist of the man in bed next to her, less to show affection than to anchor herself in time and space, and in her own mind.

\*     \*     \*     \*

Meanwhile, earlier that evening, Greg had set about executing Plan B.

He had taken to heart what Clive's cousin, the deejay Edward Harper, had said about successful music — that it was mostly about one of two subjects, societal conditions and love. Greg had already, of course, tried to inspire Lester to rap about societal conditions, with results that argued for a new definition of failure. Plan B was about love.

Which is why Greg brought his brother to the basement, sat him on the bed, put the Sugar Hill Gang's *Rapper's Delight* on the turntable with the volume on low ("Well a hip, hop, a-hippy to the hippy …"), then got comfortable on the bed himself — the better to share tales of his own amorous adventures. The cassette recorder was beside him, in case he got lucky.

"Well, where to start, Les, where to start," he said, lying on his back, head resting on his folded-up pillow, knees up, and legs crossed in triangular fashion, as if he were sitting in a chair. Lester, meanwhile, sat on a corner of the bed, gazing at Greg in that special way of his, which suggested either that he wasn't taking in Greg's presence completely, or that he was taking in that plus other things. "Might as well start with Carol, I guess." He told Lester the story of Carol, Greg's first real girlfriend and the person to whom, at sixteen, he had lost his virginity. "That gal messed me up some'm terrible," Greg told his brother. Carol, whose normally sunny demeanor could turn stunningly businesslike when it came to matters of her self-interest, informed Greg one day during the summer between his sophomore and junior years of high school that she now had another boyfriend. Greg had known, of course, that couples broke up all the time, but because the new experience of having a girlfriend had redefined his idea of romance — had taken him back to square one, in a way, even as it made him more experienced — it was only when Carol broke up with him that he realized she *could* do so; he couldn't have been more bewildered if he had headed home after school and found his house gone. It was only after he got a new girlfriend, Jennifer, that he overcame his bewilderment completely. "Now, Jennifer was sweet," he told his brother. Indeed, whereas Carol had seemed to be sweet, Jennifer really was, and while Carol's core was made of rock, Jennifer's was, if anything, even softer than her exterior. Because of how nice Jennifer was, because she was cute besides, and because he had been burned once, Greg had some trouble trusting his own luck — until it ran out. Jennifer not only went away to college, but enrolled in a school in Wisconsin; the one time he scraped together the cash to visit her there, he felt acutely uncomfortable around the crowd of tie-dyed whites and fast-talking, brainy blacks she had surrounded herself with, fearing that his every word and gesture would unmask him as the hick he felt himself to be in their presence. Jennifer's break-up letter, which came the following spring, did not surprise him, though it made him sad. The hardest thing was that he couldn't blame her. Her school was halfway across the country, and to ask her to remain faithful was to expect a lot. And in the letter, in her gentle way, she accused him of things he couldn't deny. She wrote that his constant clowning, his unspoken demand that she be ready at all times to laugh at his jokes, created a strain that she wasn't even aware of until it wasn't there anymore. He couldn't say she was wrong. He *did* like attention, even he realized that — because it reassured him, and because he hadn't always gotten it at home.

"Tell you the truth, though, Les, a little part of me was kinda glad." That is because it is difficult for a young man (or woman) to keep his eye from straying when separated from a loved one for an indefinite period, and Greg was no exception. As hurt as he was by Jennifer's letter, he also felt relief — as if an invisible door had swung open, and he was free to pursue any woman who struck his fancy. A new period began, in which dry spells were broken up by three one-night stands and two mostly sex-based relationships that had ended by unspoken mutual consent, sort of like expired health-club memberships. That brought him up to the present.

"And now, Gina," Greg said, smiling. As he had all day, when he remembered the details of the previous night's date with Gina, he felt a warm, pleasing sensation in his stomach. "I'm kinda ready for a real girlfriend again, Les," he said. "I want to be with somebody I could *talk* to. Maybe it could be like that with Gina. I hope so. Tell you what, though, I had some fun with her last night. Her body felt so *good*. And I *never* had a gal move her tongue around in my mouth like she did while we were —" He stopped short, remembering why he had begun talking to Lester about his love life in the first place, and deciding that that last detail about Gina was perhaps not needed.

Thinking of Gina reminded him: she had said she would be home by eight o'clock that evening. He looked at his digital clock and was delighted to see that it was seven minutes after eight. "Awright, that's enough for today, Les. Time to call the lovely Gina." While Lester stayed still, Greg took *Rapper's Delight* off the turntable, re-settled on the bed with the phone, and called Gina.

"Hiiiii," she said, recognizing his voice.

"Hi, yourself. How was your day?"

"It was good …"

Greg was dimly aware, as he talked to Gina, that Lester was rising from the bed. It was only when Greg happened to glance up at his brother, though, that he noticed the angry look and the gunslinger stance …

> *Papa drove us to the place we got the CHRISTmas trees at*
> *Took it home to decorate it — not as SIMple as that*
> *Wouldn't stand no matter what we did to MAKE it stand up …*

Gina, laughing, said, "Who's that? Do you have a record on?"

"No, it's — my — I better call you back —"

Greg hung up. Then he remembered the cassette recorder and turned it on, to capture:

> *Used the hammer, used the saw, but it kept FALLin' on down*
> *Papa sighin', head was shakin', he was WEARin' a frown*
> *Thought he had it — it was standing — then it FELL down again*
> *Sister ran upstairs a-cryin' — Brother STARTed to grin …*

# — NINE —

On Wednesday morning Maddie sat at her dining room table, sipping coffee and thinking about her family — not the one she had raised, but the one that had raised her. In the normal course of things Maddie didn't think about them more than she could help. But she couldn't help doing so now. At the age of forty-seven, she was longing to be comforted in someone's arms; she had Pat, of course, but in many ways he was as affected by developments with Lester as she was, and if he was comforting her, then who was comforting him? No: she wanted a mother, someone older, stronger, who was fazed by her troubles only to the extent that they affected Maddie, someone whose only interest in these affairs was to make her feel better. Someone to tell her, It's natural that these rhyming bursts are transforming your affection for Lester into fear and distrust, the distrust people feel for any unknown thing; someone to say, Of *course* you feel resentful toward Lester because you're having to give up the job you love, even if only temporarily, even if it isn't exactly his fault. This was all a fantasy, since there was no one left in her original family who could say these things, and even if those people were still around, it would be hard to imagine them doing so. And that was what she was *really* thinking about.

Maddie's father, Herman Bell, was long dead; her mother, Rosa, had died three years ago; and her siblings … well. Maddie had always regretted that her own children never got to know any of their grandparents. (Pat's parents had died within a couple of years of each other in the early 1950s; Pat, still in his postwar daze, almost didn't notice.) That was why — as pointless as it seemed in some ways, even to Maddie — once a year or so, up until her mother's death, the family traveled two hours by car to the outskirts of Richmond, Virginia, where Grandmother Bell lived with Maddie's older sister, who had always been called Little Rosa, and her husband and children.

The last time had been on a Saturday four years ago, when Sherrie was nineteen, Greg seventeen, and Lester fifteen.

"So how long do we have to stay?" Sherrie said loudly from the back seat, to be heard over the air rushing in the open car window.

"Long enough to have a nice visit," Maddie said.

"No offense, but I don't see how it'll be nice. Grandma never knows who we are, and everybody else just looks at us like they can't figure out what we're doing there."

"This is one time I gotta agree with my sister," Greg said.

"Long enough to have a visit, then."

"But—"

"You heard your mother," Pat said.

Silence then prevailed for several minutes. Pat, having created it, felt the need to break it, and so he said, as they went south on the highway, "Even if she doesn't know who you are, you know who *she* is. She's your grandmother. The only one you have. It's not so important what she can *do*, it's who she *is*. We have to accept who she is."

Maddie held her breath waiting for her children's response to this argument — which was the one she had given herself for dragging them all out to see her mother, instead of just coming herself. She would not know how to feel, much less what to say, if they made good counterarguments. But there was only silence from the back seat, and Maddie relaxed, to the extent possible, the rest of the way to the house of her older sister, the stoutish, forty-six-year-old woman she still called Little Rosa.

The house was in a pocket of modest homes built on grassy mounds along winding roads and facing in various directions. A narrow dirt path, etched into the grass by years of foot traffic, led up to Little Rosa's one-story, pale green stucco house. Standing in the doorway, as the Hobbses single-filed their way with Maddie in front, was Little Rosa — her arms crossed, her neck and cheeks speckled with the tiny moles of black middle age, her expression neither unfriendly nor affectionate, but businesslike: *Well, here you are. I understand why you must be here. Let us proceed.*

Following the most perfunctory of hugs, they passed into the dim, lamplit living room, with its pleasant, lived-in smell, a record of good meals. Little Rosa's very old sofa and chairs all combined orange, green and brown in such tightly woven patterns that they formed one unnameable color; their cushions and springs had long ago given up the fight, and one did not so much sit on them as sink into them, and then, later, climb out. In one of the chairs, half in shadow, sat Maddie's mother, wrapped in a shawl (it was June), her eyes fixed hard on something that may or may not have been in the room.

Little Rosa's daughter, Sharon, stood expressionless in the middle of the floor, hands plunged knuckle-deep in the front pockets of her thigh-strangling jeans. The sound of a televised basketball game came from one of the back bedrooms. Little Rosa called in that direction, "Freddie! Freddie Jr.! Maddie and Pat are here!" Then she turned to her mother and said, "Momma, Maddie is here."

Maddie took her cue, bending over the old woman and kissing her on the forehead. "Hi, Momma. It's Maddie. I brought your grandchildren, too. Sherrie and Greg. And Lester."

The three of them approached (Lester nudged gently by Pat). Sherrie and Greg said, "Hi, Grandma," almost — but not quite — together, one voice sounding like an echo of the other. Grandmother Bell's gaze did not shift, even when Greg and Sherrie each planted a kiss on her forehead; she merely nodded and said in a soft voice (to whom, no one was sure), "Yes."

*How different that voice had been at certain moments of Maddie's girlhood. When it was at its loudest, Maddie heard it from upstairs, in the room she shared with Little Rosa. She would awaken in the dark, unsure of the time, to the sound of her mother's clear shouts alternating with — sometimes blending with — the murky, gin-heavy growls of her father, who had just stumbled home. The first sister to wake fully would whisper the other's name; the other would whisper back, "Yeah," the signal to the first to slide in bed beside her sister. The sleeve of one's wool nightgown would encircle the other's waist from behind, and they would listen as the shouts trailed off or were replaced by bumps, smacks, screams.*

*Sometimes the sisters whispered to each other. "Wish it was another man around here," Rosa once said.*

"We could get Mr. Fuller." This was their nearest neighbor, a hundred yards away on the dirt road.

*"How?"*

*"Climb out the window."*

*"I ain't breakin' my neck."*

*"We could call to him, then."*

*"He wouldn't hear. And if he did, by the time he got here Daddy woulda beat us silly."*

Freddie and Freddie Jr., Little Rosa's husband and son, came from the back room, walking slowly, looking in the direction of Maddie and her family without seeming to see them, as if they were trying to find their way across a dark room. The older man finally said, in a voice devoid of inflection, "Hey, how y'all doing."

Little Rosa said, "They were just back there watching the basketball game. Pat, Greg, you can go back there with 'em, if you want to. I'll call you when the food's ready."

The men did as they were told. Maddie, Little Rosa, Sherrie, and Sharon settled on the sofa and chair.

"So," Little Rosa said.

*The sibling who was alone during those middle-of-the-night fights between the parents was the middle child, Lester. Maddie and Little Rosa would see him at the breakfast table the next morning, where he was even quieter than usual, staring down at his food, at the yellow-and-white checkered tablecloth, from beneath large, half-lowered eyelids, his fleshy lips unnaturally still. (This was his pose, too, on those evenings when he was the target of his father's drunken taunts.) Their mother, meanwhile — sometimes with a black eye — bustled around the three children with a desperate cheerfulness, spooning out steaming grits and asking, "Did you have your history test yesterday? How you think you did? … Oh, it might not be so bad. What about your game, Lester?" The bustle, the cheerfulness, stopped only with the thuds of Herman Bell's brogans on the wooden stairs.*

"Sherrie, what are you doing now?" Little Rosa asked.

"I'm at G.W. — um, George Washington University. I just finished my first year."

"Very good. And what are you doing this summer?"

"I'll be working in their library."

"Well. I'm sure that'll be nice."

Maddie knew that Sharon was the age to graduate from high school, either that year or the next, and to find out which it was, she said, "Sharon, are you still in school?" The girl's face went from blank to sullen. Little Rosa, in a tone of controlled anger — whether at Sharon, or Maddie, or both, was not clear — explained, "Sharon had a little trouble in school this year. She was supposed to graduate, but she'll be going back to take some classes again."

"Well," Maddie began, and, not knowing what to add, added nothing.

A long silence ended only when Grandmother Bell said, "Yes."

*Maddie's mother's cheerfulness, fake or otherwise, ended for good one morning in late winter. Maddie and Little Rosa came down for breakfast on that school morning, but not Lester. No doubt he was sleeping late, as he had been doing for so long. Little Rosa was sent upstairs to wake him. A few minutes later she returned, wearing an expression Maddie would remember the rest of her life, the absent look of someone shaken beyond the ability to cry. Lester was not in his room, she announced, and neither were his pair of shoes or his three pairs of pants. He did not come home that evening, or the next, or the one after that. (He was not present, either, at the funeral that took place a couple of years later, following his father's death in a car accident; nor was he around several years after that, when his mother, by then a broken-down, forgetful woman, moved to the outskirts of Richmond to live with Little Rosa and her young family.)*

*Maddie's father could be described in a number of ways, but he could not be called stupid. He knew he was to blame for his son's departure, and he knew that every silent meal he sat through with his family was a collective finger being pointed at him. And he knew, finally, what to do about that.*

*"Maddie, guess what?" he said, as they all sat down to dinner.*

*"I was so proud of you for gettin' that 'A' on your art project, I got you something"* — a new dress. *Another night, it was, "You're turning into such a pretty girl"; another night, "It's such a pleasure to me to see you doing so well"* — all without so much as a glance at Little Rosa or her mother, as if they were pieces of furniture.

He was not saying anything he didn't believe, but he was not saying it innocently, either, and his methods were as effective as his motives were obvious. In one of the parents' middle-of-the-night shouting sessions, among a lot of unintelligible sounds, Maddie made out, *"Filling Maddie's head with all that flattery, and you got that stupid girl believing you!"* That night Maddie whispered Little Rosa's name, but got no response. She tiptoed to her bed, and again called her name softly. This time Little Rosa said in a normal tone of voice, which, in this setting of darkness and whispers, seemed to rattle the window panes: *"Go back to your own bed."* Maddie did as she was told, quietly, though she wanted to shout at her sister and mother, *"I don't ask him to say those things! And I don't want him to! I don't, I don't ..."*

When Little Rosa went to check on the food, and Maddie offered to help, the response was, "No, sit still" — which would have seemed a polite refusal of assistance from anyone else but sounded, from Little Rosa's mouth, like the words of a prison guard. Maddie stayed where she was. She, Sherrie, Sharon, and Grandma Bell were plunged again into uncomfortable silence, until Sherrie said to her cousin, "So what kind of music do you listen to?" This began an actual conversation between the two young women, to which Maddie was blissfully unable to contribute. As it went on, Maddie gazed at her sister, over the half-wall separating the living room from the kitchen. Little Rosa's face, as she concentrated on cooking, unaware of being watched, seemed to flash glimpses of its younger self, and Maddie thought what she had thought a couple of times before: that, contrary to what we assume when we are young, we do not become different people when we get older. We merely take on new layers, while, underneath, the same resentments and desires rage on, sometimes even more torturously — like an itch beneath a leg cast.

A few minutes later, just as the music discussion had run out of steam, Little Rosa announced that the food was ready. Sharon was sent to retrieve the men. Pat, Greg, Freddie and Freddie Jr. brought chairs from other parts of the house to the living room, and everyone assembled there, with plates of ham, collard greens, black-eyed peas and cornbread. The greater number of people seemed to help the conversation, which, if not meaningful, was at least sustainable: a discussion of President Ford and Tricky Dick Nixon. The talk got them through the meal before hitting its first lull. Grandma Bell ended several seconds of silence with, "Yes, indeed," after which Maddie, aware of smiling a little too broadly, said, "Well, I hate to eat and run, but I know Pat's got some work he brought home from the office, and it's a long drive …" There was no "Oh, can't you stay a while?", no "I hate to see you go"— Little Rosa and Freddie Sr. stood up almost before Maddie finished speaking. There were the same perfunctory hugs, the kisses planted dutifully on Grandma Bell's forehead, and then Maddie, feeling vague sadness and profound relief, was back on the road with her family. It was the last time she saw her mother alive, and the last time, except for her mother's funeral, she had seen or spoken to Little Rosa.

No, these were not the people to whom Maddie could tell her present troubles.

Who was there to tell, then? There were a couple of women friends, teachers she had met over the years, who had come over for dinner now and then and whose houses she and Pat had gone to. But it was rare that she talked to those women between get-togethers, and so it would be unprecedented, awkward, to telephone one of them and say, "Hello, how've you been? I'm really depressed." This, it seemed, was the price she paid for having been so focused on her family over the years, so — *insular* was the word: there was no one she felt comfortable turning to outside it, when things within it went wrong. You were bound to mess up something in your life, she thought. It was just a matter of what. Because the family she had come from had collapsed in on itself, she wanted more than anything for the members of the family she had created to get along; but they didn't, not always, and meanwhile she had no one else. Part of her wanted to call Sherrie. Her daughter was far enough away now to have a little perspective on matters, even if she had been raised in this house, and the girl was so *competent*. But that didn't seem right, either. Maddie didn't want to turn into one of those parents who wait until their children are just able to take care of themselves and then use them as crutches for the next several decades, getting back all the care they expended on their children, plus an extra dozen years' worth or so. Hadn't Maddie's own mother done that, with Little Rosa?

And so, on this Wednesday morning, while Lester doodled on a napkin at the dining room table, Maddie drifted to the living room and turned on the TV, welcoming its background chatter as she finished reading the newspaper on the sofa. When she'd gone through the sections she cared about — the front page and the Style section — plus a couple she didn't, she threw the paper down on the sofa, where it lay crumpled, used up and boring, which was how she felt herself. Now what?

Her attention drifted to the TV. There was a talk show on. The host was a middle-aged white man who had started off as a singer and performed songs on the show from time to time, making himself look, ironically, like a talk-show host trying to be a singer. At the moment he was interviewing an actress Maddie had never heard of, a girl with straight dark hair who didn't look much older than some of the kids in Maddie's art classes. Maddie was becoming absorbed in what the girl was saying — the way it's possible, in idle moments, to become absorbed in things as mundane as water going down the drain — when the doorbell rang.

When she looked through the peephole and saw Celestine, Maddie's body sagged against the door. *Haven't you been here enough?* she asked the old woman in her mind. *What more is there to find out about Lester?* But then she answered her own question: Nothing. Celestine had beheld Lester in all his rhyming glory, the gossip had been spread, the damage was done. So maybe she had come merely to be social, as she often did. Why not welcome her into your home, Maddie asked herself now. What will she be interrupting?

"Hello, Celestine, come on in."

"How you doin'?"

"Oh … I'm making it."

"Good for you, child."

Celestine entered in her usual fashion, with steps whose very forcefulness made her look unsteady, each footfall seeming to come just in time to keep her from toppling over. "Just came to see how you was. I thought you might be here, I heard Alma wasn't sittin' for Lester no more. Hi, Lester," she said, waving toward the dining room.

So the news about Alma was out, too. There was no escaping the gossip network, you just had to face that fact and laugh about it, which was what Maddie did now. "Oh, Celestine. What can I get you? Want some tea?"

"That'd be might nice. Oh, you watchin' him too," Celestine said, pointing to the talk-show host.

When Maddie returned with the tea, the two of them sat on the sofa and watched TV. "Look at that girl," Celestine said. "Ain't hardly out of diapers yet, talkin' like she got some'm to say."

"I was thinking the same thing."

"When she get to where she done learned a thing or two, and got a couple of wrinkles on her face, then they won't want her on the show no more."

"That's exactly right."

"So how you doin'? You can't teach no more, 'cause you got to stay home with Lester?"

"Well, right now. I'm hoping it's just temporary, till we figure something else out."

"What are you doin' with yourself, then? Nothing much?"

"Nothing much. The problem is, I used to be able to take Lester with me places, but now I'm scared he'll start … you know. So I can't even go out."

"Yeah, don't reckon you want him on the bus or somewhere doin' that stuff."

They were quiet as the talk-show host welcomed his next guest, the actor James Earl Jones. After exchanging the usual pleasantries with the host, Jones got onto the subject of how, as a boy, he had developed a stutter, with which he still struggled. "Once a stutterer, always a stutterer," he said. "So how is it," the host asked, "that you've had such a successful acting career, with such a bad speech problem?" "I avoid words that give me trouble," Jones replied.

"Now, ain't that some'm," Celestine said.

Jones and the host now moved to the subject of the actor's

most recent role. He had played the author Alex Haley in the TV miniseries *Roots: The Next Generations*, which was about the American descendants of an African slave — including Haley himself — and culminated in Haley's journey to Africa to find the slave's, and thus his own, people. In the clip introduced by the host, Jones, as Haley, sat among Africans in a village and listened as the griot recited tribal history. The griot wore a red head-covering, a white cloth and black leather cord as neck ornaments, and a loose-fitting blue robe, and he held a wooden staff. Speaking through an interpreter, he gave an account that made the list of "begats" in the Bible seem short by comparison: "On the big water of the upper river, Kamaru Owa Kinte left the Malik land and traveled to the village of the samba fish, and when he had twenty-five rains he married Balta, the daughter of Manin, and their children were Yaya, Bautu, and Fanta. The country did not have grass. ... Kariba Kinte went to the Gambia and lived in a village called Javaya. And when he had thirty-one rains, he married a woman called Baya, and they had a son, Omari Bota Lanu at Omaya. He married a woman called Yeesa. ... And at about that time the king's soldiers came. The eldest son, Kunta, left the village to cut a tree to make himself a drum. And that was the last time that he was seen. ..." Having nodded off after hours of listening, Haley/Jones awoke when he heard the detail about the drum. He checked his notes against the words the griot had just spoken. "You old African," Haley/Jones said, laughing and crying, when he had put the pieces of the tale together. "I found you! KUNTA KINTE! I *found* you! I found you! I found you!"

As the clip ended, and the TV studio audience applauded, Maddie asked Celestine, "Did you watch that when it was on?"

"Sure did, child. Didn't miss a night."

"Neither did I. It was so good."

"That boy" — she indicated James Earl Jones — "reminds me of a fellow from down the country. He was kinda light-skinned, too. And handsome, child? Mmp, mmp, mmp." She took a sip of her tea, leaving a thick smudge of red lipstick on the rim of the white cup. "Name was Fulton Ligon. One of his sons, Leroy, used to run with your daddy. Fulton had him a saloon and a dry-goods store — not in the town where your people was, but the next town over. He could do all that 'cause he could get along with the white folks almost as good as he did with the colored. 'Cause he was light-skinned, you see. White folks treated him a mite better than they treated other colored folks. Course, colored folks is like that, too. Yellow-skinned colored folks'll spit on you just as quick as white folks will — it was true down the country, and it's true here. Anyhow, Fulton was the big man down there. And he could be just as nice as you please, give you the shirt off his back, but you bet' not cross him or get too rowdy in his place, or he'd th'ow you out hisself, didn't have no need of a bouncer. That was Fulton. He had goodness *and* meanness in him. Look like his sons — he had two sons, Leroy, who used to run with your daddy, and Otis — look like they just couldn't be what their daddy was. One had the goodness, that was Otis, but he couldn't hardly stand up for hisself or do nothin' else, and the other one, Leroy, was just mean. Now one of them boys shoulda been able to take over his daddy's business, but they tell me Fulton told his wife on his dyin' day, 'Sell the store and the saloon. That way at least you'll get *some'm* out of it, but if one of them boys start to runnin' it, won't be nothin' left to run.' And that's what she did. Now, one of Leroy's children (Leroy wasn't married to the mother), he did all right for hisself — look like he had more of Fulton in him than Leroy or Otis did. ..."

Lester passed through the living room on his way upstairs. Celestine's eyes, Maddie noticed, followed him as she slurped her tea.

The TV host ended his show with, "See you tomorrow!" The studio audience applauded as the credits rolled. The host kept chatting with his guests, unheard over the applause and the show's theme music. Maddie always wondered what they were saying during those moments — maybe, *A few more seconds to fill here, guys, pretend to say something funny and I'll laugh … Ha ha ha … CUT!*

A commercial came on, showing a black man very excited over a low-calorie mayonnaise substitute. "Oh, I hate watching that fool," Celestine said.

"I can turn it off," Maddie said, standing up.

"No, leave it on. Might be some'm else good on."

Striking a compromise, Maddie changed the channel, settling

on 5, the local station. A youngish black woman with a short Afro was sitting on a wooden stool; the set behind her was bare, except for pastel shapes on the walls, lime green and lavender rectangles and circles that could have been either pieces of sheer fabric or projections of light. "Welcome to *D.C. Connections,*" the woman said in a voice like a warm bath, as Maddie sat down again. "I'm your host …"

Celestine said, "Is Lester coming back down?"

"He might. Or he might stay upstairs a while and do a puzzle or watch TV."

"That's good, at least you don't have to watch him every minute."

Maddie sighed. "Yeah …"

The *D.C. Connections* host welcomed her first guest, a young black man who brought out his own stool and set it next to hers.

"Now don't he look foolish," Celestine said. "Boy's on TV and can't dress no better than that?"

The young man wore a black leather vest and matching pants; sneakers; a red bandana that covered his head, with two rolled-up sections sticking out in back; a red sweatshirt whose sleeves had been cut off, possibly by small children, and whose front was all but hidden by layers of gold necklace. He was saying, partly with his hands, " … Rap music is rilly like, you know, the rhythms of urban black folks, together with the oral tradition that's been passed down for centuries. It's kinda in the spotlight now because of *Rapper's Delight* by the Sugar Hill Gang. …"

"And who are *they* when they're home?" Celestine said.

" … but it comes out of, you know, a tradition. So I'm just trying to put a little bit of hometown D.C. spin on it."

"Well," said the *D.C. Connections* host, "let's hear some!" She moved, stool and all, while the young man walked a short distance to a microphone. From somewhere unseen came musical accompaniment, and the young man, holding the microphone, rapped:

> *Old folks on their porches, talkin' 'bout kids today:*
> *"Can't do nothin' wit' 'em, they don't hear what you say*
> *Ain't like in the old days, when the kids had respect"*
> *— Old folks was the same way, they just don't recollect …*

"Plain foolishness," Celestine said.

As Maddie listened to the young man, a peculiar thing happened. He suddenly began speaking in two voices at once, the words alternately drowning out and echoing each other. She couldn't figure out how it was happening, or even *what* was happening, and she felt disoriented and a little frightened. Then she realized that the second voice wasn't the young man's at all; it wasn't even coming from the TV. It was Lester, shouting a rhyme that seemed to be about riding in a car. In place of her confusion, Maddie now felt tears spring to her eyes. She said, "Do you mind if I turn this off?"

"No, child," Celestine said, in the softest voice she had used all morning. "Go right ahead."

No more than five seconds after Maddie turned the TV off, Lester stopped shouting. Where there had been a cacophony there was now only the sound of Maddie's rapid breathing, as she stood in the middle of the room, hands over her eyes, crying. "Come on back over here," Celestine said. "That's a girl." Maddie soon had her head on Celestine's shoulder, riding out waves of sobs.

"That's right. ... It's all right," Celestine said. "What you need is to get *out*. By yourself. Or with Pat. Has he took you out lately?"

"No," Maddie said, chuckling for some reason, as her tears subsided. "You know ... I don't know why, but I was thinking ... I'd like to just go and get my hair done." She didn't know what was so appealing about the thought of having her hair done, unless it was the idea of lying back and letting someone else take over — not take *her* over, as Lester's situation had done, but simply do things for her.

"Go 'head and get your hair done, then!" Celestine told her. "I can stay here while you go."

"You *can?* Are you *sure?*"

"Sure."

"Oh, Celes— You know what? I'll just check and see if Lil"— the hairdresser she had gone to for years — "can fit me in this morning. I'll be right back." She went to the telephone in the kitchen to call Lil, who did indeed have an opening. She bounced like a teenager back into the living room and said to Celestine, "She can fit me in if I go right now. Is that all right?"

"Child, I told you it was."

"Celestine, you don't know what you're doing for me."

It was another beautiful day outside. We've been lucky with the weather this week, Maddie thought. The sky was pale blue, the clouds few and far between, and thin, like cotton balls stretched to the point of tearing; a gentle breeze stirred the new leaves on the trees and fluttered the hem of Maddie's skirt as she went, clop, clop, down the sidewalk. It was too lovely a day to cry. Part of her wanted to, the part that had gotten just enough mothering from Celestine to want more, the part that was thinking of her own mother — not the mother who had resented the attention Maddie got from her father, certainly not the senile old woman who had spent her last days at Little Rosa's house, but the one who, probably wanting to cry herself, had comforted Maddie when she was a little girl. A man walked toward her, but no, she would not wonder what she often wondered, just a little, when she saw a strange man — if he might be her brother. No, she told the man in her mind as they passed each other, as she smiled to herself and brushed a tear from the corner of her eye: you are you, and he is him, and I am me, on this beautiful day.

# —TEN—

Pat knew he needed to do two things. He just didn't know which to do first. One thing was to take his wife out somewhere, at least to dinner. The past few days hadn't been easy on her, what with the development with Lester, which they still didn't understand, and Maddie's having to stay home with him because of it. The other thing was to go out by himself, call up an old buddy and have a beer, get away from everything for an evening. But which first? There was a pro and a con to each one. Maddie was going stir crazy, which was part of what was making him uptight, and the two of them out alone together might make each other feel better — or maybe their combined anxieties would be fruitful and multiply. If they were more likely to make each other feel better, he owed it to his wife to do it as soon as possible. But maybe that wasn't more likely. Maybe he'd be more likely to cheer her up if he went out by himself first, cleared his head a little. But if he went out by himself first, then went out with Maddie, and they still just brought each other down, they'd all be right back where they started.

Does anyone else make everyday decisions in this painfully convoluted way? he wondered, as he sat in his office chair, facing the window, watching a plane approach National Airport. Or is it just lawyers? Or is it just me? Maybe he needed to simplify things.

Often, to do that, he asked himself a question: What is the *right* thing? Put this way, the matter seemed simple indeed.

"Hello?"

"Hey."

"Darling ..."

"Listen: let's go out to dinner tonight. Just us two. Who can we get to stay with Lester?"

"Oh — you're sweet. I don't think we can get anybody tonight, though. Alma's scared to stay with Lester now, as you know. And I could ask Celestine, but she already stayed with Lester this morning while I got my hair done. I just got back a little while ago."

"She did, huh? That's nice."

"Yes. She can be sweet."

"Well, what about our other son? You know, the kind of normal one?"

"You know he's been studying for his finals. And I heard him mention something about a new girl. I don't know exactly what he's doing tonight."

"Staying under our roof and eating our food, for one. Actually, that's two."

"When did you get so mean?"

"I'm not being mean. I'm just saying it wouldn't hurt him to help out with his brother once in a while."

"Honey, he does. You know Greg just sits with Lester and talks to him sometimes when nobody else does. Besides, Greg is young. He needs to have his life."

Pat sighed. "I suppose."

"How about this: let me see who can come over tomorrow night, okay? Then we can go out."

"Okay. Listen: you mind if I go somewhere after work, then? Maybe just for a beer. I know you've already been with Lester all day —"

"No, it's fine. Just going out to get my hair done helped a lot. Go ahead. Who're you going with?"

"I was thinking of calling up Stan."

"*Oh*. Been a while since you saw him. Well, have fun. Give him my love."

Pat's friendship with Stan, he had found, was the kind it is possible to have only in middle age or beyond, and was just about the only kind Pat had anymore: one that could thrive without the constant contact that seemed necessary for friendships between younger people. Pat and Stan had been in Korea together. The family ties and work lives they had built up separately since then did not infringe on their friendship; rather, they helped sustain it, gave the two men something to talk about besides their army days, kept them at a certain distance, perhaps, but also on the same level, as if they were standing on separate rooftops, chatting across the divide. Stan, too, had been married for over twenty years, had grown children, and worked for the government — in his case, the Government Printing Office; like Pat, he had a full life from which he could peel himself once in a while for a get-together. Pat sometimes wondered if there was something wrong if he did not need friendships closer than this; but then he put it down to his having been an only child, who had not had the constant company of siblings and therefore did not miss it. And, besides, he had Maddie.

Stan was free that evening, and the two met at a downtown bar Pat had been to once or twice over the years. The place was bustling with the after-work crowd, a mix of blacks and whites, some of them clearly regular customers of the Irish-looking, bulbous-nosed bartender. Pat and Stan managed to find two adjacent stools and ordered Budweisers.

"So what's goin' on, Mr. Stanley?"·

"Man, what's *not* goin' on. I'm glad you called up when you did. I got a lot to tell you about."

"Well, let's hear some of it."

"Guess I'll start with the big one first: me and Gloria are getting divorced."

Pat, who had been about to take a sip of his beer, froze with the mug halfway to his lips. He gazed a moment at his friend, who gazed back with an expectant look, almost, if Pat wasn't mistaken, a smile. Pat looked down at the bar, lowered his mug, then turned back to his friend. "*Divorced?* Why?"

"Well, it's kind of simple," he said. "I fell in love."

"Fell in …!"

Stan had a broad face whose cocoa-colored skin was rocky terrain, a mix of blackheads, pock marks and moles that somehow didn't stop him from being handsome, in a rough sort of way; his eyes were also broad, but narrow, almost the slits of a reptile, and the look he gave Pat through those eyes did indeed seem to be a smile, one of sympathy that bordered on condescension: *I've been where you are, so I know how hard it is to imagine where I am.* "I know it's a surprise," he said.

"That there is an understatement. In love with who? How'd it happen?"

"Well — you know I'm a little bit of a handyman on the side, right?"

"Yeah ..."

"Word gets around, so there was this young lady needed some work done on her kitchen sink, and another buddy of mine told her about me. So I went over to her house. Soon as I saw her, I said to myself, this is one fine-looking woman — if I was single I'd try to make some time with her in a minute. But you know how it is: you're married, you think that once in a while about a woman you see, but then you don't see her again and you don't think no more about it. But while I was working on her sink we got to talking. She was just so *sweet*, man, with this nice voice, felt like it was caressing my ears. Name's Darlene. Told me she was divorced, no kids, in her early thirties. I couldn't imagine nobody divorcing her. And I thought about her after I left, but I still didn't have no plans to do nothin' else. Then, I'm at work one day, and the phone rings, and it's Darlene. I had told her I worked at the GPO, and she knew my last name. Asked me if I wanted to come over for a drink. And that's how it started."

"But ... I mean, I guess one thing leads to another sometimes, but — what about Gloria? That's just *over*, after — what — twenty-three, twenty-four years?"

"Hey, man, a lot of things are over after twenty-three years. Excitement, for one. New shit to talk about. Things you don't know about each other. You know how that is — you been married as long as me."

"I can't believe it, Stan."

"Listen, Pat, you ain't no more surprised than I was. It's not like I *planned* to fall in love. I didn't even think it was something I could do. But that day Darlene called me up at work, man, it was like something changed inside me. Or like I grew a third eye, and I could see something I couldn't see before. A possibility. I didn't *have* to just keep on living the way I was until I died. Nice as that is in some ways, or was."

"What about Gloria? How'd she take it?"

"'Bout like you'd expect: she's mad as shit. So are my kids. The five of 'em together are like this great big pair of angry eyes staring at me. This hasn't been easy, man, I want to tell you. Matter fact, sometimes it's miserable" — the look on his face made him appear to be reliving some of the misery in his mind. "I'm not a cold-hearted man, Pat …"

"I know that. I've known you almost thirty years."

"… I'm not happy about what I'm doing to Gloria and my kids. But, at the same time… it's kinda like it's the price I'm paying for feeling *alive*. I just feel *alive*, man."

"Stan … wow."

Stan laughed and said, "Yeah, man, I know. So, how *you* doin'? What's new?"

"Well — you know. Same ol' same ol'…"

\*　　　\*　　　\*　　　\*

Sherrie, at that moment, was with one man while thinking of another. Dr. George Greer had just come to her apartment to pick her up for their dinner date. He had stepped into the bathroom; Sherrie was gathering her jacket and purse and remembering, with feelings of guilt, something she had done recently with Oscar.

He had talked her, somehow, into speaking to his third-graders. "It would be so great," he had said, as they shared pizza at a place near the Hopkins campus. "These are kids in a poor black neighborhood, some of their mothers get welfare checks, and they'd meet a *black woman* who's training to be a scientist. What could be better than that?" And so Sherrie had shown up at Oscar's school at eleven o'clock one morning, nervous, even if they *were* eight-year-olds she was going to talk to. But once she got in the classroom, something about the way Oscar dealt with the children and with her presence in the room — Oscar, who in some situations could seem so ill-at-ease himself — made her relax.

"All right, class," he said as the two of them stood in front of the boys and girls, his expression a mix of affection and firmness. "This is Miss Hobbs. She's a chemist. Who can say what a chemist is? What did we say yesterday?"

Half a dozen hands went up. "Beverly," Oscar said. The hands went down. A girl with pigtails, large eyes, and front teeth in desperate need of braces said, "It's somebody that … studies what the earth is made out of."

"Okay, that's close," Oscar said, a note of gentle correction in his voice. At that moment Sherrie caught herself thinking that he would make a good father. "Miss Hobbs, you want to take it from there?"

"Sure," she said. "Yes, you were close. A chemist studies the properties of substances. Do you know what those words mean …?"

Sherrie was brought out of that memory by Dr. Greer, who stepped out of her bathroom. "Your place reminds me of the apartment I had when *I* was in grad school," he said.

"Really?"

"Yes. Near the campus at U-Mass."

"So what brought you back to Baltimore? I know your family was here, and Hopkins had a good program. …"

"Yes, those two things. I wanted to settle here. Partly I wanted any children I had to be near their grandparents, soak up our family traditions. They're around me, of course, and they pick up my values, but it doesn't hurt to be around *my* old man some, who's the original source of so much that my family has always believed in and profited from. Are you ready? You look very nice."

"Thank you. Yeah, let's —"

Her doorbell rang.

"Are you expecting someone?" Greer said, sounding mildly put out.

"No," Sherrie said, trying to keep the panic out of her voice.

*       *       *       *

As he stood on the Metro platform, waiting for the Blue Line train, Pat tried to figure out why he hadn't told Stan what was going on — which was, he'd thought, the reason he wanted to get together with his old friend in the first place. Or maybe it wasn't; maybe he had really wanted to talk to someone about something besides work or Lester, which had been the only two things on his mind for going on a week now. Maybe that explained why, even when Stan had asked specifically about Lester, Pat had said nothing was new. And maybe that wasn't the only reason. Pat hadn't yet come up with the words to discuss Lester's situation with someone who didn't already know about it. *What's new? Let's see … well, my nineteen-year-old son said his first words. And guess what: they all rhyme. Something else, huh?* And Stan's news, which Pat was still struggling to take in, had made Pat reluctant to say anything about his own, possibly because they were such opposite kinds of developments: Pat's had drawn him even deeper into family life, while Stan's had sent him hurtling, spinning out of it. So much for regarding each other across the rooftop divide; one roof was suddenly several floors higher than the other, though he wasn't sure which.

Then again, maybe he was. After all, Stan had been where Pat was, but the reverse wasn't true. Had Pat felt awed because Stan seemed to have advanced beyond him? Was he … jealous? It wasn't that Pat wanted to do the same thing. He loved Maddie. But then, Stan would've said the same thing until recently about Gloria, at least Pat thought he would have. He couldn't be sure. What was there to be sure of, when something he thought was as solid as the ground beneath his feet — his oldest friend's marriage — was no more? Or when, for that matter, Lester had started talking?

Maybe there was a different reason he hadn't said anything about Lester, he thought, stepping onto the Blue Line train. Maybe it was simply Lester himself. Was Pat embarrassed about the whole thing? He had always prided himself, secretly, on not feeling that way about Lester, possibly because he already had two children who could speak and had normal intelligence; this one just couldn't and didn't, that was all. Certainly, if Pat had been one to feel embarrassed by his son's limitations, there had never been a shortage of opportunities. Oh, the number of times Pat had stood on line at stores or sat on benches with Lester next to him, when the boy was five, six, seven, and had some friendly stranger start talking to his son. At a certain point in Lester's non-answering, the stranger would say, "Feeling shy?" or "Don't feel like talking today?"

Pat would say simply, not in an unfriendly way, "He doesn't talk."

Thus would begin the improvised portion of the play. Some people, smiling all along, would smile even more broadly at this news, as if it were cause for celebration; they were, of course, covering their own embarrassment. Some people were openly embarrassed: "Oh, I'm sorry, I didn't know, I ..." Pat, in a strange reversal of roles, would begin comforting such people, saying, "Don't worry, it's okay." Some people, hearing Pat say, "He doesn't talk," would stop talking themselves, turning away, pretending their exchange had never taken place, sometimes giving a little smile of apology first. And then there was the special category: the do-gooders. "He doesn't talk? At *all*? Are you *sure*? Maybe he just has to be encouraged. There are books you can get. My cousin works with children as a blah blah blah, I could ask her to yadda yadda ..."

No, Pat had never felt embarrassed in those days. But now? He thought of his and Lester's visit to the Giant on Saturday, when his son had begun shouting rhymes to the masses gathered in the frozen-food aisle. Pat had dragged Lester out of the store as if both their lives depended on it. You could dress his reasons up in language as fancy as you wanted — he didn't want to cause a disturbance, he was protecting Lester's dignity, he wanted to prevent some kind of misunderstanding, etc. — but it really came down to one simple thing. The irony was not lost on Pat: he had never felt ashamed when his son didn't talk, but now ...

"Hello, darling," Maddie said when Pat walked in. "I kept your dinner warm. How was it? How's Stan?"

"Well," Pat said, furrowing his brow, "he had some interesting news ..."

\*      \*      \*      \*

"Hi, Oscar."

"Heyyyy." He was smiling broadly, his face all eagerness, the way it could get sometimes — the way it was when he brought up the idea of her talking to his third-graders. He looked like one of his own students. "I've come to *drag* you out to dinner with me. I learned a lesson the other night. Sometimes I can't just ask you, I have to decide *for* you. So. Where are we going?"

"Oh. Oscar. I, um, I can't right now, I've … got …"

As he observed her anxiety and hesitance, his face began to mirror it. Then he seemed to study *her* face again, taking in the lipstick and eye shadow. "Are you — going — ?"

"I have somebody here. We were about to go out," Sherrie said, her voice suddenly firm. "Do you want to come in, for just a minute? I'll introduce you."

"Uh … okay."

Oscar followed her inside, his expression making her want to hug him and slap him at the same time. He looked hurt, all the more so as he tried to hide it: his mouth readied itself to smile for the introduction, but the puckered skin between his eyebrows wouldn't let it happen. "George, this is my friend Oscar Thompson. Oscar, this is Dr. George Greer."

The two men shook hands and said, "Nice to meet you," in unison.

"George teaches neurology at Hopkins."

"*Oh.*"

"Oscar teaches, too," Sherrie said. "Third grade," she added, smiling as she said this, instantly regretting the smile, and hoping Oscar wouldn't notice or misinterpret it.

"Well. That's a noble field," Greer said.

"Yeah, uh, thanks."

"So," Sherrie said, as a kind of transitional noise, an introduction to … she didn't know what.

She couldn't tell what caused it — her stupid smile, or George's possibly condescending remark about "a noble field," or just the situation itself sinking in — but Oscar's hurt look gave way suddenly to one of barely suppressed rage. "Well, you're going out," he said. "Don't let me hold you up. I'll get out of your hair" — at the word "hair," his lip just about curled up. She walked behind him to the door, dreading his parting glance, but there wasn't one; he opened the door himself and walked out without a backward look.

*     *     *     *

Yes, embarrassment is what it is, Pat thought, sitting on the sofa and reading an editorial in the *Washington Post*, from which his mind had drifted. That was what had made him drag Lester so quickly out of the Giant. It had also stopped him and Maddie from going to church this past Sunday, which they normally did with Lester in tow.

Pat and Maddie belonged to the neighborhood Baptist Church, where the pastor could be counted on to scream his message of salvation every Sunday. For Maddie, who came from rural Virginia and grew up listening to country preachers, for whom speaking meant yelling, their present church was a continuation of what she had always known. Not so for Pat. His father, Christopher Hobbs, who himself had been a Baptist as a boy in the country, became an Episcopalian after his move to Washington; a career railroad porter, Christopher Hobbs was by nature an intellectual, and he preferred the "thinking man's religion" he found in the Episcopal Church — where he had also found his wife, Susie, Pat's mother. Pat had therefore been an Episcopalian in his youth.

The war changed that. In Korea Pat saw things most people couldn't imagine, things his mind couldn't completely take in because they seemed so absurd: men reduced to meat, their half-severed arms or legs or heads attached only by skin, like pieces of chicken he had pulled apart during Sunday dinner; some were men whose names Pat knew, whose voices and even laughs he had heard, men with mothers and girlfriends and little sisters, who suddenly became no different from the picked-over scraps of flesh and bone you gave to the dog. When Pat came back from seeing this, he found he had no use for the kinds of sermons he had heard as a boy, the lilting reflections on God's love and grace and His continuous presence in our lives. As a boy he had loved the story about the man who dies and goes to heaven and meets God. God tells the man that He has walked beside him throughout his life, and to prove it He points to two sets of footprints. "What about those places where I see only one set of footprints?" the doubting man asks. "Those are the times I was carrying you," God replies. This parable, which had once captured the essence of Pat's faith, came to seem no better than a fairy tale. Who had carried those men — those boys — who died in pieces on the fields of Korea? No: Pat came to believe in a different kind of God, not one who fussed about like an invisible manservant in one's daily affairs, but more of a chief executive, whose company was the universe, whose headquarters was Earth; this God let people go about their business, rewarding them at the end of their lives if they were faithful and lived well (look out, Stan!), occasionally singling one out for a special purpose, but otherwise letting them be. How else to explain what Pat had seen? This view explained the gratitude Pat felt when he made it out of the war alive and in one piece, because he didn't *have* to survive, God *wasn't* necessarily going to protect him, as many people wanted him to believe. It seemed to Pat, after his return, that such people took far too much for granted. After the war, Pat, for all his gratitude, did not respond to church teachings — until the day, during his law-school years, when he passed by a Baptist church and heard the preacher's voice carrying beyond the doors. Pat heard in that voice what he himself felt about God: not the calm assurance of the priests he had known in his boyhood, but awe, wonder, fear, and gratefulness, combined with a feeling, almost a despair, that he could not feel grateful *enough*. Pat's gratitude, the foundation of his faith, which he seldom talked about but felt every day, led him to become a Baptist. It also left him wondering why God had allowed him to live through the war, had let him have a second life. He still wondered. Sometimes he thought the reason might have to do with Lester, since his younger son's situation was the only unusual thing in his life. Maybe, Pat had been thinking lately, Lester's new speaking ability was tied to that reason. Maybe that meant that Pat, rather than being embarrassed by Lester's speaking, should embrace it, whatever that might mean.

# — ELEVEN —

Maddie arranged for Celestine and her sister, Floretta, to stay with Lester on Thursday evening while Greg did his schoolwork in the basement. That meant that Maddie and Pat could go out to dinner. They drove out to Southwest, to a seafood restaurant called the Flagship, on the Potomac River. In one of its enormous, red-carpeted dining rooms, among gleaming silverware on white tablecloths and parties of every size, they shared a table for two.

"I'm still getting over what you told me about Stan," Maddie said. "I just feel so bad for Gloria. Not like I even know her that well, but still. You've been with a man for twenty-three years, raised four kids together, and everything seems fine, and then this. I wonder if she saw it coming?"

"Wow. This is good," Pat said, savoring his salmon and mashed potatoes. "I don't see how she could have, since Stan didn't see it coming himself, from what he told me."

"It just makes it seem like such a mystery."

"What's a mystery?"

"Marriage," Maddie said. "Why some people stay together and others don't. I mean, some people shouldn't even *be* together, you can look at them and tell that. Like my parents. But the ones that seem like they belong together — why do *those* people split up? And other couples stay together?"

"You're not going to ask me to explain," Pat said in his kidding tone, "why *we're* still together, are you?"

"No. I know why we're still together. At least I know why I'm still with you. But how can you know that one day, and then the next it's all over? It just makes you feel afraid. I don't feel afraid for us, because I feel secure — I mean, I know I just said it makes me feel afraid. I guess I feel afraid *because* I feel so secure — oh, I don't know what I'm saying."

"No, I know what you mean. I feel the same way."

"I mean, what *happens?*"

"I guess anybody who gets married is taking a chance," Pat said. "No matter how happy you are at the beginning. In the beginning everything is so exciting, and then later the excitement gets replaced by habit. Or it *becomes* habit. And you don't know if you like the habit until you've formed it. And even then, maybe you're not quite the same person you were before. You know? Maybe marriage isn't something that's good until something makes it go bad. Maybe the whole thing is like a big chemical experiment. It's probably going to turn out a certain way, but you don't know how it's going to turn out until it ends." He smiled, and put his hand on top of his wife's. "Except for us, of course."

Maddie gave him back a grateful but worried smile. "It makes me afraid for Sherrie and Greg. Can you see them married? Do you ever think about that?"

"Sometimes. I can see Greg married; I can imagine some girl making him more serious to the point where he's ready to settle down and raise kids. Sherrie I'm not too sure about. I take that back — I can see her married, but sometimes I have a hard time picturing her with someone I can stand. God knows I haven't liked most of the boys she's brought home."

"Yes, I know. She *has* mentioned someone named Oscar. All I can get out of her is that he's nice."

"Well, if that's true, he's head and shoulders above his predecessors."

They were quiet a moment. Then Pat said, "You know, I didn't say anything to Stan about Lester's — new development."

"I was wondering if you were going to. Of course, he might have heard about it already, the way word got around, thanks to Celestine and Floretta."

"Hmp, I hadn't thought of that. Come to think of it, he did ask me specifically about Lester, like he was pretty interested. Maybe he *did* hear something, and that's why he asked."

"Or maybe not. Maybe it just seems to you now like he was extra interested, because I made you suspicious."

"Who knows. You know, speaking of all that, I was thinking ... I know the family agreed last weekend we were going to keep Lester's shouting to ourselves as much as possible, but since so many people already know about it now anyway, maybe we need to relax a little. You know? Things are tense enough as it is. You're affected more than anybody, since you can't teach. I wish it didn't have to be like that, if only we didn't need my salary —"

Maddie put her hand on top of her husband's. "You don't have to be sorry about that."

"Anyway, I was thinking: maybe we shouldn't worry so much. Our attitude can be, well, this is what Lester's doing now. Maybe we should even take him with us to church Sunday."

"To *church?* You really think so?"

"Why not? I mean, we can always leave if Lester starts his shouting. But we can make the 'new' Lester part of our lives."

"Maybe so. I guess we can wait and see what Sherrie's neurologist says at Hopkins tomorrow."

\*     \*     \*     \*

Later that evening, Sherrie got the telephone call she had been dreading.

"Hello?"

"Hi."

"Hi, Oscar."

This was followed by silence, which itself communicated something. *We know what we have to talk about. It is important. Our words will have more than their normal weight.*

Oscar finally said, "Listen. About yesterday. I don't want to be a jerk. I know I don't really have the right to expect anything from you, because you haven't committed to me in any way, *really.* I mean, that's been a little frustrating for me, but at least you haven't said anything you didn't mean, and I appreciate that. But I don't want to be a chump, either. The man I met yesterday, Doctor, what's his name —"

"Greer."

"Thank you. Dr. Greer." He seemed to be rolling the name around in his mouth, tasting it; Sherrie could imagine the sour look on his face. "I don't want to ask you about him. But I do want to ask about us. I know I have before, but this time, Sheridan, I need an answer. Are you and I going anywhere together? Are we going to be a couple? *Are* we a couple?"

"I don't think you should think of us as that. No."

"And I shouldn't think we will be?"

"No." In the silence that followed, Sherrie realized she was holding her breath. She forced herself to breathe normally. "No. You shouldn't think that."

"Okay. Fine. You know what, though? I changed my mind. I *am* going to ask about this Dr. Greer. You don't have to tell me anything, but —"

"No, I owe you that. What do you want to know?"

"*What do I want to know?* Well, are you involved with him?"

Following a pause, Sherrie said, "Yes."

"Oh. Okay. When did it start?"

"This week."

"This week. Are you and him — have you —"

"I said I was involved with him."

More silence. This time Sherrie ended it: "Oscar … you're going to think I'm saying this as some kind of consolation prize, but I really mean it. I think you're a decent, smart, funny, warm, and … good-looking man. You're going to make another woman very happy, and she'll be very lucky. But I don't think I'm the woman."

"Well, if I'm decent, funny, smart, and whatever else you said, what's the secret ingredient Dr. Greer came up with? How's the question go — 'What's he got that I haven't got?'"

"Oscar, it's not a mathematical equation. You can't break it down that way. I don't know. I just feel — I don't know, a connection —"

"With Greer?"

"Yes."

"And what's that feel like? How does he make you feel?"

"Oscar, this is getting kind of personal."

"Don't you know?"

"I don't know — *safe*."

The word, like the smile on her face when she said "Third grade," had been unplanned, seemed to have come from some hidden, subversive corner of her brain. As with the smile, she regretted it the next second.

"Safe," Oscar said. "Safe, like he'll protect you? Like he's more of a man than me?"

"He's not 'more of a man' than you, whatever that means. I don't even know why I said that."

"Hey, if that's how you feel, that's how you feel. You're just being honest." His voice, now, was just short of a snarl. "I'm going to say goodbye now. But listen. Whatever you do in life, don't lose your honesty, okay? Promise me that. It's your one good point."

"Oscar!"

"I'm sorry. I didn't mean that. I — whatever. Okay. Goodbye."

Sherrie put the telephone in its cradle, beside her on the sofa. Then she started to cry.

# — TWELVE —

On Friday morning the round, phosphorescent alarm clock on Pat's bedside table, giving off a pale glow like a full moon in the darkness of the room, sounded at five o'clock — two hours earlier than usual. Pat reached over to turn it off, then leaned back on his elbows, shaking his head slowly to clear it. "Unhhh … oh … Maddie …?"

"I know," she said. While Pat fumbled for his slippers, she rose slowly, retrieved her nightgown from a nearby chair, and made her way down the dark hall to Lester's room. When she turned on his bedside lamp, his head was sideways on the pillow, eyes closed, mouth open, his face showing no reaction to the light. Only when she stroked his shoulder and said softly, "Lessssterrr," did he make the face he'd always made on school mornings — one she realized she hadn't seen in a while: the who-are-you-and-why-are-you-bothering-me look, the closest Lester came to a normal person's annoyance. The look faded slowly as he sat up and scratched his head. "Bath," Maddie said. Knowing that meant "It's time for you to take a bath," Lester went slowly down the hall.

Maddie was in the kitchen, pouring coffee, still in her nightgown, when Pat walked in, wearing a suit and tie and the face of the not-quite-awake. "I think I'll just throw some clothes in the car and bathe at Sherrie's," Maddie said, handing Pat his steaming mug. "The appointment's not till ten."

They sat at the table and sipped awhile in silence. Then Pat said, "Are you nervous?"

"A little bit, I guess. I don't know why. It can't be any stranger than what's happened already."

Since Lester's appointment with Dr. Greer was in Baltimore at ten o'clock; since Pat needed to work; since no one wanted Lester to go to Baltimore via any kind of public transportation (despite Pat's advice that they make Lester "a normal part of their lives"); and since Maddie was not comfortable driving on the highway, the Hobbses had risen very early so that Pat could drive Maddie and Lester to Sherrie's apartment. He would leave the car there, take a train to his office and then another back to Baltimore after work, spend the night with Maddie at Sherrie's, then go with them the next morning to the second meeting with Dr. Greer.

All this meant that Greg had the Hobbs house to himself Friday night. When he'd heard this plan, several days earlier, he had needed all of his self-restraint to keep from dancing around the house. He could have Gina over and take full advantage of the fact that no one else would be around — as full as Gina would let him, anyway, and given the way things had gone between them so far … When he invited her over and offered to cook her dinner, she had teased him, pretending to be reluctant before giving him a mock-grudging, "Oh, all right." His week — possibly more than that — was made.

He had gotten ahead of himself in one area. He knew how to make exactly one dish — chili with meat — and if he couldn't make that, the only thing cooked would be his goose. Well, maybe not. He could come up with something else if he had to. But just to be safe, he had avoided asking her if she liked it or not. It would just be ready, or in preparation, when she showed up. And on Friday evening, he had just dropped a rock-hard pound-and-a-half of frozen hamburger meat into a pan with a *clank* when the doorbell rang.

He found, when he opened the door, that Gina's actual face still eluded the picture of her that he carried in his mind; her eyes, the shape of her jaw, were softer than the outlines in his memory, and the difference made for a surprise, but a nice one. "Hi. Welcome."

"Hi. What's cooking?"

"Nothin' mu — *oh*. You mean what's *cooking*. Chili."

"All right! I *love* chili."

Phew.

She was wearing a blue pullover blouse, a black skirt, and black stockings; she kept him company in the kitchen while he cooked, sitting at the table, her short but shapely legs crossed in a way that accentuated her calf. Greg sneaked glances at it when he turned to talk to her.

"So where did you say your family went?"

"I don't think I did. But they went to Baltimore. My brother's having some tests done at John Hopkins today and tomorrow."

"Is he all right?"

"He's all right. Least I think he is. He's taking everybody *else* through some changes."

"This brother of yours is intriguing me."

"I'll tell you all about him when we're sitting down. How was your day?"

As Greg tended to the meat, turning the frozen block over when it had cooked on one side and scraping off the browned portions, Gina talked about her day. A senior, she was continuing at Howard in its graduate program in international relations; she had had to attend a lunch meeting for students entering the program, an event she described as "kind of sad. It was like, nobody really seemed to know why they were *there.*"

"They didn't have any kind of event?" Greg asked, turning on the flame under the beans. "It was just lunch?"

"No, I don't mean nobody knew why they were at the lunch — I mean, I didn't talk to anybody who seemed to know why they were going into the *program.* I talked to a couple of people, and I told them, you know, how I'm interested in establishing more ties between the U.S. and nations in Africa, especially helping countries that have been struggling toward democracy since their independence — all the things I told you the other night. Then I'd ask them what got *them* interested in the program, and they didn't have a thing to say! Except one guy, who said he applied because he wasn't sure he could get into law school! I thought, *these* are the people being trained to think about the future of U.S. foreign relations? I don't know. Sometimes people aren't at their best at those kinds of things.

And I can get excited." This was something Greg had noticed and found endearing about Gina: the way she often pulled back on the occasional negative comment, as if she had a parent on her shoulder whispering, "If you can't say anything nice …" She reminded him in that way of his friend Clive. But she was a lot cuter.

When the food was ready they moved to the dining room. Greg lit two tall red candles, which he had put on the table along with a fresh white tablecloth. "Very romantic," Gina said.

"That's what's in my soul, girl. Romance."

"Romance and teasing. Mmmmm," she said, tasting the chili. "That's good."

"Um — good …"

"Is anything wrong?"

"No. I was just … I said I'd tell you about my brother when we sat down. I'm just trying to think of how to start."

He started at the beginning, with his memories of having Lester as a brother during childhood, when he wished for a brother who could talk and play games, like other boys had; nonetheless, he said, he had become attached to Lester. He talked about getting into fights to protect Lester, or when kids teased him about having a retarded brother. There were times, he told Gina, as he and Sherrie walked Lester to and from school, when he felt like they were his parents, because they had so much responsibility for looking after him. ("I know something about that," Gina said, referring to her responsibility for her sisters after her mother's death.) Sometimes now Greg found himself thinking about a time when he and Sherrie really would be responsible for Lester; their parents weren't old, of course, but in fifteen or twenty years they would be, and what then? Would Greg have his life together enough to take care of Lester? He hoped so. No doubt Sherrie would, but he couldn't just assume she would do it. Sometimes he looked at Lester, who was still so helpless. … At that point in his reflections, to his surprise, Greg found himself tearing up. "Damn … sorry," he said, brushing away a tear.

"It's okay. It's emotional stuff."

"I haven't even told you the strange part yet. You know how I said my brother's never said a word? Well. Last Friday … well —

you know the other day, when we were talking on the phone, and you heard somebody doing a rap in the background? You thought it was a record?"

"Yeah."

Greg said no more — he merely looked in Gina's eyes, watching as comprehension, then disbelief, blossomed on her face. "Wait a minute," she said. "That was your *brother*?"

"That was my brother."

"So, you're saying he never talked before, and now he's …"

"Rapping. Yes."

"Was he — was he repeating something he heard?"

"Nope. All new stuff. Out of his own head. Stuff about when he was little, stuff about our family, a lot of little details the rest of us forgot. All in rhyme. Sounds like something from a bad TV show, but it's the God's honest truth."

Gina sat back in her chair and laid her fork on her plate, all the while staring at Greg. She looked down a moment, then back up at him. "That's …"

"You don't believe me, right? Now you know why I didn't want to tell you before."

"It's not that I don't believe you, it's just … I can't believe *it*."

"I know. Join the club. You don't have to say anything. You can just digest it, along with the chili. Here, let me take your plate. Want to see my room?"

After he had rinsed the dishes, Greg took Gina to the basement. "This is nice," she said, looking around. She's being polite, he thought. She sounded sincere, though, when she said, "I like your Earth, Wind & Fire poster. I love them."

"Well then, allow me to put some on."

He joined her on the edge of the bed as one of the group's mellower songs, "Reasons," played. "How long have you slept down here?"

"Since the tenth grade."

"You're lucky. I have my own room, but it's a lot smaller than this."

"Prob'ly 'cause it doesn't have everybody else's junk in it, like this one does."

"Well ... I shouldn't complain," Gina said. "I'm twenty-two, and I'm living in my father's house. I'm going to look for another place after graduation, maybe just a room somewhere near the campus. I haven't told my dad yet."

"Will he be upset?"

"Not upset. Sad, I think. I don't think he ever wants any of his girls to leave." She turned toward Greg. "You know: I believe you. About your brother."

"Well. Thanks."

"Is he having tests at Hopkins so they can find out what's causing him to talk suddenly?"

"Yeah, that's the idea. My sister's in grad school there. She talked to the head of the neurology department. Black dude."

"*Really.*"

Greg laughed. "That's what *I* said. I didn't know there *was* no black neurologists. But if somebody white said that, we'd say he was a racist, right?"

"True," Gina said, and they laughed together.

"Hey, want some Asti Spumante?"

She smiled. "Are you trying to—"

"*Yes.* What do you think?" He went upstairs and returned with two glasses and a green bottle. "So, a toast," he said, pouring the clear, sparkling wine in a glass and handing it to her. He filled his own glass and held it up. "Here's to believing each other."

They clinked their glasses together and took long sips, gazing into each other's eyes the entire time. They lowered their glasses simultaneously. Still holding them, they leaned together for a long kiss, made cold but sweet by the wine. After their lips separated, with a *blick*, Greg gently took her glass, his hand shaking, and set them both on the floor. When he straightened up again and turned toward Gina, her eyes seemed wider, boring into him. He felt a surge inside him, and the next moment he entered a blurred frenzy, eyes now closed, now open, now closed again, his body on top of hers, underneath hers, his palm on the soft bare skin of her lower back, the warmth of her fingers on his bare side, down the back of his pants, their tongues battling like swords made of flesh; they fell apart to undress, her eyes heavy-lidded, drunk-looking, her lips parting as they moved toward his again.

Afterward, they held each other as they talked, joked, laughed. Then they grabbed some of their clothes — she put on her blouse and underwear but not her skirt, he pulled on his pants but not his shirt — and went to get more food. They ate on the sofa, watching television. During a commercial they started kissing again. They went to the basement to make love a second time. Afterward, they both dozed off.

Greg was awakened from a solid sleep when Gina said, "Oh! God! Greg!"

"Hunh … what? …"

"It's almost three o'clock! My father's going to be worried sick! I've gotta go!"

She jumped out of bed and put her clothes on with the urgency of a firefighter; Greg, meanwhile, blinked enough clouds away from his brain to find his pants. "So," he said, pulling them on slowly, talking even more slowly, "was he expecting you back at a certain time?"

"No, it's not that. I'm just never out this late. Or if I am, I let him know ahead of time. It's not that he asks me to, it's just that I know he worries. He never *says* he worries, but — it's hard to explain."

"Wish my dad's car was here. I'd drive you."

"Think we could call a cab?"

"I don't think they'd come out here this time of night. I'll go to the bus with you. You want to call your dad and tell him you're coming?"

"No. I don't want to wake him up in case he's sleeping. He probably isn't, he's probably up waiting for me, but … how long do you think the bus will take to come?"

"This time of night, it could take a while."

"*Ohhhh …*"

"Don't worry. I just had an idea."

The air outside had turned cool and foggy. Greg put on a denim jacket and lent Gina a hooded sweatshirt of his that was absurdly large on her, and they set off in the quiet dark.

"Where're we going?"

"To see my friend."

They stopped in front of Clive's house. Greg began scouring the grass in the front yard. "Greg," Gina said, "Um, what are you …?"

"Here. Found some." He stood up and aimed one of the small rocks he had found at a second-floor window; it struck home, with a *plack*.

"Greg, should you be —"

"It's fine." He threw a second rock. *Plack*. He was about to throw a third when the window rose with a squeal, and a voice said, "What the fuck you — *Greg?*"

"I need your wheels," Greg said in the loudest whisper possible, cupping his hands around his mouth. "It's an emergency."

"Negro, are you crazy?" Clive was whispering now, too. "That's my dad's car! You know what time it is?"

"Greg," Gina said, "You don't have to —"

"It's an emergency. I gotta take Gina home. I'll bring it right back, I swear."

There was a pause, and then Clive said, "Wait a minute."

"Is he going to get in trouble?" Gina said.

"Ain't gon be no trouble."

In a few seconds they heard the front door open. They walked up to the porch. Clive stood in the doorway, wearing paisley pajamas — and a scowl — and holding the car keys. "I didn't know you wore pajamas," Greg said, smiling.

"Boy, I like *your* nerve. I'ma be wearin' prison stripes if you don't bring this car back before it gets light."

"It'll be back way before then. This is Gina. Gina, this is Clive."

"Hi," Clive said, managing to smile at her, in spite of everything.

"Hi," Gina said, smiling back.

"Clive," Greg said, "you are a true gentleman."

"Just bring the car back, fool."

*     *     *     *

They drove through northeast Washington along wide, empty streets. They passed Union Station, then went in a quarter-circle around the U.S. Capitol, whose white stone glowed faintly in the middle-of-the-night blackness. Next they turned onto East Capitol Street. "Clive sure is a good friend, huh?" Gina said.

"Yeah. He knows I'd do the same for him, though."

She chuckled. "You're like — some kind of movie adventurer. Getting into a jam, thinking of a way out. I guess I'm the one in the jam, though."

"So you think your dad'll be mad?"

"No, I just don't want to worry him. All he does is worry about his girls."

Greg turned left onto Tenth Street. "It's the second one from the corner, on the right. Uh-oh," she said as Greg put the car in park, "the living room light is on. What time is it?"

"Three-thirty-five."

She sighed. Then she turned toward him with a sad smile. "Listen, thank you. I had a … it was nice."

"Should I come in? Maybe he'll feel better if he meets me."

"*Oh*. Well, okay."

In the front yard the moisture on the bushes glistened in the light from the street lamp. Going up the porch steps, Greg exhaled through his mouth, and though the air was not very cold, his breath formed a white cloud, as he had thought it would. Gina unlocked the door, and he walked inside behind her.

"Hi, Daddy." In a corner of the small living room, an enormous man with a short, graying Afro sat in an armchair. On the small table next to him were a lamp and a glass half-full of amber liquid. A book was open on his lap, but he was not reading; he was, rather, staring grimly in their direction, and even when Gina crossed the room and kissed him on the cheek, the stare continued — at Greg. Maybe this was not such a good idea.

"Daddy, this is Greg. He goes to Howard. He drove me home."

Greg walked up to him and offered his hand. "Nice to meet you, Mr. Bowie."

Gina's father stayed seated, and silent. He did extend his hand, which surprised Greg with its softness. He stared up at Greg, with eyes that, on closer inspection, were not so much grim as — Greg couldn't quite say what; large, yellow, luminous, they seemed almost to be asking something. Finally he said, in the bottomless voice Greg remembered from the telephone, "Sit down. You want a drink?"

"Daddy, Greg's got to go, he's driving his —"

"He can have a drink." With a suddenness that surprised Greg, the older man stood and made his way, somewhat unsteadily, across the floor. Gina looked at Greg, an apology written on her face. Mr. Bowie returned with another glass and a bottle of Jim Beam.

"You can drink it straight, like me," he said, filling a third of the glass and shoving it at Greg.

"Dad, you don't even know if he likes bourbon."

"He looks like he can handle it."

Mr. Bowie returned to his armchair. Greg sat at the corner of the sofa nearest him, and Gina sat beside Greg. Mr. Bowie said to Greg, "You got any daughters?"

"Daddy!"

"No, sir, I don't."

"You don't have to call me sir. We just talking. Got any sons?"

"No."

"Got any parents?"

"Daddy ..."

"Yes, I do."

"Do they worry? About you and your siblings?"

"Um ..." Greg chuckled. "Sorry. Yeah, they do."

"You not drinking."

"Sorry." Greg took a sip of bourbon, feeling it burn his tongue. "Wow, that's strong stuff."

"So since you got parents, and they worry about you, you can appreciate why I worry. Not trying to be mean. Just takes me a little while to come out of it."

"You don't have to explain, Mr. Bowie. I understand. I really do have to go, sir. Thank you for the drink. I'm sorry I don't have time to finish it. I'd like to talk to you another time."

"All right, then," Mr. Bowie said.

Gina walked him to the door. "Sorry about that," she whispered.

"It's all right. I like him. I'll call you tomorrow."

When Greg pulled up in front of Clive's house, Clive was sitting on the porch glider, dressed this time in jeans, a shirt, and a jacket. "You been out here all this time?" Greg said, walking up the porch steps and handing back the car keys.

"Just about. Who you think can sleep, waitin' for you to come back?"

"I appreciate it, man."

"Guess you like this gal, huh?"

"Guess so."

# —THIRTEEN—

Many hours earlier, on Friday morning, Sherrie had taken her mother and Lester by car to Johns Hopkins University Hospital, where they met George Greer. The four of them gathered first in a small examining room, where Dr. Greer's calm, friendly, but authoritative tone, his air of being unfazed by any details about Lester's behavior, won Maddie's confidence and put her at ease. Dr. Greer explained briefly that in another room Lester would undergo a painless procedure, something called a CAT-scan, and that a group of residents would be present to observe Lester and the procedure. This second room was larger, with a desk-level shelf that ran along all four white walls and was packed with equipment that looked to Maddie as if it had been borrowed from the set of a science-fiction movie. The four young residents, three men and a woman, all white and wearing white coats like Dr. Greer's, greeted Maddie stiffly; they listened with unreadable faces as Dr. Greer summarized Lester's behavior. When Lester suddenly began shouting and rhyming about his trip to the circus, Dr. Greer and three of the residents behaved as if this were perfectly ordinary — while the fourth, one of the young men, looked concerned, if not alarmed. Maddie decided that she liked this resident.

What seemed to be the centerpiece of the room was a large white machine. Part of it was an examining table, for patients to lie on; at one end of the table was what looked like a point-and-shoot camera blown up to the size of a dresser, wider than it was tall, with a hole at the center, large enough to accommodate a person's head. Maddie held Lester's hand while Dr. Greer gently guided him onto the table and Sherrie and the residents looked on; she stroked her son's leg as the machinery around his head began to hum and Lester's face took on a vaguely worried look. When it stopped, Dr. Greer showed them back to the first examining room. Sherrie left to attend a class, and Maddie and Lester sat alone for nearly a half hour. Then Dr. Greer came to get them again, explaining on the way back to the larger room that for the next test — the electroencephalogram, or something that sounded like that —Lester's head would have to be shaved. Maddie held and stroked Lester's hand while a female technician with wild red hair and long purple fingernails lathered, then shaved, Lester's head. The woman then attached sixteen (Maddie counted) electrodes to Lester's scalp with a white paste; the electrodes connected to wires that fed into a square machine, on the other side of which were instruments like horizontal windshield wipers that made thin, jagged marks on a long, rolling piece of paper.

Next, Dr. Greer wanted to examine Lester in private. Maddie left them in the small examining room, first reminding Dr. Greer to take Lester to the bathroom occasionally, as Lester didn't know where it was and could not simply go there on his own, the way he did at home; Dr. Greer assured her that he would. Maddie found the cafeteria, where she ate a surprisingly good tuna salad from a plastic container, then browsed in the gift shop, returning to the examining room in an hour, as Dr. Greer had instructed her. He was not done with Lester yet. Maddie circled the halls for another few minutes. When she peeked in again, Dr. Greer was ready for her. The three of them went to the larger room again, where the residents had reassembled. Dr. Greer asked Maddie questions about Lester's daily behavior before and after the shouting spells had begun; the residents listened and asked an occasional question themselves. Dr. Greer then asked Maddie to take Lester for a short walk while the rest of them conferred among themselves.

"Well, *this* is different, huh, Lester?" Maddie said, as they walked slowly and quietly through the halls, where more people in white coats went to and fro in hurried strides. She smiled and added, "I wonder what kind of rhyme you'll make up about this later. You know, you don't look too bad with no hair." She checked her watch; it was nearly one o'clock. They had been at the hospital almost three hours. "Well, you think they're ready for us yet?" Maddie took a chance and led them back to the large examining room, where Dr. Greer told her that they were finished for the day and that he would see them tomorrow.

A short while later, her class over, Sherrie picked up Maddie and Lester. After she had gotten over her mild shock at Lester's bald head, she drove them back to her apartment. Sherrie had bought some children's puzzles, which Lester worked at her round kitchen table, his trembling hand steadying as it picked up a puzzle piece. Across the room, Sherrie and Maddie sat on the sofa with cups of tea.

"Dr. Greer is so impressive," Maddie said. "He really makes you feel like you're in good hands. And I have to say, it gives you a good feeling to see a black man in charge like that, telling white residents what's what. He cuts a fine figure."

"Don't think he doesn't know it," Sherrie said.

"Why do you say that? Does he seem conceited to you?"

"Oh … just a feeling I get from him." She sipped her tea.

"Well … at least he's got something to be conceited *about*. He's such a good role model. I suppose," Maddie said, giving her daughter a sidelong smile, "he's married?"

"Yes, I believe he is."

"Too bad. He's good-looking, on top of everything else."

"Yep, he's a regular bionic man."

"Oh, you're so cynical. So how's Oscar?"

Sherrie furrowed her brow. "Oscar," she said, "is just a weeeee bit mad at me right now. We had a conversation yesterday about our relationship."

"Let me guess: you just want to be friends, and he wants something else."

"That's it in a nutshell, yeah."

"So what's wrong with him?"

"There's nothing wrong with him. Just because I don't want to have a romantic relationship with him doesn't mean there's something wrong with him. I like him as a friend."

"Didn't you say he's nice?"

"Yes, Ma, he's nice. That's just not enough to make me want to be his girlfriend."

"Sometimes I think you don't like boys — men — *because* they're nice. Poor Calvin Thomas, nice as he could be, just adored you, and you only had eyes for Ben—"

"Oh my God, Ma. Can we please give the subject of Calvin Thomas and Benjamin Giles a *rest*? Especially since I haven't seen either one of them in five years?"

"I'm sorry, you're right. I'll stop. Oh, look at your brother over there, with his bald head. He looks so cute! So — do you have any friends nearby, besides Oscar? Anybody else you can do things with?"

"No, not really. Which is just as well, since I stay so busy I don't have a lot of time."

"I envy you, then. Since I'm not teaching I have a lot of time and no way to fill it. Although I have been thinking about doing a little painting again."

"Really? That would be good."

"Yes. It's been so long since I thought about doing it. I used to enjoy it, and then it became so tied up with teaching that I stopped just doing it for myself. But I just might pull out my easel again."

"That sounds good. Actually, Ma, I was going to say I should go to the library for a couple of hours. Will you and Lester be okay? Do you need anything?"

"We're fine. We'll just watch TV, or something. Won't we, Les?"

*　　*　　*　　*

In spite of everything, Sherrie had been looking forward to having Lester and her parents spend the night with her. Maybe it was the prospect of having her first interaction in days that did not involve some sort of romantic/sexual negotiation. Her father would make a comment or two about the safety (or lack of same) in her neighborhood, her exchanges with her mother might have come from a textbook on the psychology of mother-daughter relations, but those annoyances were so familiar that they were comforting, like corny or maudlin or otherwise objectionable songs we probably wouldn't like if they didn't remind us of childhood. Sherrie and George Greer had agreed to keep things on a purely professional basis for the weekend, so as not to raise her parents' eyebrows; besides, he had his own family to spend time with, the dog. So Friday evening it would just be Sherrie, her parents, and Lester.

After spending the rest of the afternoon at the library, Sherrie went to meet her father's train. "How'd it go at the hospital?" Pat said, as Sherrie drove them away from the station.

"Sounded like it went okay. I was only there for part of it. I guess we'll find out more tomorrow. One thing: be prepared for Lester's new look. They had to shave his head for one of the tests."

"Oh!"

At the apartment, Pat, Maddie and Sherrie laughed about Lester's new resemblance to Jack Johnson, Lester giving a little smile as Pat squeezed his neck and shoulders and called him "Champ." Sherrie had picked up ingredients for lasagna, which she and Maddie prepared in the kitchen area while Lester watched cartoons on television and Pat perused the books on his daughter's shelf. Once, Lester stood and shouted a rhyme about some winter day years earlier, an outburst that might have been happening on TV for all the attention Pat, Maddie, and Sherrie gave it. At dinner around Sherrie's little round table they speculated about what Greg might be doing with the house to himself.

"He did say he had a lot of economics to study," Maddie said.

Pat laughed so heartily that Maddie and Sherrie had to join in. "Are you kidding? We're talking about our older son? Did you see the look on his face when he heard we were coming to Baltimore? His eyes lit up like he'd hit the number. The only thing he's studying is how to get his new girlfriend's—"

"Careful, Dad!" Sherrie said, covering her ears. "I'm an impressionable young girl!"

"Why don't we call him right now," Pat said, barely able to get the words out, "and ask him what page he's on!"

"Pat," Maddie said, laughing loudly, "you're terrible!"

Later, the four of them watched *The Rockford Files*. Then they went to bed, so they could be rested for the next morning's appointment with Dr. Greer.

*       *       *       *

At eleven a.m. on Saturday, in Greer's office at the university, Pat and Sherrie sat in chairs in front of the desk, while Maddie sat with Lester on the black leather sofa next to the wall. Greer, in a single-breasted jacket and a shirt with a collar but no tie, leaned forward on his desk, his fingers interlaced. "Well. We've finished our preliminary tests and gotten back some results," he said. "I'd like to do some further tests and observation, but I do have enough information for a theory. When Lester was a small child, he was pronounced to be simply mentally retarded, which was not inaccurate, as far as it went. But our findings, and Lester's recent behavior, suggest that there is much more at play here, and always has been. I believe that Lester's condition actually represents a convergence of different phenomena that is unusual, if not unique. As I said, Lester's intelligence, his ability to grasp ideas, is just below normal. But he also has a form of Parkinson's disease."

Pat, Maddie, and Sherrie, as with one voice, said, "*Parkinson's?*"

"Yes. A highly unusual form. In one strain of the disease, patients may actually feel as if they are performing actions at a normal speed but look to you and me as if they are not moving at all. A man might be standing perfectly still. Ask him what he is doing, and he will respond, 'Buttoning my shirt.' His brain may have sent his hand the signal to button his shirt, and it may seem to the man as though he is doing that, and indeed his hand may be making its way toward the buttons — at a speed that seems normal to the man, but which *you and I cannot detect*. It's a condition called *bradykinesia*, and it generally refers to such physical acts. It seems that with Lester, the act that is slowed to the point of stillness is his ability to speak, to translate thought into speech. You might think of it this way: each one of us is like an army, with the brain as supreme commander — General Eisenhower. Our thoughts, then, are field commanders, which makes words like foot soldiers. In Lester's case, the mechanism connecting thoughts to words is so slow that the chain of command, you might say, breaks down. If what I believe is correct, there are, and always have been, moments when Lester begins to speak. But the sound is never heard, in part because of his slowness in making the sounds, and in part because the situations he is responding to change, and so he stops 'speaking,' or rather, stops trying to speak."

"Oh, my," Maddie said.

"You mentioned, Mrs. Hobbs, that Lester often looks at you as if he is not seeing you, or as if he's seeing you and other things, too. What we think accounts for that is that the words he attempts to speak echo in his mind, even after the situations that inspire them change. And each set of words connects him to the event that inspired it. Looking at you might take him back to many sets of words and memories, *simultaneously*. So when he looks at you, he may be 'seeing' more than one of you — almost like a fly."

Pat said, "So what about the shouting and rhyming? Why that, all of a sudden?"

"That brings me to the second phenomenon, or I should say, the second part of my theory. It's that recently, Lester has been experiencing a form of epileptic seizure. With this particular type of seizure, which results from unusual activity in the temporal lobes of the brain, a memory can take over a person's mind with incredible vividness. It might be the memory of something that occurred over the course of an afternoon, or a week, or a year. In the patient's mind, it *feels* that long. In reality, the memory lasts a few seconds or a minute. My belief is that with Lester, these seizures cause two things to happen. One is that he relives events from the very distant or very recent past. The other is that these convulsions in his brain actually stimulate his speaking ability, which is usually slowed down by his form of Parkinson's. So when he begins to shout, he is in effect narrating the events he is reliving. And, if he's not exactly talking to *you*, it's because, in his mind, he's not where you are. He's in the past."

Sherrie said, "But why the *rhyming?*"

"Basically, because he can. In those moments, when he has the seizures, Lester's brain is operating incredibly quickly. In his mind, the events he describes — which he relives — are happening in what's called 'real time.' To us, it's a matter of seconds or a minute, but to him it's much longer. That's why, in seconds, he can translate his experiences into rhymes that would take you or me half an hour or more to think up."

Dr. Greer leaned back in his chair, loosely gripping the armrests, allowing the Hobbses to take in what he had said. The Hobbses, for their part, stared with puzzled faces into the middle distance, as if straining to see an object there — all except Lester. Pat said, "So — we've always known he could understand some words that he hears over and over, almost like a dog does. But, obviously, he's taken in the meanings of a lot of words. I mean, we've always tended to talk in front of him like he can't understand most of it, but you're saying ..."

"He understands quite a lot of it, yes. Maybe not as much as you or I, but much more than you've probably thought up until now. How deeply he thinks about it is another question. From what you've told me, and from the little I've observed, he shouts about things that have happened, but doesn't comment much on them. Which doesn't suggest a great deal of self-consciousness, which is where higher intelligence comes into play." Smiling slightly, Greer added, "He's more of a reporter than an editorial writer."

"So," Sherrie said, "what now?"

"That's largely up to you. We can't really prevent seizures. There is, however, a drug for treating Parkinson's patients: L-dopa. In many patients it counteracts the kind of slowness that affects Lester's speech."

Maddie, her eyes wide, said, "You mean if he took it, he could *talk*? To us?"

"*Maybe*," Greer said. "But there is something to keep in mind. I mentioned that the seizures very likely stimulate Lester's ability to speak. The process works in reverse as well. That is, the Parkinson's acts as a kind of slowing device on the seizures. During the seizures, as it is, Lester's brain is in a tumultuous state. Without the slowing effect of Parkinson's, we can't be a hundred percent certain what will occur. Probably nothing extremely dangerous — millions of people suffer from epileptic seizures and live otherwise normal lives. But we couldn't say for sure. If you think of your brain as an electrical system — basically, that's what it is — a seizure is like a short-circuit, an overload. They're a nuisance, but they don't usually leave you without power for very long."

"So," Maddie said, "if Lester had a seizure without the Parkinson's to kind of guard against it, he could … pass out?"

"Pass out, blank out. Much of the danger from seizures is not from what happens in the brain, but *when* it happens. If you're standing, you can fall and hit your head. If you're on the steps … you get the idea. But that's not to say that the seizures pose no risks *with* the Parkinson's. They just haven't seemed to be dangerous *yet*."

"And," Pat said, "taking that risk into account, if he takes the — what is it —"

"L-dopa?"

"Yes. If he takes that, there's a good chance he could … talk to us, *communicate* with us, like a … normal person?"

"Yes. I would say so."

Pat, Sherrie, and Maddie began looking around at each other as if to say, *Can this be true? Are we dreaming?*

"Why don't we do this," Greer said. "Think about what I've said. I'll schedule Lester for more tests next week. If you decide you don't want to try him on L-dopa, then the tests can simply be to shore up what I already believe. If you decide you want to go ahead with the L-dopa treatment, it can begin that day, and we can begin to observe the results. And again, this will cost you nothing. I'll arrange it with the hospital. What we're learning from Lester is worth much more than the costs of the testing." This brought a chorus of *thank you*'s from the Hobbses. "How about next Saturday, then? A week from today?"

Pat, exchanging nods with the others, said, "Next Saturday it is."

*    *    *    *

They drove back to Sherrie's apartment without saying much, all of them trying, separately, to take in the implications of what they had heard. When they got to the apartment it was lunchtime, and they made sandwiches. It was not until they were seated at the little round table that Pat said, "Well, we should at least consider trying the L-dopa, right? If it'll give Lester the chance to speak, I mean, normally, after all these years?"

Sherrie nodded. Maddie said, "I'm excited about that, too, but what about the risk? From the seizures?"

"Dr. Greer said it probably wouldn't be all that dangerous. And we don't know that he isn't *already* at risk because of the seizures. I know we should think about it and talk about it some more, but right now I feel like we should do it."

"I guess I do too," Maddie said.

After lunch Sherrie hugged and kissed her father, mother, and brother, who got in the car to head back to Washington.

"You know," Maddie said when they were on the highway, "what if we're thinking of taking this risk, but we're not appreciating what Lester already *is*?"

"I think we have the chance to finally find *out* who he is," Pat said. "And, more importantly, I think we have the chance to give Lester to himself."

"I liked him the way he was before."

"Yes. But he isn't like that anymore."

# — FOURTEEN —

Beulah Baptist Church, the Reverend Marvin Briscoe, Pastor, occupied a short block roughly a third of a mile from the Hobbs home. The church was surrounded by houses with small front yards, where the grass was like the hair on the heads of old men — more on some than on others, with shapeless, curious bare patches here and there. By contrast, the yard of Beulah Baptist, bisected by a concrete walkway, was completely covered by grass of an almost startling green, thanks in part to the chest-high wire fence that protected it from the feet of the neighborhood children. The church building itself, like many of the houses around it, was made of red brick; but unlike the brick of those houses, which had darkened to a blackish purple with years of dirt that the rain had not completely washed away, the outer walls of Beulah Baptist were periodically hosed and scrubbed, their brightness restored, a process that involved hired men, scaffolds, and pole-handled brushes. Such care made the church stand out among its neighboring buildings like an audience member at a sold-out show with a spotlight trained on her.

Wide, white stone steps led to the glass double doors of the church's entrance. The visitor passed through these into the lobby, whose most prominent features were two large, framed paintings, one a portrait of the church founder, the other of the current pastor. The church offices were to the left. To the right were more double doors, wooden and several inches thick, polished to a gleam, requiring the same effort to open and close as barn doors. These opened onto the chapel, where Pat and Maddie, with Lester between them, sat in a pew near the back, waiting for the start of the service.

The other worshipers in the small congregation filed in, mostly people Pat and Maddie's age and older, or couples with teenagers or young children — little girls with white stockings and buckle shoes, their shiny hair pulled back into buns whose tightness looked painful, little boys with bony arms and elbows hanging from enormous white or powder-blue short sleeves. The older women wore hats, many with veils, and from beneath these, as they tottered down the red-carpeted aisle, they aimed looks of undisguised curiosity at the Hobbses, looks that Pat met with a smile and a nod as he thought, *Lord, what have we done.*

On Sundays when the weather was good, as it was today, the Hobbses enjoyed walking to church instead of driving. But this morning's walk, for all the sunshine and pleasant air, had been marred by anxiety that Pat began to feel even before they came in sight of the church — and that Maddie began to feel, too: he could tell, because she had helped him keep up an almost desperate chatter about anything at all that didn't involve Lester. Now, in the pew, Pat told himself, *It's all right. If he starts up, you'll leave, that's all. The whole point of doing this was to feel normal. So feel normal.* This silent pep talk helped him for about a minute, after which, like a New Year's resolution in the third week of January, it was forgotten. Reverend Briscoe and Deacon Woodard took their seats behind the lectern; to the right, the choir began to sing "The Old Rugged Cross" (*On a hill, far away, stood an old rugged cross/the emblem of suffering and shame …*); the congregation joined in, somebody's high, bad voice rising above the others. As these rituals took place, Pat felt like a bus passenger who has to go to the bathroom, passing familiar landmarks viewed now through a lens of desperation: *Please don't let me wet myself/Please don't let him start shouting. …*

To distract himself, Pat thought, ironically, of Lester — of the proposed treatment, of the possibility that the boy could speak normally. He remembered something Maddie had said a week or so ago: that in a way Lester had been a baby who had never stopped being a baby. But speech would perhaps put an end to that; his personality might well emerge, just as those of very young children did — only, in this case, the parents of the young child would be nearing fifty. Were he and Maddie ready to become parents again? Was that what would happen? What part of Lester's hidden self was contained in the words he had never used until now? Might he become defiant? Would the whole process of parenthood really begin again — the discipline, the arguing, the things most parents signed up for when they were young and energetic, not middle-aged and tired?

At the invitation of Deacon Woodard, several new visitors to the church, scattered among the worshipers, stood and spoke. "My name's Winston Banks, I belong to Ebenezer Baptist Church, I'm here today with my cousin and his family, I'm very happy to be with you on this beautiful ..." Throughout his adult life, with some decisions, large and small, Pat had been able to simplify matters by asking himself, What is the *right* thing? But here was yet another case in which there were two answers. The right thing, of course, was to go ahead with the L-dopa treatment Dr. Greer had mentioned, to pursue the possibility that their grown child Lester might finally be able to have something approaching a normal life. Except, of course, that the right thing was actually to protect their child, to avoid any possible risk to him from the seizures Dr. Greer had described, which might result in God only knew what.

"Thank you, it's always good to see new faces. A few announcements: the bus for the picnic next Saturday will leave the church promptly at ten a.m. Anyone who is planning to attend who has not spoken to Sister Jenkins about bringing food, please do so after the service. ..."

Something made Pat glance toward Maddie, who in turn smiled at him with her lips closed and eyebrows raised, as if to say, *So far, so good, we'll see.* He peeked at Lester, still vacant-looking in his jacket and tie; and his worries about this service, which had never really left his mind — as the thought of peeing stays with the bus passenger even as he thinks of other things — came back into focus. *It'll be all right*, he told himself again. *The second he starts, if he starts, you'll grab his arm and go. Nothing else to it.* So what made him keep worrying? Perhaps it was his forty-eight years of living, which had been filled with instances when he had figured on a certain number of possible outcomes, only to witness the one he had not thought of. Ah, to be young, to be sure you could predict things, to be … Greg. Greg's response to the news about Lester had been predictable — predictably free, that is, of anything serious. "Me and Les could finally go talk to girls together! 'My name's Greg, this is Lester, he just started talking. Say some'm to the ladies, Les. Help him out, ladies     what rhymes with *Hello*?'"

While the choir started on "Rock of Ages" ( … *let the water and the blood/from the wounded side which flowed* … ), the ushers came down the center and side aisles with collection baskets; in charcoal suits and white gloves, their faces unmoving, they were like Secret Service agents, like caricatures of seriousness, as they passed the baskets down each pew. Pat reached for his wallet and pulled out his usual five-dollar bill. Good gracious, *would* Lester start talking about girls? As far as he had been able to tell, the boy had little or no impulse in that direction, though Maddie had said that on a few occasions Lester's underwear had been damp with something that seemed like … What kind of wet dream could the boy have, anyway? Would he be able to talk about them now? Would Pat have to sit him down to talk about sex? Maybe not. Or maybe he could talk Greg into doing it. …

Now came the sermon. The burly Reverend Briscoe, his black robe flowing, black hair shot through with gray, took his place behind the lectern. "Good morning, brothers and sisters," he said in his resonant voice, sober as a network news anchor. (The church answered with "Good morning" or "Good morning, Reverend.") "I wanted to tell you a little something about the day I had yesterday. …"

"Tell us, Reverend. Mmm-hm," called one of the elderly ladies in a pew near the front.

"I ran an errand or two, the kind of thing you do on Saturday — you know what I'm talkin' about: took my clothes to the dry cleaners, took a package to the Post Office, had to rush to get it there before it closed. I made it, though."

"Good for you, Reverend."

"Then I came home, because the basketball game was on,"

Reverend Briscoe went on, in the same dry tone. "And as I was watching, congratulating myself on having run my errands, gotten my clothes to the cleaners, taken the package to the Post Office on time, as I was preparing to enjoy the game, something occurred to me, and I said to myself" — here it was, Pat could feel it coming: the rise in the Reverend's pitch, the moment when the news anchor stood up and began to shout — "I said, *Have I THOUGHT about the LORD yet today?*"

"Amen!"

"I said to myself, I'm worried about gettin' to the Post Office on time, but am I thinking about the *Lord's* office, the one where he keeps his *book*, with the names of the *sinners* and the *righteous*?!"

Several ladies' hands shot into the air, wrinkled brown fingers outstretched, immaculately painted nails reaching toward heaven. "Amen!" "Hallelujah!"

"Oh, I know how it is," the Reverend said in a quieter tone. "I know what it is to be so caught up in your daily affairs that you forget about the Lord. You get so good at what you're doing, you start to think to yourself, Well, I'm pretty good at this. I'm pretty good at that. But do you think that it's the LORD that's MAKING YOU SO GOOD AT WHAT YOU DO? That it's the LORD that helped you get to the Post Office on time?"

"Yes, Lord!"

"Oh, yes, I was looking forward to watching the basketball game. Like many people, I wanted to see Elvin Hayes drive to the basket, I was ready to be one of the people shouting 'Eeeeeeeee!' when he made a lay-up. But when we're shouting 'Eeeee,' are we thinking that it's the LORD that gave the boy the TALENT and the HEIGHT to make the lay-up? The LORD that ENABLED that boy to slip past the defenders on the other team, to DRIVE to the BASKET for GLORY, the glory that rightfully belongs to the LORD?! When we're shouting 'Eeeeeeeee,' are we thinking 'Looooooooord,' as we ought to be thinking?!"

"You know we ought to be, Lord!"

"This is what I'm trying to say today: it's all right to get on with your life. The good Lord knows we've all got things we've got to do. We've got jobs to do, to put food in our mouths and the mouths of our families; we've got children to raise, bills to pay, chores to do at home — we've got to do these things, and the Lord doesn't want you to neglect your duties, brothers and sisters, oh, no. And once in a while, there's nothing wrong with sitting back a little bit and *enjoying* yourself, brothers and sisters, enjoyment is the Lord's creation, laughter IS his invention. But when you're sitting back, brothers and sisters, enjoying yourself — can you SHARE some of your ENJOYMENT with the LORD?!"

"It's yours, Lord! You made it! Hallowed be thy name!"

"The LORD, who GAVE you the GIFT of laugher, brothers and sisters, the GIFT of ENJOYMENT? Can you SPARE just a LITTLE BIT of your HAPPINESS, for Him who is ETERNAL HAPPINESS? Because when we GLORY in the LORD —"

For the first time since he had come into the church this morning, Pat's attention was focused fully on the service. He was not responding out loud to Reverend Briscoe's sermon, or rising and falling in his seat, like the ladies in the front pews; but in his quiet way, he was absorbed by the minister's message of gratitude, the gratitude that Pat himself had felt at the bottom of his very being since the war, that he sometimes struggled to feel even more. It was during this moment of total absorption, when he relaxed his vigilance, that the thing he had feared came to pass.

"Pat!"

His head swung to the left. He saw Maddie's frantic face, and in the next instant he realized that Lester was standing. And the instant after that …

> *Momma standin' in the doorway when we GOT home from school*
> *Momma said "How was your day?" and Brother SAID "It was cool"*
> *Sister goin' to do her homework, Brother WATCHING TV*
> *Momma said "Greg do your homework," Brother ROLLS eyes at me …*

For several moments, Lester was the only person in church making a sound. Reverend Briscoe had gone silent in mid-sentence, his mouth open, his eyes trained on Lester, as were those of everyone else; wherever the worshipers sat, their heads were twisted toward him, the congregation becoming a collective swirl, with the angry-looking, shouting boy/man as its vortex.

*Brother goes up to his room and takes his BOOKS from his bag*
*Says he'd rather go outside and play some FOOTBALL or tag …*

The first to move was Pat, who stood, grabbed his son by the inside of his elbow, and tugged. But something was wrong. Lester was completely stiff, more so than he had been last Saturday in the Giant, and his feet were planted wide apart. He could not be made to walk. "I'm going to need help," Pat told Maddie. "Get one of the ushers."

Maddie made her way past other worshipers toward the end of the pew. That movement seemed to serve as a signal to others. Reverend Briscoe found his voice again: "Brother Lester Hobbs is talking, brothers and sisters, not just talking but making *rhymes*! Do we need any more proof of the wonders of GOD? I say, when we WITNESS this boy who has never said a WORD, and suddenly he has FOUND his VOICE, do we NEED more PROOF??"

"Don't need no more proof, Lord!"

*Brother grumbled 'bout his homework while he GOT in the bath*
*"Don't know why we got to study all this ENGLISH and math"*

"Praise His name, he has seen FIT to give this boy the POWER to exercise his MOUTH, his LUNGS, to talk about the FAMILY that has CARED for him these long years —"

*It was my turn after Greg to wash mySELF in the tub*
*Got my body good and soapy, then I STARTED to scrub*

The heads of the worshipers, like those of fans at a tennis match, swung this way, then that way, then this way again, from Lester to Reverend Briscoe and then back. The most agitated of all were the ladies in the front pews. While some of them merely made themselves dizzy, looking rapidly back and forth, a few — seeing God's hand in the wonder of Lester, feeling the Spirit move in them as a result — began to sway, rock, jiggle, and moan. As Pat waited helplessly for Maddie to return with the usher, Lester shouting rhymes in his ear, he saw one of the ladies, in a wide-brimmed red hat with a feather, lurch backward in her seat. Head back, she began to make strange noises, sounds that seemed to be words in another language, except that they were too rapid for anyone's comprehension; and Pat realized, as the Reverend's words rang from the pulpit, as Lester poured out rhymes about a bath he had taken a decade ago, that the lady was speaking in tongues.

The usher arrived. Pat stepped out of the pew to let the usher in. When they were on either side of Lester, they each grabbed an arm and lifted. Necks craned, parents held their children back, and shouts of "Hallelujah!" and "Lord, Lord!" followed Pat and the usher as they carried the still-shouting Lester toward the heavy wooden doors at the rear of the church. Maddie stood there, waiting, her face blank with shock, a look much like the one usually seen on Lester.

# — FIFTEEN —

The first time that Celestine Johnson and Floretta Childs heard Lester rap in person, they lost no time in telling others about it, spreading the word face to face and over the telephone. Between them the sisters talked to upwards of two dozen people, singly and together. The news they shared, being the kind that made hearers want to repeat it, was spread over an impressively large portion of the D.C. metropolitan area and even made its way to several faraway points elsewhere in the southeastern United States. An aerial view of the paths of communication, if such a thing were possible, showing lines connecting the communicants, might have resembled an enormous pyramid, with Celestine and Floretta at the top — a pyramid full of criss-crossing lines, as the many paths of communication intersected other paths, down, across, and diagonal.

The communicants were all sorts of people, with all sorts of relationships to one another. A teacher told her fellow teacher, who shared the news with her brother, who ran a dry-cleaning shop; the dry cleaner told a regular customer with whom he was friendly, and this customer, a dentist, passed it on to one of his patients; and so on. People had several reasons for passing on the news. Some simply had the desire, which most of us have, to be the agent of surprise or astonishment in another person. Some, not sure if they should believe such a wild story, repeated it to others to gauge those people's reactions and, in that way, to help form their own; they might start out by saying, "You know what I heard? I'm not saying I believe this, but …" and then carefully observe the expression on the listener's face.

In these ways, the news about Lester Hobbs (whose name was invariably dropped at some point along each line of communication) reached adults and children, the educated and the uneducated. Some, as noted, were teachers. Others owned small businesses. Some were police officers, others check-out clerks in supermarkets or clothing stores. And one of them had a more unusual job.

\*     \*     \*     \*

On Monday morning Maddie was up as early as Greg was. While he took a shower and bustled around in the kitchen, getting ready to go to work in the Howard University cafeteria, she was getting comfortable in the living room in front of her easel. The previous afternoon, after recovering from that unqualified fiasco of a church service (she had to admit that Greg's uproarious laughter about the whole thing had helped — that, and a nap), she had dug up a piece of acrylic board. Then she had sketched the outline of the house across the street, visible through the living room window. That had been in preparation for this morning, when the sky behind the house was the shade of blue she wanted to capture: the just-short-of-dark blue of the sky just beginning to get light, when the tree limbs in relief against it were black silhouettes. These were the blue sky and black limbs of her girlhood, when she had walked to school with Little Rosa and Lester before the sun was up. She and Little Rosa were usually full of talk about who in school liked whom, always ready to tease Lester, who walked quietly beside them, rolling his eyes. Sometimes the talk was all the sillier on a morning after one of their parents' brawls, and particularly if they had spent breakfast watching the spectacle of their mother and father competing to see who could be more silent and angry-looking. Those moments on the way to school, she realized many years later, had been the happiest of her childhood.

She mixed colors on her palette, blue, black, a touch of white, to get the shade right. There, that might be it — she began filling in the space to the right of the house and above it. Those walks to school … Maddie had always been the sillier of the two sisters, at least it always started out that way. She would say ridiculous things about their schoolmates, just to watch the expressions they brought to her older sister's face; Little Rosa would begin by looking askance at Maddie through her narrow eyes, the beginnings of a smile on her lips, as if to say, *I don't have to laugh at you, you know. But you're so silly you make me want to.* And from there Little Rosa would begin making jokes of her own. Then the two of them would turn on their younger brother: "I know who Lester likes," Maddie might begin. "And who is that?" "Ginny Johnson"— a girl Lester had never talked to or thought about. "Oh, now you mention it, I *thought* I saw him lookin' at her the other day." Lester bore this as he did everything else, in silence, with an occasional mock-disgusted shake of his head. He would occasionally join them in their silly songs, like the rhyme they had learned from their mother and set to a tune of their own: *There was a little chigger/he wasn't any bigger/than the point of a very small pin/But the lump that he raises/Itch like the blazes/And that's where the scratch comes in.*

"See you later, Ma." Greg was leaving the house to go to his job.

"Bye bye. Have a good day."

No ten-year-old girl, walking to school in semi-darkness on the heels of a fight between her parents, would think to herself, These are the happiest days of my childhood. No, time was needed for that, time and circumstances that would set such days apart from what came later. What came later, after their brother's disappearing and their father's driving a wedge through his remaining family, was that Maddie and Little Rosa walked to school in unbroken silence — until the day Little Rosa, with no announcement, began leaving for school without Maddie. But before that were the good days, when Maddie had her sister by her side, laughing and joking, their little brother in tow, on the way to school under the almost-dark-blue sky and the black limbs of the trees.

She had painted in the sky. She squeezed some black onto her palette for the tree limbs. Her old life with Lester — not her long-lost brother, but her son — was perhaps similar in a way to those mornings on the way to school: maybe she had not always appreciated it fully when it was happening, before all this shouting and rhyming business. Oh, she had long ago accustomed herself to Lester's retardation and his lack of speech, she had always loved him, but did she appreciate before how special it was to have him, not in spite of his difference, but because of it? She had said to Pat, as they talked in bed a week or so ago, that she had always loved having a baby who never stopped being a baby. But was that really true, or did she just want to think she'd felt that way? Was she really just projecting a feeling backward in time, a feeling she wanted to have had? It was so hard to know even what was in your own mind, sometimes. Well, even if she hadn't fully appreciated every past moment with Lester — and who could have done so, really? Who could actually live her life that way? — she *remembered* those moments. She used to read to Lester when he was small, and he always seemed to enjoy it, leaning against her and gazing up as she went through the well-worn picture books, not so much reading as reciting, so many times had she read those stories; and unlike with Sherrie or Greg, who would sometimes break the mood of intimacy ("Mommy, don't keep reading when you yawn!" "That's not how you read it yesterday!"), Lester's presence was all warmth and closeness, even if he wasn't taking in much of the story. (Though, according to Dr. Greer, maybe he was after all.) Later, even after Lester got big and gangly, Maddie still sometimes had the urge to fondle the back of his nappy head, the soft skin of his neck; and unlike Greg, whom she also wanted to stroke in this way but who would have bristled under such displays of affection, Lester submitted until she had had her fill, until *she* decided to pull away.

"You're up early this morning." Pat was coming down the steps in his robe.

"Good morning. I wanted to do some painting. The coffee's made."

She took a sip of hers, which was barely warm now, then continued to paint the limbs. Then it occurred to her that she should leave this for later. Right now she should try to capture the early-morning dark gray, like the almost-black of a shadow, that lay over the front of the house across the street, before it faded — as it was already beginning to do. It had to be a dark but watery gray, which could lie atop the red of the brick without completely hiding it. The house belonged to the Alexanders, a family the Hobbses knew only well enough to say hello to, despite having lived across the street from them for two decades. The irony was that often, when Maddie thought of her own house, what she pictured was the Alexanders' home, because that was what she saw from her own window. She laid down the red, let it dry, then put the gray over it. Yes, that would work. She was working from memory now, re-creating the early-morning view from the window even as the morning became fully lit. There was much more of the painting left to do, she had really only begun, but she had caught what she set out to catch. A good morning's work, she thought, as Pat kissed her goodbye.

She rose, stretched, went upstairs to check on Lester. His eyes were still closed. She let him sleep a little longer while she bathed, dressed, ate more breakfast at the kitchen table. She thought of what was coming up that week. She had to buy some groceries, because Greg had asked if his new girlfriend, Gina, could come to dinner Tuesday night. Saturday they were going back to Baltimore, of course. ...

She had just finished eating when Lester came downstairs in his pajamas. "Well, hello, sleepyhead," she said, giving him a hug and kiss. She realized she had lost her fear of the "new" Lester, as they settled into their routine, with Lester's occasional rapping just a new wrinkle. It was possible to get used to anything, it seemed. Lester poured some cornflakes in a bowl, spilling some, then poured in milk, spilling some of that, too. Maddie had scooped the stray flakes into her hand and thrown them in the trash, and was wiping up the spilled milk, when the telephone rang.

"Hello?"

"Hello, is this Madelyn Hobbs?"

"Yes ...?"

"Hello, my name's Pamela Armstrong. I'm an associate producer for Eyewitness News — Channel Nine."

\*      \*      \*      \*

After half an hour on the phone with Pamela Armstrong, who was almost as friendly and warm as she was insistent, Maddie went straight to the sofa to lie down. (As she did so, she was half-consciously aware of the stain left there by the tea she had spilled during Lester's first outbreak of rap.) She stared up at the ceiling. It was too much, all of it, in too short a time: Lester rapping, the diagnosis from Dr. Greer, the choice of whether to pursue treatment, and now this phone call. Pamela Armstrong said she had heard a story from her mother about a young man who had never talked before and then started reciting poetry; her mother had heard the story from their family doctor. So Pamela had called the doctor, to find out where he had heard it, then called that person, and so on, until she found Maddie. Eyewitness News was interested in doing a segment about Lester, in which they would talk about the scientific implications of his condition and its effect on the Hobbs family. Pamela asked Maddie a number of questions, then asked more questions based on the answers. Could she have Dr. Greer's telephone number, so she could ask for his cooperation? Could she have the number of the school Lester attended, just so she could check a few facts independently? Pamela understood that Maddie and her family would have to think it over, that went without saying, and she hoped they would forgive the intrusion, but here was what Eyewitness News had in mind: Pamela herself could come to the Hobbs home one evening, meet Lester and the rest of the family, and ask a few questions, to give the eventual on-air interviewer an idea of which areas would be good to explore. She gave Maddie her work and home telephone numbers, saying that she could call her anytime at all with questions or concerns.

How was anybody supposed to make sense of it all? Well, at least Maddie didn't have to try to do so alone. She went to the kitchen to call Pat. She could picture him with his eyes wide and mouth open as she recounted her conversation with Pamela Armstrong.

"Good gracious," Pat said, and they were both quiet a few moments. Then he said, "You know ... after what happened at church yesterday, at first I just thought, well, *that* was hard, *that* was embarrassing, what did we do *that* for. But you know, nothing is easy that's worthwhile, and I think it's worthwhile to keep Lester as a regular part of our lives, even with his new condition. Not only that, I think we should embrace what's special about him. It's hard, but maybe it's a test."

"So you think we should let them do the story on us?"

"Well, why not? Goodness knows, there's nothing left to hide. If there was, it got out in church yesterday."

"And you think we should go ahead with the treatment? The L-dopa?"

"Well, here's what I've been thinking about that," Pat said. "It's a slight risk, because of the seizures. But having a child and letting him grow up is a risk. Letting a child walk to school by himself for the first time is a risk. Should he just stay home, because it's too risky? Lester might be able to *talk*, honey. Really converse, after all this time. Maybe it's up to us to take the risk for him. He can't ask us to do it. But if we do, he might just be able to thank us."

# — SIXTEEN —

Gina rang the Hobbses' doorbell at exactly six o'clock on Tuesday evening. Greg, visibly nervous as she came in and met his parents, talked non-stop, spouting jokes that Maddie and Pat waved away as they welcomed the young woman with smiles and hugs. Greg relaxed some as the four of them (Lester was upstairs) sat down in the living room. Maddie asked how Gina's parents were ("Oh, dear, I'm sorry," she said when Gina explained about her mother), then asked where they had come from originally. When the answer was Culpepper, Virginia, Maddie said, "Oh, I grew up not too far from there. I know some people from there. I wonder if your father knows the Gaineses — the family that owned the …" The two women carried the conversation into the kitchen, where Gina helped Maddie with dinner. Pat and Greg stayed in the living room and drank beer from bottles.

"She seems nice, son." In a lower voice, he added, "Pretty, too."

"Thanks."

"How'd you get her interested in *you?*"

"Ha ha, you're funny."

"Just joking. That's what your grandfather would say if I brought home a girl that didn't look like she'd escaped from the zoo. Or even if she did."

"So you're passin' on the tradition, huh? Lucky me."

"Got to, son. I was an only child — nobody else around to do it."

Soon Maddie called to Greg from the kitchen, asking him to set the table and then go get Lester from upstairs. Pat went to pick out dinner music. It would be jazz — just a matter of which jazz. Pat usually put some on during dinner, and he nearly always did when there were guests; it made for pleasant background music. That, anyway, was how other people usually responded to it, if they noticed at all. Pat loved the music for itself. He had first become interested in jazz during his college days, in the early and mid-1950s, when a fellow student had introduced him to records by the likes of Lucky Thompson, Clifford Brown, and Charlie Parker. It was at about the time Pat became a confirmed jazz fan that Parker and Brown both died, within little more than a year of each other, in 1955 and 1956. Pat kept listening, though, buying records, exploring the music of the survivors — Dizzy Gillespie, Charlie Shavers, Howard McGhee — and the guys who stepped to the forefront, notably Miles Davis, Thelonious Monk, and John Coltrane. (He didn't know so much about the stuff Davis had done the last decade or so, but he still played the trumpeter's records from the Fifties and Sixties.) Sometimes, during stressful periods, listening to the music late at night with a beer or something a little stronger helped to keep him on an even keel; during Maddie's bout with depression after Lester was pronounced to be retarded, when Pat worked during the days and became two parents in the evenings, he sometimes stole a few minutes 'round about midnight to sit near the record player, glass in hand, and lose himself in the dreamy trumpet lines of *Clifford Brown with Strings*. (He sometimes felt he was being untrue to the music by enhancing its effects on him with alcohol, until he found out what some of the musicians themselves had ingested when the records were being made.) Listening to mellow trumpet solos in ballads, or to intricately woven saxophone statements in up-tempo recordings — beautiful music with no words getting in the way — Pat found his mind transported to other, surer, more elegant planes.

Pat put on a Hank Mobley record, and they all sat down to dinner. "Gina, this is Greg's brother, Lester," Maddie said.

"Nice to meet you, Lester. I've heard a lot about you."

Lester aimed a vacant but pleasant look more or less in Gina's direction as Greg put potatoes on his brother's plate. "You have to forgive him for not answering," Maddie said.

"It's okay. I , um — heard."

"Did Greg tell you that Lester's seen a neurologist, and there's a possibility he could talk to us, for the first time ever?"

"Yes, he did. It's very exciting."

"Hey," Greg said, "he's talking already. Right, Les? He's turned into the family historian. Lester'll get up in the middle of anything and start talkin' 'bout stuff the rest of us forgot."

"I think," Pat said, "your mother meant we could actually have *exchanges* with him. Up to now," he continued, addressing Gina, "conversation with Lester's been kind of a one-way proposition. We've always talked to him, and lately he's started talking to us, but we've never talked to each other."

"Although," Maddie said, "Dr. Greer told us it hasn't been as one-way as we thought. He understands a lot of what we say. He must, if he can make rhymes about conversations we had years ago. I've had to remind myself of that the past few days. I'm so used to thinking out loud in front of Lester. Don't you find that's true, Pat? Pat?"

Pat's attention seemed to have shifted elsewhere. "Sorry," he said. "I was trying to remember who's playing piano on this record. I think it's Wynton Kelly."

"God, Dad."

"Forgive my husband. He's a jazz nut."

"It's okay," Gina said, laughing. "I think you'd get along with *my* dad, Mr. Hobbs."

"Really?" Pat said. "Who does he —?"

"*Hey*, Pat, guess what?" Maddie said. "Gina's advisor is Samuel Steen. Wasn't he that government professor you always used to talk about?"

"Good gracious, is Sam Steen still at Howard?"

"He sure is. I think he'll be there as long as there *is* a Howard. He's so smart. I don't think if I had two lifetimes I could learn as much as he knows."

"Gina's going to continue at Howard to get a degree in international relations," Maddie said. "Isn't that interesting?"

Pat didn't have a chance to respond.

> *Brother took me to the basement, started TALKIN' to me*
> *Told me all about his women — told me ALL about three*
> *Carol Carol was so nice, at least that SEEMED to be true*
> *Then she told him it was over, broke his HEART right in two*

All eyes shot toward Lester, except Greg's, which were on Gina. She was staring up at Lester (for he was now standing) with a mixture of fascination and fear, as if he were a force of nature, an approaching funnel cloud — which, in a sense, he was.

> *Jennifer was so much sweeter, nice and PRETTY to boot*
> *Brother couldn't quite believe a girl who LIKED him was cute*
> *Then she went away to college, left him HERE all alone*
> *And one day he got a letter, hurt him RIGHT to the bone*

Greg had a sudden, bad feeling about what was to follow, and his fear was soon confirmed. When Gina heard her own name from Lester's lips, her expression changed, moving from awe to curiosity and then to — Greg didn't know what, he was too scared to look at her anymore. ...

> *Gina Gina, so good-lookin,' put her TONGUE in his mouth*
> *Wiggled it from side to side before she PULLED it back out*
> *Oh her body, Brother told me, felt so GOOD Brother said*
> *While he had his tape recorder next to HIM on the bed*

Lester's seizure passed. For a moment he stood where he was, blinking, then sat and began eating as if nothing had happened. From that point, the dinner proceeded like a car with four flat tires — and not much gas. Gina concentrated on her food as if it were a tightrope on which she was balancing. The eyes of Greg, Pat, and Maddie sought each other nervously and then, like billiard balls, bounced apart on contact. No one talked. The only sounds were the scraping of knives and forks on plates; that, and the sax solos on the Hank Mobley record. When he could stand it no more, Pat smiled and said quietly, "This record always reminds me — I went to see Hank Mobley once, when he was in D.C. It was in the early Sixties. It was a good show, I think Lee Morgan was in his group then. I don't know why I think about it, maybe just because it's something that happened a long time ago now, and things were different. Not that they were better, but there's just something about days that won't come again, even if they weren't all good, I don't know. ..." His voice trailed off. No one else's followed. Maddie gave him a small, closed-mouth smile: *That was a valiant try, honey.* They finished the meal in silence.

After the plates had been cleared away, Gina said, in a tone struggling to stay even, "It was nice to meet you, Mr. and Mrs. Hobbs."

"It was nice meeting you, Gina."

Greg followed her to the door. "Let me walk you to the bus," he said quietly.

Her reply, just as quiet, ruled out further discussion: "No, *thank you.*"

Greg locked the door behind her. When he turned around, his parents' faces were like big question marks. "Don't ask, OKAY?" he said, rushing past them to the basement.

Thick fingers interlaced behind his neck, he paced at the end of his bed for several minutes. "God damn mother fucker ... God damn ..." Then he turned on his TV. He found every show he turned to more inane than the last, until he turned the set off and put on some music. He paced some more. Then he took the needle from the Bootsy Collins record, nearly scratching the vinyl, and headed back upstairs. In the hallway he passed Lester and his stupid, blank face; he restrained himself from punching it and went out the door, letting it slam behind him.

It was still light outside, which surprised him, for some reason. He walked past girls jumping rope on the sidewalk. He looked, half in hope, half in dread, toward the bus stop on the other side of the street farther down, but Gina wasn't there; just a woman with her young daughter and younger, wailing son. Greg kept walking, hands in pockets, until he arrived, having only half-consciously decided to go there, at Clive's house.

His mother answered the door. "Oh, hi, Greg. Clive's not here, he ..."

Of course — Greg knew, he'd just forgotten: Clive was finally going somewhere with that girl Robin he had been talking about. "Okay, thanks. See you later, Miz Tompkins." Back down the porch steps, to the street corner, where he paused. Where to now? He walked until he spotted the Brookland Metro station. Why not? He was going nowhere, but the train would get him there faster. Down the steps, through the turnstile with his pink student-discount Farecard, up the escalator to the above-ground platform.

He stood gazing across the tracks in the direction he had just come from, watching the buses enter the lot in front of the station, discharge some passengers, pick up others, head out again. Lester, he thought. How long have you been messing up my life? My whole life, except the two years I was alive before you were born, and those don't count, since I can't remember them. It's all about Lester. Mother and father always worrying or happy over Lester. What about me? The one that got beat up trying to protect his retarded ass? When the rapping began, Greg had felt it start up again: oh, praise God, Lester's talking. Greg thought he was going to drown in it all. And so he grabbed for a life preserver, a way to get just a little attention for himself — by trying to record some of Lester's raps, trying to do something with them that could bring him a little credit. Nobody else was thinking about doing it, were they? But the first attempt had failed, and the second had just blown up in his face, driving away the one person who had taken Greg's mind off all of it — Gina. All thanks to … Lester!

The train came, bound for Silver Spring. Greg got on. The train continued above ground; he looked out the window, down at the streets, houses, outdoor shopping malls. His whole life … He thought back a dozen years or so, to his nine-year-old self. By then he had gotten to be a fat boy. He could still remember the feeling of always wanting food, like a little two-legged brown shark. At times when he was bored, when Sherrie was doing her homework, when Daddy had work he had brought home from his office, when Mommy was busy talking cute to Lester, *like she always was*, he would see what was in the refrigerator. There were a couple of other chubby kids in his class at school, but unlike those kids, who avoided drawing attention to themselves, Greg sought it in every way he could think of. If something funny happened in class, he would laugh louder than anyone, purposely falling off his chair; the teacher would yell at him to get up, but he had already gotten what he wanted: some girls nearby had laughed. When the teacher asked a question, he would raise his hand whether he knew the answer — which was about half the time — or not. Once, after he had given three wildly wrong answers in a row, a boy at a nearby desk said to him, "Why you keep raisin' your hand, fat boy? You don't know nuffin."

"Know more than you, ya crooked-tooth motherfucker."

"Nigger, I'll knock *your* teeth *out*."

"You just want 'em for yourself. How you gon put 'em in, with some glue?"

That made some of the kids laugh. This was one thing Greg could hold his own at: joning, or trading insults. (His parents sometimes called it "signifying.") After school that day, while Greg was waiting for Sherrie and Lester, the boy with the crooked teeth started shoving him. A crowd formed around the fight. Greg lost — but he had gotten some attention, at least.

The teachers' comments on his report cards during those years were variations on a theme. *Greg is intelligent but lazy and undisciplined. Craves attention.* On one parent-teacher night in fourth grade, Sherrie stayed at home with Lester while Greg and his parents waited their turn outside his classroom to talk to Miss Taylor, Greg's teacher. When their turn came, Greg, seated between his parents, listened as the young, pretty Miss Taylor spoke with a smile about how Greg might focus and work just a little harder, to earn the grades she knew he could get. Then she asked Greg, with a bigger smile, if she could talk to his Mom and Dad in private for just a minute. Hovering just outside the door, Greg heard Miss Taylor say, "I was just wondering if there's anything going on at home. Greg is a nice boy, but he does really seem to need to be the center of attention."

"Well," his mother said, "Greg's brother is retarded. Sometimes that takes a lot of our attention."

"Yes, I know. I was also noticing that Greg seems to eat a lot. I know sometimes that's a sign that a child is craving some kind of comfort."

"Oh, *is* it now?" Greg heard his father say; it was the only time he could remember hearing his father's voice become bristly with someone outside the family.

"Pat," his mother said. "She might be right."

For a while after that night, Greg noticed that his mother would ask him to play a game, just the two of them, or his father would ask Greg to walk with him to the store. He couldn't bring himself to enjoy those times, because, not being stupid, he knew what was behind them; and he never had much to say during them. After a while they stopped, and it was back to life as usual.

Greg eventually took up karate, weight-lifting, and all the rest of it, figuring that if he was going to keep fighting — to defend Lester, or to defend himself against the results of his own trash-talking — he might as well learn how. Before that, though, every day of walking to and from school with Sherrie and Lester had brought with it a fresh chance for disaster. "It's the retarded family! Hey, retarded family!" a boy would yell loud enough for the whole block to hear; he would keep at it until he got what he wanted, a response from Greg, which would give him an excuse to throw a punch. All because of Lester. Then there was the time ... oh, he didn't like to think about that.

The train stopped at Fort Totten and then Takoma before pulling in to Silver Spring, the last stop. Greg stayed put while the other passengers got off, waiting for the train to go back in the other direction. The sky had darkened. And now, Les, you messed things up with Gina, too. Or you and I did together. That little insight didn't make him feel any better. What to do now? Maybe Gina had cooled off some. Maybe he could call her now. Better still, he would go to her house. In a few minutes the train began to move. He rode it to Union Station, got out and walked toward her house. The other night, in the car, the distance between Union Station and her house had seemed like nothing, but this was a real hike, across traffic circles, then down long, long East Capitol Street. It was nearly nine o'clock when he got there. Gina's father answered the door.

"Hi Mr. Bowie. I'm Greg, we met Saturday night. Is Gina at home, please?"

"She's just gone to sleep," Mr. Bowie said, looking grave.

"Oh." He wondered if this was true, but then, as far as his

chances of seeing her went, it probably didn't matter. "We had a misunderstanding, I was kinda hoping I could clear it up."

"Well, try her another time."

"Okay. Thank you, Mr. Bowie."

He began the hike back to the Metro, strolling in the dark back down East Capitol, under the newly blooming leaves of the trees, those wide trees whose branches stretched far beyond the curb, meeting the branches of trees from the opposite sidewalk, forming a roof over the street. He felt … no, not better, but calmer. Maybe he was just tired. He would study when he got home, though; his economics exam was in the morning, after his work shift. He had never thought he would look forward to studying econ, but it would give him something else to concentrate on. Anything was better than what he was thinking about now.

*    *    *    *

In the cafeteria on Wednesday morning, in his white paper hat and apron, Greg kept the counter supplied with pastries and fruit, walking back and forth between the counter and the kitchen, handing students what they asked for, clearing away the dirty dishes that were brought back in — all while going over economics in his head and trying not to think about Gina.

"I said the *apple* tart. The *apple*, boy, are you deaf?"

"I'm not deaf. I'm not a boy, neither. Maybe *you* are, punk."

"Come from behind that counter, I'll show you who's a punk."

What followed could only charitably be called a fight; after the first punch, or attempted punch, which the other man had been foolish enough to throw, he didn't get a chance at another. Greg would feel bad about it later, but in the moment, as the other man picked himself up from the floor, as the women from the kitchen yelled at Greg and threatened to report him, all he felt was anger — at himself, at the other man, at Lester, at his parents. He felt like the nine-year-old boy he had once been, and whom, not far below the surface, he still was.

# — SEVENTEEN —

Sherrie had remarked to Oscar recently that her parents tended to repeat anecdotes, little happenings that had no particular significance, years after they had occurred — treating them not only as if they had just happened, not only as if they were actually memorable, but as if the listener or listeners (usually Sherrie and/or Greg) had never heard them before. There was this to be said for her mother and father, though: the stories never involved bragging. They were just reflections on the humor, wonder, or exasperation of life, stories in which her parents themselves were usually not the main characters.

Sherrie came to appreciate this quality in her parents' stories on a Wednesday evening, while sitting in an old-style Italian restaurant in Baltimore — one with red-and-white checkered cloths over solid, heavy wooden tables, cheap bottles of good red wine, bread in wicker baskets, and heaping plates of spaghetti served by olive-skinned, black-haired waiters. Across the table from her was George Greer. In the nine days she had known him, Sherrie had not only learned certain bits of information about him, she had heard them repeated several times, leading her to realize that they were not merely the facts of his life, but its themes. "It reminds me of that fellow I met once in high school, who went to a different school and didn't know much about me," Greer was saying now — and Sherrie thought how significant it was that on this, the second Wednesday of their relationship, she knew which fellow he was referring to, and what Greer was going to say about him. "I made the casual remark that I had to play a football game across town that would coincide with my school's awards-day ceremony, and that I couldn't get out of the game, since I was the team's starting quarterback," he said. "And this fellow said to me, 'Well, what does it matter? You're not going to get any awards, are you?' He just assumed I wasn't, without knowing anything about me. No doubt because he didn't think anything of himself, and so it was hard to relate to someone who was focused on accomplishment. And I tell you, if that's your attitude, you never *will* get anywhere in life. You think I could have done any of the things I've done with that attitude? No, indeed. You can't think that way and be a starting quarterback, finish at the top of your class in high school and college, head up the neurology department at a major university. No, indeed. And then there's always the excuse that 'the white man won't let me do this, the white man doesn't want me to do that.' I always say, until you forget what the white man wants and figure out what *you* want, and make up your mind to get it, you'll never get anywhere in this life. No chairmanship of a neurology department to be had if you're always thinking about 'the white man.'"

How had she gotten involved with this guy? And how did he get these sentences out of his mouth? It was not that she disagreed with what he said, and it was one thing to *think* such things, but to say them to someone else, over and over, to take other people into this orbit of self-worship — did he even realize he was talking out loud? She sipped her wine as he went on. She thought: If I disappeared right now, faded away in front of his eyes, I wonder if he would notice. He was not interested in what she thought about anything; that was clear at this point, and it was true on a couple of levels. It was not just that he hadn't asked her any questions about herself (apart from those about Lester) since their first dinner; he didn't seem to care how she *felt*, or else it hadn't occurred to him to wonder. She had been waiting for him to raise the subject of where she fit into his life, exactly what their relationship was to be, since he was already a husband and father. She nearly brought it up herself once. But she was beginning to think there was no point. Their relationship was probably where he wanted it already. He could, she thought, go on like this indefinitely, fucking her and talking her ear off a couple of times a week, until she married someone else or had a cerebral hemorrhage, at which point he would simply find another victim. She wondered how many women he had done this with already, the creep.

He asked the waiter for the check. "Can I take you to my friend's place?" he asked her, referring to the efficiency apartment he rented without his wife's knowledge.

"You know," she said, "I think I'm just going to head home. I'm kind of tired. I hope you don't mind."

"Oh. Of course not," he said, though she had clearly upset his plans. Poor man, he might be forced to go home to his wife and children. "Well, let me drive you home."

"That's okay. I drove here. I finally got my car out of the shop. So, I guess I'll see you Saturday, when my family comes up."

She was not, she realized, in any position to feel moral indignation. That was the worst of it, she thought, turning cautiously from the side street where she had parked onto a major thoroughfare. She had gone into the relationship fully aware of what she was doing. Which brought her back to her first question: how? How had she become involved with a man who betrayed his wife without a second's hesitation, whose favorite activity — ahead of sex, even — was talking about himself? Oscar had asked the same question, why she preferred Greer over him, what Greer made her feel. And she had surprised both of them by saying, "Safe." Ever since, she had wondered about that response.

She stopped at a red light. Oh, how she hated driving in the dark. She would get used to it as she did it more, no doubt, but for now she was still in the stage of being terrified of it. Tomorrow, when she drove to D.C. to take part in that interview with the news producer, she would make sure to leave well before the sun started going down. (She couldn't quite fathom why her parents wanted to do this, but if they were determined to go through with it, she'd better be there.)

"Safe." Her mother was right that George Greer had an air of authority that put you at your ease, made you feel that nothing too bad could happen while you were with him, that you were … well, safe. Maybe that was what she had sensed the first time she saw him, or, rather, the first time he saw her, when he looked at her with those wolf's eyes. If he could go after what he wanted with such confidence — ferocity might be a better word — and operate with such sureness in the world, then she could move with sureness, too, if she were in his company. This was an attractive quality, no two ways about it, one that Oscar, for all his sweetness, lacked; and it was a quality that, in George, had blinded her to some of his other qualities. (And, if she was to be honest, his looks hadn't hurt, either.) Her previous boyfriends, all of them, had had more of Greer than of Oscar in them, though Greer, without a doubt, was the Greeriest. Why did this quality seem to attract her more than others?

In her apartment, where she had arrived, thank God, without ramming anybody from behind or running over any children, she approached the question a different way. She thought of the times in her life when she had felt *un*safe.

She remembered that late August night when the Hobbs family went to the drive-in, back in '67, when Sherrie was twelve, Greg ten, Lester eight. She and Greg had talked in low voices about walking to school, which was starting up again in a few days; they had discussed how far Sherrie would go with her brothers, now that she would be in junior high school, and how Greg and Lester might protect themselves. Their voices turned out not to be low enough, as her father yelled at them to be quiet. He had felt bad about it in the days that followed, quizzing them in vain, poor Daddy, about what they had been discussing. It was hard to say why she and Greg weren't more forthcoming. Then again, maybe it wasn't. If they explained the problem, what would he do? Quit his job and walk them to and from school every day? There was nothing he could do about their problem, and the more he knew about it, the worse would be the look of helplessness on his face. Sherrie hated it when her father seemed at a loss for what to do.

Then, on the first morning of her seventh-grade year, her father announced with a satisfied smile that he would begin driving them to school in the mornings, before he went to work. He couldn't pick them up in the afternoons, but maybe, he said, they'd be okay on the way home. Poor Daddy — he had forgotten what school was like: kids never did anything bad on the way there, when they still had school, and thus the consequences of their actions, to face. It all happened *after* school, that lawless hour of escape into the open.

One afternoon in late September … oh, she didn't want to think about that … but she should. One afternoon in late September, Sherrie left school and got to the corner of 14th and Otis, where she had been meeting Greg and Lester on the way home. They showed up a few seconds later, and she could tell right away something wasn't right. Greg told her later what had happened: he had gotten into a joning contest with another boy. As usual when that occurred, Greg had left the other boy looking stupid and feeling angry. And as sometimes happened, the other boy refused to take such feelings lying down.

She could still see the scene. It was a beautiful day. On that residential street the late September sun was dappling the sidewalk, shining through leaves just beginning to yellow at the edges; the air was the air of a pleasant summer day, not too hot. Greg and Lester came toward her down the cracked sidewalk, Lester walking in his side-to-side way. Not far behind them was a crowd of boys, some of them moving in an exaggerated version of Lester's walk; where he was staring ahead blankly, they were making cartoon versions of idiots' faces, crossing their eyes, sticking their tongues out sideways. One of them, eating a banana, made a show of chewing it like a cow, mouth opening wide with every bite, lips curling. The boy in front, the biggest in the group, was walking normally. His name, Sherrie learned later, was William, and though he should have been in Sherrie's grade in junior high school, he was in Greg's, having stayed back twice. As Sherrie remembered it, his eyes made him look crazy, eyes a dull yellow like those of a grown man who drinks too much; he smiled, white teeth standing out in a dark face. "Hey," he called to Greg. "Where you goin'? Wanna finish what we was talkin' about?"

"You finish," Greg answered without turning around. "I'm goin' home."

"Not yet you ain't."

Very quickly after that, the boys, half a dozen of them, had Greg and Lester surrounded. Lester looked vaguely confused. "This your brother?" William said. "What they be teachin' him in that school? How to suck some dick?" He put his palm on top of Lester's head. Lester looked worried. "Come here, retarded boy, suck —"

Next came the only good moment in the whole episode, the one Sherrie would hold onto. Greg aimed a straight jab up at William's face, connecting solidly on his jaw, knocking it sideways for one sweet second, wiping away the smile. William forgot about Lester and charged toward Greg. Then one of the other boys shoved Lester from behind; his head shot backward as he stumbled toward a third boy, who shoved him back the other way. Sherrie rushed toward them, yelling, "Leave him alone!" One of the boys pushed her away. William was punching Greg's head. The boys kept shoving Lester, who tried to hide by closing his eyes. Sherrie charged toward the boys again. Again she got shoved back. Across the street she caught a glimpse of Greg's friends Clint and Darnell, who watched the scene for a moment blank-faced, and then walked away. Sherrie ran as hard as she could toward Lester; this time she got shoved hard. She stumbled back, out of control, and fell down. As she watched, getting to her knees, one of the boys broke off a piece of the banana and smeared it over Lester's face. Greg, blood streaming from his nose, tears in his voice, yelled, "Sto-o-o-o-p!" William hit him in the stomach. Then someone punched Lester's face. Blood ran from his nose, thin red rivers snaking through the yellow mashed banana. Someone hit him again. And again. Greg was on the sidewalk, getting kicked.

When William and the other boys moved on, laughing, Lester was sitting up on the sidewalk, rocking back and forth, his nose, eyes, and lips swollen beneath smeared blood and banana pulp, mucus and silent tears. Sherrie walked, Greg crawled, toward him, both crying. They each took an arm and lifted him gently. "Come on, Les," Greg said, his voice choked, and Sherrie saw that Greg, too, had a swollen and bloody nose and lip, as well as a lump to the side of one eye. Greg pulled out a handkerchief, Sherrie some tissues, and they cleaned off Lester's face as well as they could. Then they walked home, slowly, Sherrie and Greg on either side of Lester, without words, sniffing.

At home there was no way to hide what had happened. Their mother, screaming, crying, called their father, who came straight home. Sherrie, meanwhile, rushed to the bathroom and vomited, the image of Lester's blood- and banana-smeared face bright in her mind. (She was never to eat a banana again, and it would be years before she could watch anyone else do it.) There was not much to be done. Their father called the school principal, who promised to "have a talk" with William. Unsatisfied with that, he called William's home. He managed to get out of the boy's mother that there was no father in the picture; other than that, the woman was barely coherent. William seemed, for all practical purposes, to be raising himself. Sherrie wished her father would go find William, put his hands around the boy's throat, threaten to kill him if he touched his children again. But the idea didn't seem to cross her father's mind. Or he thought it wouldn't be right.

\*          \*          \*          \*

On Thursday the undergraduate chemistry class for which Sherrie was a teaching assistant let out at 3:45. From there she left straight for D.C., heading south on I-95. The traffic was already heavier than she liked. As she drove, squinting against the sun, she remembered the William episode, over a decade ago now. She recalled how, in the days that followed, she thought less about William than about Clint and Darnell, Greg's friends who had walked away from the scene; she imagined them as they did so, making excuses to each other, feeling better about themselves with every step they took, every justification that came sheepishly from their lips. They had been at the Hobbses' house the weekend before, both of them, eating sandwiches fixed by Sherrie and Greg's mother, thanking her so politely, those two cowardly, useless, nice boys.

That, she thought, was why she liked niceness only to a certain extent: she could never be sure about what it was covering, what was at work underneath it. And it occurred to her that her interest in chemistry, in knowing how things work at their most basic levels, came in part from a desire for safety. What she understood, she didn't have to fear.

She pulled up in front of her parents' house at a little before five o'clock, well before the sky began to darken, well within the zone of safety.

# — EIGHTEEN —

Pamela Armstrong of Eyewitness News was twenty-four years old, a proud product of the D.C. public schools, the oldest child of parents who had come to Washington from points further south. She had attained such an important position at one of the city's four news stations with her two strongest assets: her intelligence, which was above average, and her drive, which had inspired envy, awe, and flat-out disbelief. In high school Pamela had been valedictorian, editor of the yearbook, president of the student council, first clarinetist in the band, and the fastest runner on the track team. At George Washington University, where she had majored in broadcast communications, she had been valedictorian, editor of the yearbook, president of the student council, first clarinetist in the band, and the fastest runner on the track team. (Her long limbs had helped. Pamela was mostly limbs, in fact, with very dark skin and big white teeth thrown in.)

It was Pamela's feeling, when people expressed disbelief at all she did, that they simply didn't want to believe it; accepting that one person could do all those things might call into question their own failure to do as much, and it was much easier to accuse Pamela of exaggerating than to accuse themselves of being lazy. Such reactions were the things Pamela hated most in life. Normally friendly, Pamela could nonetheless flash fire when provoked. She had actually told one woman, her head moving from side to side as it did when she was angry: "Look, just because *you* can't do something, don't try to tell me *I* can't."

For that reason, Pamela was careful, in her own reactions to what she heard, to avoid committing the same type of offense. And that was one reason, in turn, why she reacted as she did on first hearing the story of the rapping mute. Another reason had to do with her job. She loved being an associate news producer, because the job's rapid pace, its demands that she think on her feet, gave her multiple outlets for her considerable energy. If a news story broke — a murder, a big fire, a local political scandal — *bam*, she was on the way, feeding the on-air reporter questions he/she should ask on the scene as they sped there in the van. At the scene she directed the camera people, pointing them with her long index finger toward the courthouse steps to get a shot of lawyers hurrying away, or toward a shot of a mother holding her rescued daughter. Back at the studio she edited footage for that evening's broadcast while simultaneously composing copy in her head. In the beginning it had been a pure thrill, reacting to so much every day. But she had begun to feel lately that reacting was all she did. In school she had had to *think*. There had been time to explore subjects, not just aim a camera at them. She had been wanting, therefore, to produce a feature all her own, something she could devote a little time to. The story of the mute young man who suddenly began reciting poetry, if it were true, might just fit the bill.

"So," Pamela Armstrong said, pad in her lap. She sat in the middle of the Hobbses' living room, on a wooden chair pulled from the dining table. "I guess the first question I'd like to ask is for the two of you, Sheridan and Greg. Tell me about having Lester as a brother. Do you think it's affected the other relationships you've made in your lives?"

Greg, on the sofa next to his parents, began to snicker loudly. From the armchair, Sherrie said, "How did I know he wouldn't be able to take this seriously."

"It's not enough seriousness in the world to please you," Greg said, still laughing, "so why try?"

Pamela's gaze shifted back and forth between them. "Well, let me try a different question. How has it affected your relationship with each other?"

This quieted both of them. Sherrie, for her part, couldn't think how to begin answering; she might have been asked how many times she had sneezed in her life.

"Or to put it another way still: what is your relationship *like*?"

"What're you," Greg said, his laughter drying up, "a news producer or a psychologist?"

"Greg!" Pat and Maddie said together.

"I'm only trying to figure out ways that Lester's condition might have affected you as a family. Before he began talking. But if that makes you uncomfortable I can start with some less personal questions."

"No, we can answer that," Sherrie said. "Or I can. Our relationship's not that close. I mean, on the surface. Greg and I love each other —"

Greg smiled. "We do?"

"— but," Sherrie continued, glaring at her brother, "it's not the kind of thing where we tell each other every day. We're very different. You can probably tell."

"What do you love about your brother?" Pamela smiled at Greg. "I'm going to ask you the same thing about your sister in a minute."

"I don't know," Sherrie said. She shrugged. "He's my brother."

"I love my sister because in addition to being very beautiful, she is extremely intelligent, wit-ty, and full of the joy of living. And tell me, have you seen her backhand?"

Sherrie shot her parents a look that said, *What did I tell you?*

"Well, I can tell you," Maddie said, "they *used* to get along *great*. When they were children. I don't know what happened."

"Well, I was trying to get at something," Pamela said, "but maybe I'll just ask it straight out. Did you, Sherrie and Greg, ever form any kind of particular bond because of your brother? Or did it not really affect your relationship?"

For a moment no one spoke. Then Sherrie said, "Well … we shared some unpleasant experiences that had to do with Lester. Mostly involving bullies. I think a lot of what I think about, when I think about Greg, is tied up with those memories, and a lot of them were unpleasant, like I said, so …"

Pat, Maddie, and Greg all turned toward Sherrie, Greg looking serious for the first time since they sat down. In the dining room, Lester drew on a napkin.

"If you don't mind my asking, what were those experiences like?"

Sherrie shrugged. "Like I said. Bullies."

"Okay." Pamela scribbled on her pad. "But you would say those experiences made it harder for you to relate to each other, rather than easier?"

Silence. Pat said gently, "Maybe there's no more oil where you're drilling."

"Well, maybe we'll come back to it," Pamela said, smiling. "So let's move to the two of you, Mr. and Mrs. Hobbs. How has being Lester's parents been different from being the parents of your other children? What have you done differently?"

Greg chuckled bitterly and said, "Can I answer that one?"

"Greg," Maddie said, "will you please stop being so —"

"Sorry," he told her, looking annoyed.

His mother told Pamela Armstrong, "Well, it took some getting used to, in the beginning, when we first became aware of his condition. I definitely struggled with it. But I think we came to appreciate Lester for what he was and what he had to offer, even without talking and having, you know, normal intelligence."

"And what has he offered you?"

"I think appreciation is a big thing. He just seems so open to anything you do for him. He can't say it, of course, and sometimes you have to look closely. But if you stroke him, he'll give you a little smile, and he's happy when you put some food in front of him. Or a puzzle. I was saying to my husband the other day —" She remembered again that Lester did, in some way, take in words; she glanced toward him, and then, seeing that he was still drawing on a napkin, not looking in her directon, she went on: "Lester's almost like someone who was born and then never stopped being a baby."

Sherrie: "Hmp. You talking about Lester, or Greg?"

Greg: "Oh, that's funny."

Pat: "Come on, now, both of you."

Pamela: "Sherrie mentioned bullies, but for you, Mr. and Mrs. Hobbs, what about the reactions of other people to Lester? Has that been a major issue for you?" Pat explained that no, other people's reactions had never been a big problem; there was occasionally explaining to do, but they had never felt embarrassed about Lester.

Maddie, meanwhile, was thinking about what Sherrie had said: *A lot of what I think about Greg is connected with bad memories,* or something like that. Maddie herself remembered so well the day the children came home after being beaten up by the gang of boys, Greg and Lester — Lester! — so swollen and bloody. Both their noses, it turned out, had been broken; for a couple of weeks they walked around like twins with their bandaged faces, breaking her heart every time she looked at them.

"What's almost funny," Pat was saying, "is how often, when you're out with Lester, you find yourself comforting other people because of their discomfort when they find out he's not quote-unquote normal."

Oh, the worrying she and Pat did after that, Maddie remembered. And the precautions: enrolling Greg in self-defense classes, at his request; calling around to acquaintances, explaining the situation, seeing which older boys could accompany the Hobbs children at least part of the way home each day.

"Are there," Pamela Armstrong was asking, "lessons you've learned over the years as Lester's parents, that you would apply if you could go back and do it again?"

Pat said, "I suppose, after talking to the neurologist at Hopkins, we now wish we'd been more aggressive in terms of finding out earlier what was actually going on with Lester. Of course, a lot of the same information wasn't available at the time, so it might not have made much difference."

The beatings had been, Maddie remembered, the same year as The Change, the decline of their fun Saturday mornings, when they had all sat around the dining room table, talking and laughing about this and that. Suddenly Greg and Sherrie just went their own ways. Maddie had put The Change down, in the end, to the fact of her children's getting older; that had been the year Sherrie turned thirteen, Greg eleven, so of course their differences would start to come out. But also, of course, *A lot of what I think about Greg is connected with bad memories.* A bad thing happens, and the children it happens to begin to take their feelings out on each other. And why not each other? Who else had seen their defeat, their shame, as it transpired (who else who could talk, that is)? How, Maddie thought, did I fail to put those things together before now?

"So your advice to other people raising children who are not quote-unquote normal would be to aggressively pursue a second opinion?"

"Well — yes. Although as I say, a second opinion or a different opinion might not have been available at the time when Lester was small. But in general I would say that's a good idea, yes."

Should Maddie even trust her memory? She remembered the Saturday mornings as being wonderful, a time when the family enjoyed each other's company. But the tone in Greg's voice just now: *Can I answer that one?* Did he have a completely different story to tell? Did it have anything good in it?

"So," Pamela said, "we've touched a little on the subject of Lester before he began his — rapping, I guess you would say. I'd like to ask a little about everyone's reactions to the rapping. Greg, Sherrie, when you first heard that your mute brother was doing this, or when you first heard him do it yourself, what was your reaction? Could you believe it?"

Sherrie: "I was stunned. That's the only word for it."

Greg: "That's one thing we agree on."

Sherrie: "Greg called me in Baltimore and told me about it, and I was surprised then, of course, but then seeing it for myself was something completely different. I can't really describe it."

"And what has it made you think about Lester? Either of you."

"I guess what I think about Lester is still in the process of change," Sherrie said. "We're still finding out things, seeing what he might be capable of."

Maddie was brooding — Pat could tell, he knew that look. It had to be because of the arguing between Sherrie and Greg. She never could harden herself to it.

"And you, Greg?"

"Yeah, I feel like I'm just kinda waitin' to see what's gonna happen muhself."

On the other hand, maybe I'm *too* hardened, Pat thought. Well, no, not hardened. *Accepting* might be a better word. He had never had siblings himself, but he just assumed all along that brothers and sisters argue with each other as they grow up, as part of the natural order of things. It hurt Maddie to watch it, because her original family had collapsed, poor woman, and she didn't want her second family to do the same. It was different for Pat, who had been an only child, always on his own, in his own world — kind of like now, really; God knows he would rather be listening to some music, alone with his thoughts, than enduring this interview, even if he had been the one to say they should do it. And so maybe he had been more oblivious to his children's arguments than he should have been. They weren't children anymore, and still they bickered. Was that his fault?

"Speaking of Lester's new abilities, it certainly would be interesting to hear him," Pamela Armstrong said. She looked back toward the dining room, where he sat. "I know he doesn't do it on demand, though."

"I can help you out some there," Greg said. "Be right back." Pat, Maddie, and Sherrie exchanged looks as he headed toward the basement, and again as he returned, carrying a small cassette recorder. "Got a little bit of Lester on tape," he said, pressing the "play" button. "... Used the hammer, used the saw, but it kept FALLin' on down / Papa sighin', head was shakin', he was WEARin' a frown / Thought he had it — it was standing — then it FELL down again / Sister ran upstairs a-cryin' — Brother STARTed to grin ..."

Grinning herself, Pamela Armstrong said, "What's he talking about there?"

"One Christmas a few years back," Greg said, smiling like a second-grader describing his new toy to his teacher. "We had this tree that —"

"I think you're about to see the real thing," Pat said, nodding in the direction of the dining room. Everyone's head turned. Lester was standing, feet apart, hands ready to draw pistols.

*Sister came up to my room, sat on the EDGE of my bed*

*"You are causing quite a stir, you know"— that WAS what she said*
*Then my Mama and the ladies came upSTAIRS to see me*
*Then I started talkin' to 'em just as LOUD as could be*

Pat watched Pamela Armstrong, who looked as if she were watching a professionally staged, spellbinding magic trick. Then he glanced at Greg, whose face was flashing hatred.

"Wow," Pamela Armstrong said as she turned back around, blinking. "So, he just — suddenly does that, and —" She turned around to see Lester again. "— And then goes right back to, to —"

"To being Lester," Maddie said. "Yes."

"Well." Pamela stared down at her pad, as if it would give her back her bearings. "The question I was about to ask, to all of you, is, do you miss the 'old' Lester? From before the rapping started?"

There was a quiet moment. Then Maddie said, "I do miss him. But I think my husband's right: I'm trying to think of what's going on now as finding out not only who Lester is now, but who he's been all along."

"Very good. Well, as I said, these are just questions to help give the on-air interviewer an idea of topics to explore. I think we've made a good start."

\*　　\*　　\*　　\*

When Pamela Armstrong had gone, Maddie said, "I saved some dessert for after the interview, so we could relax and enjoy it. It's chocolate cake." This was met with mild enthusiasm from Pat and Sherrie and silence from Greg. Pat put on a pot of coffee as Maddie went to the kitchen to get the cake and Sherrie got forks and plates. "Twice in two weeks I have my whole family together," Maddie said brightly, setting the cake dish on the dining room table. She lifted the heavy glass top, and a warm, sweet smell wafted into the room.

When all of them, including Lester, were eating, Maddie said to Sherrie, "Pamela said she went to George Washington, too. She graduated the year before you. Do you remember seeing her there?"

"You know, I *thought* she looked familiar. I do remember her. She was always walking somewhere really fast. Always in a hurry."

"I can believe that," Maddie said.

Pat studied the napkin Lester had been drawing on. He had made ink stick figures of people, three of them, one shorter than the others. The proportions of the body parts were off — the circular heads too big, the lines representing the torsos too long, the legs far too short, like tiny, upside-down V's. All of which made it strangely interesting. If some white college professor's son had drawn it, Pat thought, they'd hang it in a museum. Not that Lester would lack publicity once this news feature aired. He pictured Lester in front of a news camera. The image made him remember something. "So Greg," he said, "You've been recording Lester?"

Greg shrugged, looking irritated. "Yeah, why not? I figured somebody should get it on tape. Just to have it. What if he stops?"

"That's a point, I guess," Maddie said.

Sherrie shot Greg a suspicious glance. Greg shot her back a look that said, *Don't fuck with me.*

Pat nearly asked Greg if his tape-recording had anything to do with Lester's dinner-killing rap about Gina, given the curious last line of Lester's rhyme that evening. But he thought better of it.

Greg finished his cake and said, "I gotta make a phone call."

As he headed toward the kitchen with his plate, Maddie said, "Greg, do you ..."

He stopped. Maddie stared at him a moment, a wistful expression on her face. "Do I *what*, Ma?"

"Never mind. It's not important."

Greg went to the basement, sat on the edge of his bed, and dialed Gina's number. He had tried calling her the evening before, at the end of a day that had seen him flatten another student in the cafeteria and take his economics final in a distracted state of mind; he had gotten her father, who said, "She's out right now," in that distant-thunder voice that made him sound as if he were saying, "The court sentences you to ten years."

This time, though, Gina herself answered. "Gina, it's Greg."

There was a slight pause, during which Greg could hear his heart beating. "Hi," she finally said, in a civil but frosty tone.

"I'm sorry about the other night. I can explain it."

"Okay, well, I'm listening," she said in the same voice. Then the voice suddenly changed, and she asked, a spark of anger amplifying the words, "What *was* all that? Were you talking to Lester about — you and me — and recording it on a tape? What am I supposed to think about that?"

The tone frightened Greg but gave him some hope, too. This was not the cool, later-for-you attitude of someone who had already moved on in her mind; underneath the anger, she was trying to understand. "It's a long story," he said, "but let me tell it." As stupid as it sounded now, he explained, he had thought there might be money to be made if he could get some of Lester's raps on tape. He told Gina about the visit to the home of Clive's cousin, the deejay Edward Harper, and about Edward's advice to rap about either love or social conditions. Greg told a condensed story about the visit to the projects, which had been meant to inspire socially conscious rap from Lester. "So when that didn't work, I tried the love angle," he said. "I told Lester about some of my past girlfriends. I didn't talk about sex, and I didn't have the recorder on. I was just trying to give him ideas for a rap. Then, when I started talking about you, I felt so … excited, and happy, I kinda forgot what I was s'posed to be doing. That's when I mentioned the thing about … you know … your … tongue."

"Well, I felt really embarrassed. In front of your parents!"

"I know. I'm sorry."

"And — so your brother starts talking, *rapping*, after never saying a word, and the first thing you do is see how you can get some money and fame out of it? Did you really drag him to the projects?"

"Look, I'm not proud of it, awright? I didn't want to tell you about it. I was just trying to be honest."

She sighed. "I don't know, Greg."

"You don't know what?"

"I better go. I have to get up early."

Upstairs, the rest of the family ate cake and sipped coffee. Maddie said, "So I guess Saturday, Eyewitness News will have some cameras at the hospital where Lester is. Pamela Armstrong talked to Dr. Greer."

"Now, that's going to be a circus," Sherrie said. "Boy, we did a one-eighty here, huh? The last time we sat at this table, we all agreed to keep Lester's rapping a secret. Now it's going to be on Channel Nine. That's what I call a change of plan."

"I think we have to call it rolling with the punches," Pat said. "Lester's condition just turned out to be something you *can't* keep a secret. People were bound to find out. Of course," he chuckled dryly, "once Celestine and Floretta saw what was happening, folks found out a little faster than they might have otherwise. But they just sped up what would've happened anyway. It's like a force we can't stop. We're just riding out a wave."

"I thought we were rolling with the punches."

"Eat your cake."

They cleared away the plates and cups. Maddie retired to her room, to half-read the new *Ebony* magazine and half-watch TV, and Lester went upstairs to brush his teeth and go to sleep. Pat and Sherrie split the dining room table, Pat covering his side with papers from work, Sherrie using hers to grade undergraduate chemistry tests. After an hour or so Pat kissed his daughter goodnight.

Sherrie graded tests a while longer. These poor students ... Sherrie had come to understand, in a way that she hadn't as a college freshman, that the introductory chemistry classes were in part a weeding-out process, and here she was now, one of the gardeners. So many of the students had no chance, because they viewed it as just a lot of confusing interactions between drawings of molecules, not as what it was in a larger sense: a way of getting to the bottom of things, finding out how life really works.

When she finished grading tests she went to the sofa to read *Atlas Shrugged*. She remembered that the last time she had sat on this sofa, reading this book, Oscar had called to see how she was doing. She wondered what he was doing now.

When Pat had turned out the bedroom light and gotten settled under the covers, Maddie said, "We tried, didn't we, honey?"

"What do you mean?"

"With the children. We did our best, didn't we?"

In the dark, Pat drew his wife toward him, put his arms around her, rubbed her back. He sighed. "We tried our best," he told her. "We did that, if we didn't do anything else."

# — NINETEEN —

On Friday morning Sherrie drove back to Baltimore. Early Saturday morning, Pat, Maddie, Lester, and a reluctant Greg headed there too, meeting Sherrie at Johns Hopkins University Hospital. For a few minutes the Hobbs family and George Greer crowded, standing, into the smaller of the two rooms where Maddie had been before. Sherrie introduced Dr. Greer to Greg; Dr. Greer said a hearty "Nice to meet you" and offered his hand, which Greg shook, mumbling, "You too." Pat then explained that the family was ready for Lester to try the L-dopa medication. Dr. Greer nodded. He would give Lester the medicine right here, he said, in pill form. Greer and others would then simply observe Lester, periodically performing tests — the same ones as last week — to monitor the drug's effects. The pill needed to be taken with food, to prevent an upset stomach, so Dr. Greer telephoned the nurses' station and asked for someone to bring a muffin. While they waited, Dr. Greer explained that the observation would take place in the larger examining room. A couple of people from Eyewitness News, a cameraman and another technician, were in there already, waiting. They would spend most of their day waiting, he said, smiling and shaking his head; he hoped they weren't bored easily. A nurse brought in a muffin and handed it to Dr. Greer. He gave it to Maddie, who held it in front of Lester and said, "Eat." When he had eaten some, Dr. Greer gave Maddie a purple pill and a paper cup filled with water. Maddie held them in front of Lester. "Swallow."

The Hobbses and Dr. Greer then went to the larger examining room. There, a collision between two forms of technology seemed to have taken place. In a space already full of neurological equipment, including the EEG machine and the CT scanner (as Maddie had learned that the big white machine was called), there was now a TV camera with the Eyewitness News logo on the side and, mounted on a tripod, an umbrella-like object with an intensely bright light, like a piece of the sun, at its center. Two young men, one black, one white, in decidedly non-medical clothing (jeans, T-shirts, a baseball cap), sat chatting behind the camera. When the Hobbses entered, the two men introduced themselves in friendly tones. Soon two residents came in. The scene was suddenly like a cocktail party minus the drinks, with everyone talking and little room to move around.

Greg quietly told his mother that he was going to find a place to study and would come back in a while. Around the corner, in the middle of a long hall, Greg found an area with several low, heavy chairs with plaid patterns of clashing colors. He sank into one of the chairs and pulled his sociology textbook and spiral notebook from his backpack. He read and made notes for a while. Then his mind wandered. He thought of Gina's last words, or near-last words, two nights ago: *I don't know, Greg.* She didn't know about what he'd done, trying to get Lester on tape, dragging him to the projects and telling him that ridiculous stuff about his love life, just so Lester could blab it all during dinner? Or she didn't know if she could be with Greg anymore, since he'd acted so stupid when it came to Lester? Or maybe she had meant both. Funny how both had to do with Lester. That's who everything is about for me, he thought. What do you do when you can't get mad at the person who makes you maddest? All his life, storming off because Lester was getting all the attention, only to come back and find Lester doodling or working a puzzle, looking so sweet and innocent, making Greg want to protect him. From whom? Himself? It was like chasing the grinning kid who had pelted your eye with a rock, then finding in his place a big-eyed, whimpering puppy. What do you do with your anger then? Besides hate yourself for it?

Because, often, he did want to protect him. That was why he had taken those karate classes, built himself up. It wasn't so he could beat up other boys. It was so they couldn't hurt Lester. The day those boys smeared that banana on his face … a thousand, ten thousand times, in his mind, Greg had cut those boys' hands off. He had felt like Lester's father sometimes, the way he worried, strategized about how they would get to school. And sometimes, when they were alone together, Greg found himself talking to Lester the way he imagined a mother would talk to her baby when they were alone — thinking out loud in loving tones. "Don't know why they gotta give me all this math homework, Les. What's geometry gonna do for me when I'm outta school? Do you know, Les? Me neither. … You believe she said that to me, Les? That's what happens when a gal doesn't hear nothin' all her life but how pretty she is. Thinks she can do and say any damn thing she wants. … It's some kinda cold out there, Lester. We better dress warm. …"

He took a break, packed up his books, walked around the halls. Then he thought he should go see what was happening with Lester. Through the open doorway of the examining room, as he approached, he saw Pamela Armstrong smiling and chatting with one of the news technicians. Then he turned into the room.

Lester was seated. Above him, the bright light shone down.

The other technician was rubbing something on Lester's face. Lester had his eyes shut, as if trying to hide.

This scene horrified Greg, for reasons he couldn't put his finger on. He went up to his parents and said in an urgent whisper, "*What are they doing?*" At that, Dr. Greer and one of the residents, who had been discussing something with their backs to the Hobbses, turned around to look at Greg.

"It's makeup for the camera," his father said quietly. "They're trying to get rid of the glare on his face."

"What're they filming him for? He's not doin' nothing!"

"Dr. Greer is trying to coax him to speak. They want to get it on camera if he does."

"Dr. Greer," Maddie called out, "maybe it's time for Lester to go to the bathroom."

"Okay. Good idea."

Maddie turned to Greg, smiling. "It's okay, Greg honey. Do you want to take your brother to the bathroom?"

Greg sighed. "Okay. Come on, Les."

They went back around the corner, past the section of ugly chairs, to the men's room. As they peed in adjacent urinals, Greg studied the side of Lester's face. The stuff the technician had put on was tan, a shade unlike any skin color Greg had ever seen; it reminded him of the makeup someone had clumsily put on Grandma Bell for the open-casket part of her funeral, as if she were going off to some masquerade party for the dead. "What are they doing to you in there, Les? First they shave your head, now this?" They washed their hands and left. They turned right, heading back toward the examining room, the TV news technicians, their makeup, and all the rest.

Then, suddenly, Greg stopped. He understood what he had felt — remembered — as he watched the technician putting the stuff on Lester's face.

Bananas.

Lester stopped beside him.

*     *     *     *

Pat, Maddie, and Sherrie stood together in the hall outside the examining room. "My heart was pounding when Dr. Greer was saying things to Lester," Maddie said. "I think if he starts talking, really talking to us, I might faint."

"Well, Dr. Greer said it might take a while to happen, and it might not happen at all," Pat said. "I think we just need to be calm."

"It's really something to watch Pamela Armstrong with those news people," Maddie said. "She's so sure of herself. You forget how young she is."

"She actually seems brighter than that reporter who was interviewing Dr. Greer."

"Yes. He's not making me want to switch to Channel Nine for my news. I don't know why Pamela's not on the air. She'd do a better job, I think."

"Maybe she just likes it better behind the scenes. Less fame and glory, but you probably get to use your head more."

Sherrie said, "Shouldn't Greg and Lester be back from the bathroom by now?"

*    *    *    *

Greg and Lester went past all the ambulances, cars, and buses in the hospital's rectangular front lot and turned left, only to find another hospital building, and another beyond that, and still more on the other side of the street. The sky was overcast, gray. Clouds and the big, dull buildings blocked out the sun, and Greg felt as if they were walking around in an old black-and-white movie. They crossed Monument Street, then Madison Street. Finally they came to different buildings — homes. This was not the way they had driven. Greg was surprised by how small and shabby the houses were. Wasn't Johns Hopkins a famous hospital, with lots of money? He had just assumed that the whole neighborhood would be nice, but — wow, that building on the corner looked like public housing. "Better watch ourselves, Les."

They found the neighborhood's commercial street, such as it was. There was a little, run-down grocery store whose produce, sitting outside in plastic bins and milk crates, looked like an assemblage of the picked-over rejects from stores in better areas. A drugstore was next to that; and, next to that, a liquor store. (Why do poor neighborhoods have liquor stores when they don't have anything else? Greg wondered. Then he thought, the question almost answers itself.) Across the street, on the corner, was a small coffee shop; Greg could see its little counter through the window. "Want some'm to eat, Les? Come on." They crossed the street. Then Greg stopped. "We gotta wipe off your face first," he said, taking his handkerchief to Lester's cheeks, with only partial success.

"Ah, fuck it." He put the handkerchief, now smeared brown and useless, back in his front pocket. They went in. The place had booths in back, small tables up front. It seemed almost like a senior center: there were seven or eight customers, all but a couple of them men, every single one well past fifty. The shop was as worn down as they were, or vice versa — the white linoleum floor tiles hadn't seen a mop in a while, and the tiles overlapped the bottoms of the five stools at the counter, as if the stools had burst through the floor from below. Greg sat at the counter, and Lester did the same. Behind it, a woman with tired eyes and hair in pink curlers poured coffee. She gave the cup of coffee to the gray-haired man in the brown fedora who sat on the other side of Lester. Then she approached Greg and Lester. "Want a menu?"

"Yes, thank you. Just one." She handed him a well-worn piece of beige cardboard, with eggs, sandwiches, and other items listed at absurdly low prices, some of which had been crossed off with blue ink and replaced by new amounts, written in a childlike hand. "Let me get two plates of scrambled eggs, coffee for me, glass of milk for him." She took the menu back, shifted a mildly curious gaze from Greg to Lester, and went to pour the coffee and milk.

Guess he could start rapping in here, Greg thought. Then again, maybe the medicine will stop that. Whatever. He wasn't going to worry about it.

The man in the fedora said to the woman behind the counter, "See that picture that was on T-V yesterday? The one wit' Di-ana Ross playin' Billie Holiday?"

"Naw, I ain't see it. Was it good?"

"It was all right. That gal ain't no Billie Holiday, though. Didn't sing nothin' like her." He sipped his coffee loudly.

The woman brought Greg and Lester's eggs, coffee, and milk. The man in the fedora said to Lester, "Ain't too often I see a grown man drinkin' a glass of milk." Lester ignored him and ate his eggs.

"He doesn't talk," Greg said.

"Oh. Why don't he?"

"Just doesn't. Born that way."

"Oh." The man slurped his coffee. He said to the woman, "Di-ana Ross sound like every other gal on the radio. Billie Holiday had some'm *special* about *her* voice."

"Yeah — she couldn't sing," said a man behind them, at a table by the wall. "Now, Ella Fitzgerald, *that's* who could *sing*. Billie Holiday start singin', you think your record done got scratched."

"Man, whatchu talkin' 'bout? Billie Holiday just sounded *different*, that's all. Don't mean she couldn't sing. Maybe she ain't wanna sound like every other gal — Ella Fitzgerald and all the rest."

"You sayin' Ella *Fitzgerald* sound like every other gal? *Now* I *know* you crazy."

"If I'm crazy, and you sittin' here talkin' to me, what's that make you?" Both men laughed at that.

Greg looked over at Lester, to make sure he wasn't spilling too many eggs. He seemed to be doing okay. Greg turned back to his own food. The eggs were surprisingly good, for a place like this — light, fluffy. He sipped his milk-heavy coffee; he was getting toward the bottom, where all the sugar was.

He heard Lester say softly, "Milk."

Greg's head whipped around. Lester, who had a milk moustache, stared down at the empty glass in his hand.

The man in the fedora said, "I thought he didn't talk."

"Lester." Greg's heart was hammering. "Say that again."

Lester turned toward his brother, looked him in the eye. Greg was frightened. Lester was not staring through him, or past him, or seeming to look at Greg and see something or someone else. *I know you*, Lester's eyes appeared to say. What he said aloud was, "Milk. More."

Greg stood from the counter and backed up a step, eyes never leaving Lester. He was aware, at the periphery of his mind, that everybody was watching them. He didn't care. The weight of what was happening, of what he had done, was falling on him. "Jesus," he said. "We gotta go back." He pulled out his wallet and found a five-dollar bill, which he knew would cover everything, and tossed it on the counter. He grabbed the inside of Lester's elbow and pulled him, gently but firmly, toward the door.

They retraced their steps: back across the street, past the block with the projects, across Madison, back on the black-and-white-movie street. Greg was still holding Lester's elbow, pulling him along, the two of them walking briskly. "Oh, Lester. Oh, man." Up ahead, a woman in black pants and a red blouse was coming toward them, purposefully. "Les, is that —" It was: Sherrie. He called her name, picked up his pace. She walked more quickly, too. Up close, her face was a mask of fury. She didn't slow down as she neared them. Instead, she ran up and slapped Greg's face. "Where have you *been?!*"

"Listen — he's *talking*."

Sherrie seemed not to know who to look at. She turned from Greg to Lester and back again, twice; her lips were forming words that wouldn't come out. Until: "What were you doing? Don't you know he has to be examined, monitored —"

"I know. I was coming back. Let's go back."

Sherrie started to turn around, then stopped, staring at Lester. Greg watched him, too. He was staring at Sherrie as he had at Greg. He said, "Mommy. Daddy."

"Oh," Sherrie said.

Lester's face puckered, as if he were about to sneeze. He closed his eyes. Then his face relaxed. He opened his eyes. Only the whites were showing. Sherrie screamed. Then Lester collapsed, having said all he would ever say.

# PART THREE

## THE SCORE

# — TWENTY —

One winter night when Pat was ten years old he went to bed with chills and a slight fever. His mother tucked him in, kissed him goodnight, turned off his bedside lamp, and left the room, and Pat settled into a comfortable position under his thick covers. Gradually his chills subsided. In the darkness, as warmth spread over him, he could see the glow from the streetlamp through his window across the room. His eyes closed. Half a second later they opened again. The morning sunlight streamed through his windows, and his father sat on the side of his bed, reading the newspaper.

His eyes had been closed for longer than half a second, of course. But in his mild illness he had slept so deeply, his mind plunged so fully into a dreamless state, that the hours were compressed into nothing and passed in what felt, to Pat, exactly like the blink of an eye.

Time performs a similar trick even when we are awake. The minutes, the days, the years pass, and while much occurs, we feel much the same inside. Our memories of the events that have formed us do not change. The older we get, the more we find this to be true.

See Pat, on a Thursday morning in late November 1999, sitting in a leather armchair in the larger of the two rooms where his children once slept. Under his checked flannel shirt, his arms are thinner, his shoulders less thick, than they used to be, his once protruding belly now sagging, expanding his shirt at the bottom like sand in a half-filled bag. Under his thick green corduroy pants his legs are smaller, too, thin ankles sticking out of worn brown leather shoes. He is nearly seventy now — but his thoughts are what they have long been.

His wife knows this, and her knowledge is the tool she carries with her into the room where Pat sits. Maddie, who was slender as a young woman, is slender now, and that sameness has given her the illusion of barely having aged at all — that and her face, whose youthfulness comes partly from her sunny demeanor, partly from a near absence of creases. She is one of those women whose mostly gray hair seems an incongruity, a mistake on someone's part.

"Pat, honey," she says, taking the chair from the rolltop desk (this room is now Pat's study) and setting it down next to the armchair. She places her hand, with its slender, smooth fingers, on top of his, with its wrinkles and veins. "Everybody's downstairs now. Greg and his kids are here."

"I know. He came up to see me."

"Why don't you come down?"

"I will in a little while."

She rubs his hand. "Pat, why do you torture yourself so? It's been almost three months. And — you know nothing really changed. It's the same as before. It's been the same for twenty years."

"I know. I know it in my head. I just can't get to where I *feel* it. And, you know, Thanksgiving. I wish it was a different holiday. Jewish people have a day of atonement. Or maybe it's a week. I wish we had one. Wish *I* had one."

"Pat, you've atoned. Past the point where you had anything to atone for. Can't you see that's true? We all have to forgive ourselves. It was nobody's fault. Not really. We have to get on with things. God knows Greg tortured himself, but he's moved on."

A dry, soundless chuckle jiggles Pat's upper body. "Greg should be up here with me," he said.

"Pat! You don't really believe that."

"No, I guess I don't. Listen: I'll be down soon."

She pats his hand, leaves him, and goes down the hall to the bathroom. When she comes out and starts downstairs, she hears music coming from his study, one of the innumerable jazz records he keeps in there along with that ancient turntable and the shelves of books. She shakes her head as she descends the carpeted steps.

Her morning began at a little after six. She woke up without an alarm — she always wakes up so early now — and went to the living room to do some painting. For years now the early morning has been her favorite time to work, ever since that one painting she did right before Lester's collapse, the one that has always seemed too personal to include in any of the group shows that feature her work: the painting of the house across the street at dawn, the sky behind it that special shade of almost-dark blue, the color of her childhood mornings. Maddie has a theory now as to what inspired that painting. She wanted to capture that blue from the happiest moments of her childhood, which were gone, along with anyone who would rejoice with her at memories of them. And the view of the house across the street: that was the perspective she had at the time she was painting, a time that she also felt — on some level — was about to vanish, because Lester had started his rapping, a thing that would take them in a direction no one could predict. It was all about preservation, that painting. Capturing time. Maybe she would call it that, if she ever decided to put it in a show and needed a title for it.

After it turned light she stopped painting and peeled potatoes, cut green beans, got the turkey ready to go in the oven. Sherrie arrived around nine to help with the greens and cornbread. They had a pleasant talk in the kitchen, just the two of them, before everyone else came. Sherrie, forty-three years old, starting to look like the middle-aged woman she was. And what, Maddie thought with wonder, does that make me?

Now, as she comes downstairs, her three grandchildren watch the Macy's Thanksgiving Day Parade on television in the living room. She passes through there into the dining room, where Greg and Oscar sit at the table, laughing about something. They look up at her expectantly. "Pop's not budgin', huh?" Greg says.

"He said he'll be down. He's just not quite ready yet."

"He's so easy-going," Oscar says, "but he's got a stubborn streak, too."

"Like you?" Maddie says to her son-in-law, smiling, as she sits down.

"*Au contraire*, Momma."

"He must have a stubborn streak," Greg says, "to put up with Sherrie for twenty years."

"I heard that," Sherrie calls from the kitchen, where she and Theresa are working on the sweet potatoes.

"Oscar, I thought you were a modern husband," Maddie says. She points to Greg and adds, "I wouldn't expect any better from this one here —"

"Thanks, Ma."

"— but how come you're out here while the women are in the kitchen?"

"I *was* in the kitchen. They chased me out. No man can do right in the kitchen as far as women are concerned. At least not *these* women."

"Well, you can do something for this old lady. Pour me some scotch." She holds her thumb and index finger an inch apart. "About that much. With some ice."

"Ma," Greg says, "I'm shocked."

"It's almost twelve o'clock. And it's Thanksgiving."

"Since you put it that way," Greg says, turning to Oscar, "get me some, too."

"Who am I, Jeeves the butler? Come with me, ya lazy bum."

Greg and Oscar head to the kitchen. Maddie, alone, listens to the discussion her grandchildren are having in the next room. "This show is kinda stupid," says Quentin, Sherrie's son, who is sixteen.

"Why you been watchin' it for two hours then?" This comes from Greg's daughter, Karina, seventeen. (It was Karina who dubbed Maddie "Grammaddie," long since shortened to "Gram," the name all her grandchildren call her.)

"I didn't say I didn't like it," Quentin says. "I just said it was stupid."

"That says it all, right there."

"Shut up."

"Gram, Quentin told me to shut up."

"Good."

Karina sticks her tongue out at Maddie. Maddie sticks her tongue out at Karina.

Greg and Oscar come back in, carrying three glasses of scotch between them. Oscar says, "You think he needs some company up there?"

"No. He just needs to get himself together. He'll be down."

Oscar sips his scotch. "We went by the cemetery Saturday before last. They planted a little tree not too far from Lester. It looks nice."

"Yes, Sherrie told me. I need to go see it myself." Maddie sometimes surprises herself with how blasé she is about her own son's final resting place. Maybe that is because she did her real grieving long ago, when he entered the coma he would stay in for two decades, hooked up to all that equipment at the hospital's expense. (Dr. Greer arranged that, no doubt to avoid a malpractice suit, as Sherrie never tired of saying at the time.)

Back then Maddie entered a period of tears and listlessness matched only by the one she had gone through when Lester was pronounced retarded and mute. The difference was that she didn't have Pat to pull her out of it; he was too mired in his own guilt. (Greg was in even worse shape, despite the evidence that what had happened to Lester would almost certainly have happened anyway, without Greg's interference. And it didn't help him that, in spite of the evidence, everyone was furious at him.) Then she emerged from her grief enough to start painting again, and that became her rope, the means by which she pulled herself back into life. After a while she returned to teaching, but she continued painting, too: rural landscapes, mostly, dirt roads and trees and the occasional lonely house, inspired by memories of the surroundings of her youth. For a time she would put her easel on the front porch and create paintings based on what was in front of her, making changes where necessary — putting a dirt road where the paved street and sidewalk were, leaving out the cars, putting trees or sky in place of some of the houses. Then, after a time, that began to feel like cheating, and one morning in the middle of the week in late summer she took a two-and-a-half-hour busride to her hometown, camera in hand.

She walked around on that sunlit day, taking pictures of a barn whose side was a vast stretch of peeling gray-blue paint, of a muddy pond with a fallen tree branch sticking out of it, like the arm of some giant undersea creature coming up to attack humankind. She ran into people she hadn't seen in thirty years, old schoolmates still living near where they grew up, and she hugged and chatted with them and took their pictures, too. She felt a slight unease in the laughing she did with them, as if this were the pleasantness before the unpleasantness, a friendly chat with a nurse before the doctor probed uncomfortably in private areas. Then she realized she felt this way, and as she walked alone up a rock-covered dirt incline, with a farm on one side and tall trees on the other, she asked herself what she was dreading. The bad behavior of her drunken father, who had died over three decades earlier? Tension with her mother, who was also dead, or her sister, who didn't live there anymore? She stopped walking. Head back, she breathed the clean air and looked at the sky, feeling light enough, suddenly, to float up and join the drifting clouds. She stayed in the town another hour or so, taking more pictures, talking to a couple more people, and then she boarded the afternoon bus back to Washington — taking her hometown with her, in the form of photographs, and leaving it behind, in a way she hadn't as an eighteen-year-old.

Back at home she painted what was in the photographs, including the people — women, mostly. How they smiled, those women: theirs were not the frozen features of people thinking *Hurry up and take the damn picture*, people whose faces would return to sour repose the second after it was snapped; no, there was an openness to those smiles, as if she had caught the women doing what they were doing anyway, a look she saw mostly on people in or from the country. Those smiles were, she realized, much like her own, one fashioned by where she grew up, which even her father, mother, and sister had not managed to ruin completely. She tried to capture these smiles with her brush. One day a couple of years later, reading the *Post* Style section, she read about an open call for art by D.C.-area women who were fifty or over. She made slides of her paintings, both portraits and landscapes, and sent them off, then forgot about it. A few weeks after that she got a call about the first of what would be many group shows around the city to feature her work.

"Even though I saw the grave," Oscar says now, "I feel like Lester's still over at Johns Hopkins."

"I know what you mean," Greg says.

"That's because nothing really changed, in a way," Maddie says. "That's what I just tried to tell your father."

"I guess for me," Oscar says, "it's because I never met Lester."

Maddie looks at him. "I guess you didn't, did you?"

"No. All of that happened before I met you. I already knew Sherrie, but it was before I met the rest of you."

Sherrie and Theresa come in from the kitchen, each sitting in the chair next to her husband. "Theresa, how's work?" Maddie asks. "How do you like being a boss?" Theresa, a psychologist who has had her own practice for years, recently moved to a new building and hired two therapists and a full-time secretary to work under her.

"It's an adjustment. I'm making it, though. I wasn't born to be a boss. I'm not sure anybody is. You know, your impulse is just to be nice all the time, but you can't." If anybody was born to be a therapist, though, Theresa was; Maddie has always thought so. There is a quiet groundedness to the woman, a solidity that has nothing to do with her body, which is long and willowy. You get the feeling Theresa wouldn't move in a tornado, as if she has her own private gravity. Who else could have rescued Greg?

In the living room, Karina, Quentin, and Justin have a debate about what to watch on TV, now that the Thanksgiving parade is ending. They flip through several channels, settling on one that shows a black man wearing several long braids, pointing this way and that and talking in rhythm to loud music.

"Lord, it's that Snoop Dogg," Sherrie says.

Maddie says, "What kind of dog?"

"Snoop Dogg. He's a rapper. I don't know what kids *see* in this stuff. Every other line is F this and F that, or about shooting somebody and calling women every name in the book. And it barely even sounds like music." Raising her voice, Sherrie says, "Can we not have that on *today*?"

"Okay," comes the weary response from the living room. Quentin flips the channel with the remote, stopping at a rerun of *The Cosby Show*.

"I don't know what they see in it," Greg says, "but it doesn't seem to be goin' anywhere. Kids'll go around with their earphones on and their heads boppin' to that stuff if they don't do much else. I was in class the other day, standing at the front of the room talking, and I hear this loud tinny sound coming from the back. So I walk back there, and there's Kachomba Williams —"

"Kachomba?" Maddie says. "What kind of name is that?"

"Don't ask me."

"Boy or girl?"

"Boy. Man, really, or old enough to be one. He's stayed back twice already. This is his fifth year in high school, okay? So anyway, I go back there, and there's Kachomba with his coat on, sitting back like he's settling down for a nap, except he's got the earphones on under his knit hat. Now, I could hear it from the front of the room, so I don't even want to think about what it's doing to his ears. So I say, nice and loud so he can hear me, 'Kachomba, turn that off.' Kid looked at me like I was talkin' about his mother. He's as big as me, maybe bigger. I thought, this is it, it's gonna be me and him, right here. But then he turned it off."

Oscar, smiling, says, "You know what we played for Quentin not too long ago. One of the *original* rappers."

Maddie is confused for a moment, and then her eyes widen. "You mean —"

"Yes." Several years ago Greg came across the tapes he had made of Lester. He discovered, he said, that he was now strong enough to listen to them, and that the sounds were surprisingly clear, considering that they had been recorded on cheap cassettes seventeen years earlier. He had Lester's raps burned onto CDs and gave them to his family. "Sherrie told him the whole story first," Oscar says. "I don't think he quite knew what to make of it—"

"Still don't," comes Quentin's voice from the next room.

Maddie says, "Well, it's a hard thing to believe." She pauses. "Or live through." This makes her think of Pat, and to Theresa she says, half-jokingly, "So do you have any professional advice for how to get my husband down here?"

Theresa smiles politely; Maddie has the feeling that the people her daughter-in-law meets socially often come at her with phrases like "your professional advice," "your expert opinion." Maddie herself usually tries to refrain from it — in part so she can avoid the faint whiff of being condescended to, like the one she is picking up now. Fear of this whiff is the only thing that makes her uncomfortable about her son's wife. She wonders if it ever bothers Greg. "He'll come when he's ready," Theresa says.

"Or when he's hungry," Greg adds.

"Speaking of which," says Sherrie, "let me go check on those sweet potatoes."

Her head feeling ever so light from the scotch, Maddie follows her daughter to the kitchen. When Sherrie pulls the glass baking dish of candied sweet potatoes out of the oven, Maddie peers into the open door to have a look at the turkey, the heat making her eyes tear up slightly; she checks the skin for that golden-brown tone, which it doesn't have just yet. She thinks how odd it is that though her head is slightly abuzz with alcohol, she can know that it is, and at the same time she can examine the skin of the turkey with perfect competence. The brain is a strange thing, she thinks. (If Lester hadn't taught her that, he hadn't taught her anything.)

"These are almost done," Sherrie says. "You peeled the potatoes, right? I can put them on to boil."

"Okay, thanks." As Maddie leaves the kitchen, Theresa goes back in. When Maddie sits back down, Oscar is saying to Greg, "I saw some guys on TV the other day talking about rap music and how it's all about violence and hating women, blah blah blah, and one of them had a good point. He said that when people talk about getting rap off the airwaves and off MTV because it's so objectionable, it's like finding somebody who's been shot, and the first thing you do is clean up the blood. He said the lyrics in rap music are just a symptom, and the real problem is we've raised a generation of young men who think this way about violence and women. He said instead of getting rap off the airwaves, we should play it twenty-four hours a day, with big speakers next to the White House and the Capitol, so people in power can hear what's going on." Greg nods his agreement vigorously. Meanwhile, in the kitchen, Sherrie and Theresa laugh about an exchange their teenage children just had. Maddie thinks, not for the first time, how nice it is that her children have not only found mates but given each other a brother and sister. Sherrie, who never had a sister growing up, gets along well with Theresa, and Greg and Oscar, as different as they are in some ways, are even closer; their friendship has even helped Greg and Sherrie relate to each other a bit better.

One day about twelve years ago Maddie answered the telephone and heard, "Madelyn, this is Freddie." For a few seconds she had no idea who was on the other end; she didn't recognize the voice, and who was Freddie? The man paused, waiting for her to respond; she silently racked her brain; and she came up with the answer at the same time that the man gave up waiting and said, "Rosa's husband." If Maddie was confused before, she was stunned now. Her sister's husband was calling her, when Little Rosa herself never called or sent so much as a Christmas card? This could mean only one thing. "Is Rosa —"

"She's all right. Well … she's sick. We thought I should call you."

On the chilly Saturday morning in October when Pat drove her to Little Rosa's house in Virginia, Maddie barely ate. On the highway they passed through some pretty stretches of trees, with red, yellow, even purple and orange leaves, but her stomach was too full of butterflies for her to appreciate it. Here she was, fifty-five years old, as anxious as a teenager. Little Rosa, whom she hadn't seen since their mother's funeral, eleven years earlier, had stomach cancer; she was undergoing chemotherapy, which left her too weak and sick to do much besides lie in bed between treatments. Maddie was afraid of both how her older sister would look and what she would say. But she had to go. And so they made their way through the hilly, winding streets of Little Rosa's neighborhood until they got to the one-story, pale green stucco house.

Maddie had focused so much on how Little Rosa would look that she wasn't prepared for the change in Freddie. In her mind this man, whom she had never so much disliked as not known, had always had a blank face. It was not blank when he answered the door. His face seemed smaller, more skeletal, as if it were boiling down to its essence, which was a permanently pained expression. His hair was both considerably grayer than she remembered and longer, almost Afro-length — but uneven, not as if he were trying out a new style, but as if he could no longer be bothered to think about his hair. The smaller face, the longer hair, made Maddie think of one of those shrunken heads in cartoon drawings of witch doctors. In the living room Freddie asked about the drive down, and they talked about how chilly it had gotten; no matter how mundane a thing he was talking about, Freddie's face never changed: the same crinkling in the corners of his eyes, the same slightly curled upper lip, almost like part of his body was aching. Maddie thought that the word *careworn* might have been thought up to describe this man, her brother-in-law. She glanced around the living room, with its haphazard stacks of newspaper and several half-drunk cups of black coffee, white cups with dark rings on the inside, above the surface of the evaporating liquid. Here was a room that had not felt a woman's touch in a while.

Soon Freddie led Maddie to the back bedroom and knocked gently on the open door. "Maddie's here." While Freddie went back to the living room, where he and Pat would talk about God knew what, Maddie walked slowly toward the bed where her sister lay. Her sister: Maddie couldn't believe that's who this was, this bone-thin woman with the long gray hair that was so sparse you could see her scalp. It was a job to keep the surprise off her face, so much so that she didn't speak for a moment. She sat at the edge of the bed. "Hello, Rosa. It's good to see you."

Rosa regarded Maddie through those narrow eyes of hers; their narrowness had often made it difficult to read her expressions, even when the sisters were girls, and the years had only added to their unreadability. Finally she said, just above a whisper, "Now don't start off by lying."

"Freddie called me and said you talked about me coming." She didn't know why she had said this, unless it was to offer an excuse for her presence, her existence.

"I was just lyin' here thinkin' about the old days," Rosa said.

Maddie smiled. "Yeah? What about them?"

"You thought you were some'm else. Daddy's little girl. Daddy didn't care nothin' about his *other* girl. Just you. And you'd go around tryin' to look like you wasn't happy about it."

In her whole life Maddie had never felt the combination of emotions that took hold of her now. Her bowels felt as if they were turning to ice, the feeling she'd had as a girl when a grown-up yelled at her for something she knew she'd done wrong. At the same time, she felt angrier than at any time she could remember. "I DIDN'T —"

She thought about where she was, what was going on, and lowered the volume of her voice, though not its intensity. "I didn't do any such thing. It was just Daddy trying to get you and Momma mad at me, so you wouldn't be mad at *him*, and you and Momma were stupid enough to fall for it."

"Never heard you tell him to stop. 'Oh, Maddie' this. 'Oh, Maddie' that.'"

"You — *this* is what you wanted to see me for? After all this time? Well I'm not gonna sit here and listen to it." She stomped out of the room.

In the living room, Pat and Freddie were facing each other, making conversation in lazy fits and starts, occasionally nodding, as if in acknowledgment of their mutual discomfort. They looked up simultaneously when Maddie walked in. "We should go," she told Pat, doing her best to keep the tears and anger out of her voice. "Thank you, Freddie." As they got their jackets on, she saw her husband and brother-in-law exchange confused looks — their one moment of bonding in thirty-odd years. In the car, as they pulled away from the curb, Maddie checked her watch: after their two-hour drive here, they had stayed seven minutes.

So when she got Freddie's second call, a week or so later, she was almost more surprised than she'd been the first time (though now she at least recognized his voice). "She's sorry about your last visit," Freddie said. "She understands if you don't want to come back, but she'd like to see you again." The position Maddie was in made her resentful; given how sick Rosa was, Maddie couldn't refuse to go back, no matter what unpleasantness awaited her, and Rosa must know it.

Maddie couldn't ask Pat to drive her down again, so on a Thursday, when she didn't have to teach, she got up early and took the bus. It was a wary woman, her emotional defenses up, who entered Rosa's bedroom that day. She didn't even say hello; she just sat on the edge of the bed, and waited. Rosa didn't say hello, either. She regarded Maddie through those narrow eyes again, then said in the same feathery voice, as if she were on the edge of sleep, "I think I had to get that meanness out of me."

Maddie didn't know how to respond. But she was beyond feeling the need to fill silence with words, any words. So she sat quietly, and Rosa lay quietly, until Maddie laughed. "I'll say this for you. You know how to keep somebody guessing."

"Freddie's been saying that since 1950."

Maddie laughed harder. "Okay. So you got your meanness out. Now what?"

"Maddie."

It had been years, maybe decades, since Maddie had heard Rosa speak her name, at least it seemed so to her; and they were definitely children the last time she had said it with such tenderness. "Rosa. I'm fifty-five, and you're fifty-seven, and the two of us here fighting about what our Daddy did when we were twelve and fourteen."

"That's why I had to get it out. You got anything you want to get out?"

"Oh, Rosa, we don't have time to waste on that." Oops. "I mean, I didn't mean —"

"No, you said it right. I don't know ... how it's been with you."

"Well ..." Maddie told Rosa about Lester — the seizure and the coma; the rapping seemed like more of a story than Rosa could handle in her condition. Rosa said, "I'm sorry to hear it," a response Maddie could have expected from a complete stranger, but one that meant something coming from Rosa, who spoke no empty words. "Thank you, Rosa," Maddie said. "Rosa ... why has it been so long?"

"I guess it was my pride. But being sick like this doesn't leave you with much of that."

"Our kids should have gotten to know each other. When they were little. We should have been sitting at the table talking and laughing while they were playing together." Maddie felt tears start at the backs of her eyes. "That's what I always wanted. They should have played together like we used to."

Rosa's thin, thin hand reached for Maddie's; the untrimmed nails gently raked the back of Maddie's hand before the palm settled, warmly, on top of it.

They reminisced. It felt a bit like navigating a river in a canoe, steering clear of certain memories, the jagged rocks of their father's divisiveness. But it wasn't so difficult — this river was wide, full of good memories, too: they talked about their walks to school in the near-dark, when they had laughed and discussed who liked who and teased poor quiet Lester; they recalled how they would sit in church once a month when the preacher came around, with Maddie whispering to Rosa, trying to make her giggle, and their mother whispering to them angrily when Maddie finally succeeded. They even sang, quietly, the song they remembered from more than forty years earlier: *There was a little chigger/he wasn't any bigger/than the point of a very small pin/But the lump that he raises/Itch like the blazes/ And that's where the scratch comes in.* At the end they laughed.

After a while Rosa began to look tired, even for her. Maddie said maybe she should go. "You don't have to. Stay with me a while." So Maddie sat quietly. Soon Rosa was asleep. Maddie stood and looked around the room. She went over to Rosa's dresser, with its white lace doily, combs and brushes, and pictures of her children at different ages. There were none of Maddie, or any others from the old days. But it's all right, she thought. I'm here now. She turned back around to see Rosa, who was now breathing audibly, evenly. She crossed the room and lightly kissed her sister's forehead. "I'm going to let you rest." Rosa made a tiny sound of assent. Maddie left the room.

The third and final call from Freddie came about a month later. Maddie, Pat, Sherrie, and Greg all drove down for the funeral, which was well-attended; Rosa, it turned out, had gotten to know quite a few people in her community over the years. A number of them stood up to talk about their deceased friend, the adult Rosa whom Maddie had never really known. Maddie felt a little jealous of these people, of the knowledge of her sister that she would never have now, but mostly she felt happy. In spite of everything, her sister seemed to have had a good life.

So many funerals, Maddie thinks, sitting at her dining room table on this Thanksgiving morning. Celestine passed the year after Rosa, at age eighty-two, and Floretta, without her sister, followed not long afterward. And Lester was buried, three months ago. So many funerals to attend, if you live long enough; so many, on the way to your own. But she is not so worried about that. She has her family around her; she even made peace with her sister, a thing she had stopped hoping for. Now if only her husband can be persuaded to come downstairs.

*        *        *        *

Sherrie's Thanksgiving morning began almost as early as her mother's. In her split-level home in Prince George's County, Maryland, just over the D.C. border, she awoke when the sun illuminated her and Oscar's bedroom window, even through the closed blinds. She rose quietly and slipped into her white terry cloth robe, then went to the kitchen for coffee. Once in a while she liked being up before everyone else, to have time to herself, to think. Sitting at her kitchen table, the steam from her mug rising and warming her face, she went over the coming day in her mind: rouse Oscar and Quentin in another hour or so, if they weren't already up; fix breakfast for them all, not just the usual cold cereal but something solid, since they weren't likely to have another full meal until Thanksgiving dinner, which would fall between where lunch and dinner normally came; then shower and drive over to help her mother with the food, with Oscar and Quentin to follow later in the minivan. She heard the newspaper land outside the door and went to get it, spreading it over the kitchen table. Elizabeth Dole was talking about running for president; so were Dan Quayle and Bill Bradley and, of course, Vice President Gore. He would probably win — the economy was humming along, no wars were happening. Some Republicans had already raised money so George Bush's son, the governor of Texas, could run. That stupid Pat Buchanan was going to try again, too. There was an article about how to prepare for Y2K, in case the computer disaster some people were predicting came to pass. (Sherrie and Oscar had already bought flashlights, a ton of batteries, canned food, and several gallons of water; beyond that they weren't going to worry about it.)

At a little after seven she heard Oscar knocking around. In a minute he came in the kitchen in his dark green bathrobe, eyes sleepy behind his square, wire-frame glasses. "Happy Thanksgiving, Mr. Thompson," Sherrie said — her little joke, ever since he had become principal of his elementary school a few months ago.

"The principal needs his coffee."

"I made some. I put the rest in the thermos." He kissed her, went to pour his coffee, and joined her at the table, her forty-six-year-old, slowly graying husband of eighteen years.

They had married in June of 1981, two years — almost to the day — after she received that letter from him. The letter was their first contact after the telephone conversation in which he had said that honesty was her one good point. It came just a couple of weeks after Lester's collapse, which was only part of the reason it caused her to cry so. She still had the letter, written in his marvelous, neat schoolteacher's hand.

*June 7, 1979*

*Dear Sheridan,*

*I must start off by apologizing to you. The last time we talked I said something very mean, but worse, it was also untrue. You are indeed honest, but that is far from being your only good quality. In addition to being beautiful and smart, which are things you don't have control over, there are the wonderful things that are in your power. You are so thoughtful and caring, and you're even funny, when you let yourself be. My comment was unfair to you, and I prefer to think it was unworthy of me.*

*It was also unfair because what I was really upset about was not your fault. I wanted us to be closer than we were. I would still like that. But I respect that you don't feel the same. All I ask now is that you allow me*

*to continue being your friend, or, if you don't think that
will work, that you not think badly of me. I miss your
friendship.*

*It is a little painful to reflect on the qualities that I
may be missing, and whose lack may be keeping us from
being closer. But I also believe that we have to be who we
have to be, and that if I change myself it has to be for me,
not for another person. Maybe there are things I have to
improve on. In the meantime, as I work on figuring that
out, I wish you all the best, whatever our relationship
will become.*

*Love,
Oscar*

When Sherrie got the letter she had already told George Greer that she could not see him romantically anymore. (She got the feeling, as she told him, that he was only half listening.) After she got the letter she called Oscar, and they agreed to have dinner, a meal between friends. Over dinner she told him all about Lester, from the beginning of the rapping to the collapse outside the hospital. He listened with quiet astonishment; he responded with compassion. And it struck Sherrie, suddenly, what a good man, what a mature, decent, gentle human being, was sitting across the table from her. After another dinner, a few nights later, he accompanied her home and kissed her goodnight outside her door. For the first time ever, she responded passionately, not holding anything back; her eyes closed, and her universe reduced itself to their mouths, moist lips meeting and parting. Somehow they made it inside her apartment, where the most memorable night of her life unfolded — one of sexual excitement and emotional closeness, a closeness that grew out of her budding love for Oscar and was tinged, maybe even heightened, by her grief over Lester.

From that time on, Sherrie's life was not about just her anymore — it was about her and Oscar. The way she saw things in her mind's eye, there was a single, vertical line moving up to a certain point, where it was joined by a parallel line. They made decisions together — about the move to the D.C. area, for example, where he taught at Nalle

Elementary School and she at American University. The irony was that in forming a life partnership with Oscar, she felt that she was, at last, taking charge of her own life. No more meeting a man and then turning the wheel over to him for the next few miles; it was not in Oscar's nature to try to take charge of her. He merely stood beside her as she did it herself. Sometimes it was frightening, with nothing between her and events she could not foresee. But she learned, she was still learning, not to be afraid. She became comfortable with driving in the dark.

Quentin, her lanky sixteen-year-old, a physical replica of his father at a younger age, came in the kitchen in his baggy checked pajamas. "G'morning, Mom. Morning, Dad." He reached in the cabinet for a box of cereal.

"I'm going to fix some real breakfast," Sherrie said.

"Okay. I'll eat that too." He filled a big white bowl, poured in milk, and disappeared to the TV room, below. Quentin, this boy, this near-man she loved so, was a curious mix of things. He looked just like his father, and acted like him, too; he was unusually considerate for a teenage boy. That quality made his occasional moments of utter recklessness all the more surprising. "Quentin Thompson!" she would yell at him then, more in surprise than in anger, followed by some variation on, "What in the world were you *thinking*?" There was the time a couple of years ago, for example, when Sherrie, Oscar, and Quentin watched that PBS special about Evel Knievel. Sherrie and Oscar should have known better, given one or two other things their son had done before. On the Saturday afternoon following the documentary, Quentin came home trying to hide a limp. When Oscar asked him about it, Quentin said it was nothing; when Oscar felt around his son's knee, the boy screamed in pain. Slowly, it came out: Quentin's holding his friends spellbound with descriptions of what he'd seen on the documentary; the boys' ideas for how they could, hypothetically, perform such a feat themselves — each idea a step forward, an advance to a position from which none of them wanted to be the one to retreat; and, finally, the act itself. They set up a wooden ramp near the bottom of a grass hill. One by one, on their bikes, they came flying down the hill and up the ramp, spent one glorious, gravity-defying moment hanging in mid-air, and then —

well, fell to the ground. Quentin spent the next couple of weeks limping around with his leg wrapped from shin to mid-thigh in a tan bandage. (When Sherrie found out that a couple of the other boys were nursing similar wounds, she felt glad that Quentin wasn't the only sucker, then felt guilty for being glad. Oscar remarked, not for the first time, that this was the drawback to raising a kid in the suburbs. For all the dangers in the city, there just wasn't *room* to get into this particular kind of trouble.) At these times Quentin reminded Sherrie of no one so much as the boy's favorite uncle — Greg, whom he even resembled at odd moments, when he turned his head a certain way.

When enough time had passed for her to laugh about it, Sherrie considered that the moment of biking off the ramp was not a bad metaphor for parenthood: both were full of risk and gave you the feeling sometimes that there was nothing beneath you. It was certainly an adventure.

And it had led her, indirectly, to some others. Ten years ago, when Quentin was six and Sherrie was thirty-three, she began feeling that she should be more involved in her son's school. So one weeknight she attended a meeting of a half-dozen parents at a nearby split-level house much like her own. Sherrie didn't know any of the other parents there (Oscar had always picked up Quentin from the after-school program), but she did recognize one of them as soon as she walked in the living room. She'd heard that Jerry "Jackhammer" Beard, the former undisputed light-heavyweight boxing champion, had a child in the school, but because she didn't know anybody who knew him, she'd thought it was just a rumor. Yet that was no rumor sitting on the couch in the muscle-hugging gray turtleneck. He was every bit as boyishly handsome as he looked on television, with the added quality that his big brown eyes were now on Sherrie, following her to where she sat down, across from him. Sherrie and Beard were the only two black parents present; he was the only man. Their hostess, Barbara, was a peroxide blond in a loose-fitting, floral-patterned blouse who laughed continually at her own jokes. She led their discussion of how to publicize some of the upcoming fund-raising events at the school. As everyone but Beard put in their two cents, leaning toward the coffee table to immerse their carrot sticks in Barbara's homemade dip, Sherrie wondered if the others were as aware of the boxer's presence as she was — if their pauseless chatter about school matters was a kind of negative acknowledgment of the famous man sitting silently among them like a muscle-bound Buddha. Then Beard broke his silence. He said that he had met people at local radio stations and newspapers — he had had contracts with promoters of his fights, after all; he would be happy to talk to some of those people, if someone could sit down with him first and help him figure out exactly what should be stressed in each publicity spot. He was looking at Sherrie when he said it. Sure, I can do that, she said, before she thought about what she was getting into.

And so on a Friday afternoon, when she wasn't teaching, she found herself driving to the home of Jackhammer Beard. It was somewhat smaller than she thought it would be, though very tastefully decorated, and larger than her house, of course. He was there alone, wearing khaki pants, very expensive-looking leather shoes that were halfway to being slippers, and a black T-shirt that was clearly meant to accentuate his build — and did an admirable job of it. They talked in the living room, and for a time they focused exclusively on school matters. But that didn't take long, since the ideas they came up with were no-brainers, and when that was done, Beard came immediately to his real purpose. The seduction was completely one-sided, which Sherrie had known it would be, and which was the only reason it worked at all. That, in fact, was the point. Her desire for take-charge men was like other people's need for alcohol: she had overcome it, but she hadn't lost it.

The guilt that set in afterward was like an illness, an emotional flu. She nearly told Oscar about it, but then decided against it — not because she was afraid of his reaction, but because she concluded that it would be selfish to make herself feel better by making him feel worse. She had done this terrible thing; she would suffer the consequences by herself. Step one in her redemption was to make a clear break with Beard. And so the following Monday afternoon, in her tiny office at American University, with her door closed and her heart banging against her chest, she dialed his number.

"Hello?"

"Jerry, this is Sheridan Hobbs."

"Well. Hel*lo*."

"Listen, Jerry, I'm sorry to do this over the phone, but … listen, I can't do — what we did — anymore. It was a mistake to let it go so far. I hope you understand, we're both married — "

"No, uh, it's cool." He sounded surprised. Not upset, though. And it occurred to her, after she had hung up, that he wasn't surprised that she was breaking things off; only that she had bothered to call him about it. Clearly, in his mind, this had been an afternoon version of a one-night stand all along, and she was just now figuring that out. So, she thought, crying bitter tears in her office chair. *I'm not just a slut, I'm a stupid one.*

Sherrie's desire for redemption led her — though she didn't put it that way to herself, exactly — to try to have another child. She and Oscar had been talking about it for a while, but somehow the timing never seemed right, and the years had slipped by. Now, at Sherrie's initiative, they tried with all they had. After her second miscarriage, though, they stopped. If she wasn't careful she could let herself think that the miscarriages were God's judgment on her for sleeping with another man; but the God Sherrie believed in was not that petty. Besides, she had seen people get away with worse.

There was, for example, Dr. George Greer. After Lester collapsed from the seizure, Sherrie had suggested bringing a malpractice suit against him; she knew that her affair with Greer might well be exposed that way, but she didn't care. Her father, however, had surprised her and everyone else with how adamantly he opposed the idea. Exacting payment from Greer, he said, would amount to benefiting from what had happened to Lester, for which the family shared the blame, and it wouldn't do a thing to help him. Greer, for his part, insisted that the kind of seizure Lester had suffered was one of the risks he, Greer, had warned about, though Sherrie didn't remember hearing him say this. Greer not only got away with his reputation and his bank account intact: he later made a fortune, and became very famous, by writing a book called *The Rapping Mute and Other Neurological Tales*. He changed all the names for the book, which did nothing to quell Sherrie's outrage; its flames were fanned anew every time she came across an article by Greer in the

*New Yorker* or saw his stupid face on the Discovery Channel. She wondered how many women he had boinked on the side along the way. (It occurred to her, after the Jackhammer Beard episode, that she had had adulterous, clandestine affairs with two very famous men. She wondered what the record was for that dubious feat, then consoled herself by deciding that she couldn't be anywhere close to holding it.)

On this Thanksgiving morning she got up from the table and started on breakfast. She emptied a box of link sausages into a pan and turned on the flame; as they began a low sizzle, she cut off a quarter-inch of butter from a stick, put it in the center of another pan, turned on the flame, and watched as it began to melt.

"Want some help?" Oscar said from behind the newspaper.

"No thanks."

"So." He put down the paper. "Did you say Karina will be there?"

"Yeah. I think this is the year she has Thanksgiving with us and Christmas with the Bowies. Or maybe the Pottingers, I can't keep it straight."

"The who?"

"Gina's husband's family."

"Oh, right. I can never remember his last name."

"I know you can't."

Sherrie cracked six eggs, two at a time, and dropped the contents into a mixing bowl. She couldn't think of what it would be like to have children with two different people, as Greg did. Of course, she didn't know what it was like to have children — as opposed to child — either. When Quentin was six, seven, all she had thought about was giving him a little brother or sister, and she'd spent a lot of time convincing herself that the two kids would play together, that Quentin wouldn't be too old, at least not for a while. But then her plans came to nothing, and as time passed, and Quentin got older, he seemed to grow into the space that would have been occupied by his sibling. Now she could no more imagine having two children than she could imagine a sky with two suns.

Quentin came up from the TV room now, no doubt lured by the smell of sausages. He actually had his cereal bowl with him and placed it in the sink. What do you know: a decade-plus of saying "Don't forget to take your plate/bowl/glass/cup to the kitchen" was beginning to pay dividends. She nearly said something about it, but he sometimes bristled at being complimented for things like that; he seemed to think he was being patronized. Instead, she said, "Come here."

He looked at her suspiciously, but he came. Scrambling the eggs on the stove with one hand, she put her other arm around his shoulders and kissed his cheek. He grimaced. "Good grief, Mom."

"That's all right. One day I'll be dead, and you'll miss my affection."

"Spoken like a mother," Oscar said from behind the newspaper.

After breakfast she showered, dressed, and drove to her parents' house. *My parents' house*, she thought, pulling up outside it. The house still looked like it always had — same brick steps leading up to the porch with the black metal rail around it, same glider, painted some shade of green with a white trim every few years. But where it had once been her house, now it was her parents', which, of course, it had really been all along. She had simply come to see it that way, that was all. She had last lived there when she was twenty-two, and she was now forty-three, which meant that in another year she would have been gone from it as long as she'd called it home. She was like a plant that had grown as tall as the pot it was in. When she got to a certain height, her center of gravity would shift, and then *plop*, she would fall over, dead, having gone too far from where she started. Weren't senile old people always talking about their childhoods, thinking they were with their parents again? They weren't completely crazy, those old people; they were just trying to get back home, before it was too late, before they got too far from their roots and toppled over. She had come to understand the impulse. Back when she was trying so hard to have another child, and she envisioned life with two children, the picture in her mind was of sitting around the table, talking and laughing with Oscar, Quentin, and little whoever. It wasn't until after she had gotten over the second miscarriage that she realized what she'd been trying to create, or, rather, re-create: her own childhood, when she had sat around the table, talking and laughing with Greg and her mother and father, while Lester sat quietly among them. A time before her defenseless brother had been beaten horribly, before she and Greg had started their cat-and-dog routine, before Lester had fallen into a coma, before she had cheated on the world's most wonderful husband. Maybe adulthood came when you understood, really understood, that you were never going back. Some people probably understood that long before others — people who fled abusive, alcoholic parents who had never cared about them anyway. Maybe they were the lucky ones, in a way. They didn't waste time trying to get back what was gone forever.

Or maybe the lucky ones were those who figured out the value of what they already had, before that was gone, too. A loving husband; a wonderful son; a job she enjoyed. She knew she shouldn't take those for granted. She pulled out the key to her parents' house as she went up the steps, and she laughed, a bit derisively, at her next thought: It is, after all, Thanksgiving.

\*     \*     \*     \*

Karina showed up at Greg's apartment on Capitol Hill after dinner on Wednesday, the day before Thanksgiving, carrying a canvas overnight bag and looking startlingly like her mother. "Hey, Dad." She kissed his cheek.

"Hey." She had a puffy parka on her short, somewhat plump body, which made her look plumper still. No hat, though. "How come you're not wearin' a hat? It's cold out there. Most of your body's heat —"

"Escapes through your head," Karina said, rolling her eyes. "That fact won't escape from *my* head, as long as you're around."

"Well, what about it, then?"

"It's not that cold. You just feel it more 'cause you're old." She looked like Gina, but she had inherited Greg's smart mouth. Hers might even be worse, which was saying something. She passed by her twelve-year-old half-brother, who was on the sofa playing with his Game Boy.

"Hey, Jus."

"Hey." He didn't look up.

Greg followed her into the kitchen, where she hugged Theresa, who was washing the dishes. "Hey, honey," Theresa said. "Did you eat yet?"

"Yep. Ellsworth was testing out the new deep-fryer he bought." Greg had no trouble picturing that. He had promised himself he would refrain from making jokes about Karina's stepfather in her presence; two years on, and he still found it difficult. His name said it all, as Greg had told Theresa more than once. Any other forty-five-year-old man named "Ellsworth" would have long ago adopted a nickname, Buddy or Mac or Doc, which he would be called so universally that it would take the place of his real name everywhere but his driver's license and checkbook. But Gina's husband wasn't even called "Elzie." Nope, it was Ellsworth, and actually, it fit. He could almost hear the most dignified Ellsworth Pottinger, Jr. describing the features of his new deep-fryer as if he were delivering a lecture on the writing of the U.S. Constitution, explaining what it could do that an ordinary oven or broiler couldn't, how you could taste the difference in the meat, etc., etc., etc., until your jaws ached and your eyes watered from the yawns you were holding back. It took a complex woman to run around for several years with Greg and later end up with that certified public stick-in-the-mud. But then, Greg thought, if he had been deeply involved with a person like the one he'd been in his early twenties, he might just seek a radical change, too.

Greg wiped off the dishes Theresa had washed and handed them to Karina, who put them in the cabinets. Theresa said to Greg, "So you went to the video store, right? What did you get?"

"I got a couple, just in case we were feeling energetic. *The Great Escape* and *The Magnificent Seven*."

"What's this," Karina said, "Old Folks' Night at the Movies?"

"Ha ha haaaa," Greg said, making his face a caricature of a jolly smile while putting a headlock on his daughter, who yelled, "Aaaaaagggghhhhh!"

The four of them watched *The Magnificent Seven*. The funny thing was that Theresa, Justin, and even Karina, for all her griping, got involved in the movie, while Greg found himself distracted. Maybe he had finally seen it once too often; even during his favorite scenes and lines ("It seemed like a good idea at the time"; "I was aiming for the horse!"), his mind wandered. He thought about his twenties. In his mind, the decades of his life — his twenties, thirties, now his forties — were like objects in a funhouse mirror, stretched out or shortened to unusual lengths. His twenties, for example, had lasted three years. They began on the day Lester collapsed, even though Greg was already twenty-one then.

That was twenty years ago now, and he remembered it as if it were last week. When Lester fell, he was in front of another wing of Johns Hopkins University Hospital. Greg and Sherrie shouted for help, and orderlies were with them in seconds, getting Lester to the emergency ward and paging Dr. Greer. The seizure, Greer and the others determined, had brought on respiratory arrest, and Lester would have had to be moved even if the seizure had occurred while he was with Greer; then, after Lester reached the emergency ward, he couldn't be made to breathe right away; and the respiratory arrest brought on the brain damage that resulted in his coma. In the end it was pronounced "almost certain" that what happened would have happened anyway, even if Greg hadn't sneaked off with Lester to that diner. It was the "almost" that messed Greg up. Maybe there was one chance in a hundred that Greg had contributed to his brother's death — and that one chance buzzed around in his brain like a loud, belligerent fly.

He was furious with himself. His family was furious with him. He was furious with his family. (His father never found out how close he came one day to being knocked off his feet.) The one thing they all agreed on was that Greg could not live with his parents anymore. Pat spoke with an old law-school acquaintance of his, a fellow who was now a partner at a downtown firm, and that was how Greg got a job with the firm as a messenger. He wasn't paid much, but he made enough to move into a room on the top floor of a house near RFK Stadium, owned by an extremely upright, half-deaf old black lady. The fall of 1979 rolled around, and he didn't go back to school. He spent his days delivering envelopes, running between floors at the huge, overwhelmingly white firm or walking the streets of northwest D.C., in hot weather and cold.

One fortunate thing during this time (or the least fortunate — who could say for sure?) was that Gina got back in touch with him.

They hadn't had much contact since her dinner with Greg and his parents, but she decided she should be more forgiving, and they restarted their romance — one that was marred by Greg's bad moods, during which he either yelled at her or teased her until tears came to her eyes, then begged forgiveness. He told her about Lester's collapse and coma, but for a year or so he couldn't bring himself to tell her about everything that had happened on that Saturday in Baltimore, about how he probably hadn't killed his brother but wasn't absolutely sure. When he finally told her, she was upset that he hadn't done so earlier, and they had their second, but not last, breakup.

Meanwhile, it was day in, day out in the messenger room at the law firm. The room was L-shaped. At the top of the L was the door where the mail was brought in; just inside the door, the mail was sorted into wire bins. At the other end of the L was another door, and just inside it was the desk of the white, portly, middle-aged, mustached Mr. Nye, who was in charge of the room. In the corner of the L was the round wooden table where the messengers sat, waiting on assignments. There were about ten messengers working there at any one time, wearing light-colored shirts with collars and neckties. All were black; most were about Greg's age. At any given moment of the day, three or four of the messengers were off delivering envelopes or packages; one or two were reading at the table; the rest (including Greg) talked, about last night's basketball game, or the latest action movie, or the argument a messenger had had with his girlfriend, or a sensational news story. Sometimes they raised their voices or laughed loudly. At that point Mr. Nye would look up from whatever he was doing, filling out a report or staring into space, and say, adopting the calm, mildly put-out tone of a very reasonable man confronting an unreasonable situation: "Fellows, please. What would the managing partner think if he passed by and heard all this ruckus?" Then things would get quiet for a while, the messengers avoiding each other's eyes.

Shortly after Greg started working at the firm, Clive returned to Howard for his senior year, and between his schoolwork and new girlfriend, and Greg's having left the neighborhood, the two got together less and less often. The following fall, Clive enrolled in a graduate program in American literature at a school in Pennsylvania, and Greg barely heard from his old friend after that. Meanwhile, he had begun spending time with a couple of the other messengers. Each year when late August rolled around, a few of the messengers returned to college, replaced by new full-time guys. Two of the messengers who stayed put, in addition to Greg, were Carlton and Melvin. They became his running buddies. Neither of them was a Rhodes Scholar, but they were company; and anyway, Greg reasoned, if he himself was so smart, what was he doing here with them? Melvin was a shortish guy who seemed bigger than he was, mainly because of his very large, oval-shaped head, with its sleepy eyes and fleshy lips. Melvin's passions were playing video games and collecting stereo and other electronic equipment. He would laugh at just about any joke, and though he talked about all the women he met, he never seemed to get past telephone conversations with any of them. Where Melvin was affable, if a little pathetic, Carlton had a cynical air and a hint of menace. Tall and slender, dark-skinned and slant-eyed, Carlton laughed not from his belly but from somewhere in his throat, making a smoky, gurgling sound that was not so much an expression of mirth as an acknowledgment of how fucked-up the world was. Once, when the messengers were discussing a newspaper article about a man who killed his two-timing wife — a story no one else found particularly funny — Carlton laughed that laugh of his, which seemed to say, *Shame what these bitches out here'll drive you to.* He once brought in a book he had made of "Chester the Molester" cartoons from *Hustler* magazine, one-panel drawings that mostly showed Chester snatching an underage girl after having bashed some guy's head in with a baseball bat. Greg flipped through the cartoons, chuckling politely, while Carlton looked over his shoulder, laughing from his throat. Greg handed the book back to Carlton without a word, then blocked it from his mind.

Carlton always seemed to know where to score some reefer and where a party was happening. He also had a car. Sometimes on Friday and Saturday nights Greg and Melvin rode with Carlton to some unknown person's house, where music could be heard a block away, where a lot of people danced, some gambled in a corner, others fucked in upstairs bedrooms or closets, and nearly everyone looked drunk or high or both. Sometimes Greg left these parties with a girl, went a short distance to where she lived, and fucked her; sometimes they did it right there at the party. (What Gina couldn't see, he told himself, wouldn't hurt her.) Lying back on other people's coats on a strange bed, with a big-breasted woman astride him rocking back and forth, Greg could summon the illusion that he was enjoying his life; he could even, for a time, silence the fly buzzing in his brain.

Then there were the times he talked to Walter, the oldest of the messengers and the one who had been there the longest. Greg had figured out from something Walter had said once that he was in his late thirties. In the messenger room Walter usually had a book with him; sometimes, when the other guys had exhausted the subjects of sports, action movies, or local killings, one of them might ask Walter what he was reading about. Walter would happily put down his book and talk about that and other books he'd read on the same subject, sounding as authoritative as any professor Greg had had at Howard. The book could be about space exploration, or the Underground Railroad, or the political witch hunts of the 1950s.

One February day, when Greg had worked as a messenger for about a year and a half, Walter sat at the table reading a book called *Black No More* and chuckling occasionally. On the other side of Greg, Melvin and Carlton were talking.

Melvin: "Boy, you shoulda saw this gal I was talking to at that party. She was pretty as shit. Friendly, too. I got her telephone number. I'ma call her tonight. My cousin said when you get a girl's number, don't call 'er right away, give 'er a chance to start wonderin'. That's what I'ma do."

Carlton: "Shiiiit. Only thing she was wonderin' was how to get away from your ass. I saw you talking to her. Saw a lot of other dudes talking to her, too. Go home and call her, see if she ain't give you the number of Popeye's Fried Chicken."

Greg, who had heard numerous variations on this exchange over the past months, turned to Walter and said, "What's that book about?"

Greg had once heard Walter say he'd been in the army, and he had an upright posture and trim but muscular build that might have been a holdover from that time in his life. For a moment after Greg spoke to him, Walter's eyes stayed on the page he was reading; he smiled subtly, scratching his forest of black and gray beard with long fingers, their nails stained brownish yellow with nicotine. Then he answered in his low voice, "It's about a man who comes up with a way to change black people into white people on demand."

"Guess he becomes a billionaire," Greg said.

"Yeah," Walter said, laughing, "but it has some other consequences, too."

"That book just came out?"

"No, it was published in 1931."

"Oh. I thought it was by a black dude."

"It is."

"Writing back *then?*"

For the first time during this conversation, Walter looked at Greg, and his eyebrows rose. "You never heard of the Harlem Renaissance?"

"Yeah, I did, but I thought it was — later. I don't know. Nineteen-fifties." He was dimly aware of Mr. Nye's telephone ringing.

"No, man. Started in the *Twenties.* You never heard of the writers from that time? Arna Bontemps, Claude McKay, Rudolph Fisher, Countee Cullen, Sterling Brown?"

A couple of the names sounded vaguely familiar to Greg, who said, "I guess—"

But Walter had gathered some momentum now. "That was a rich time for black writers, man. Lot of stuff came out back then. Some books were better than others, just like with any literary or artistic movement, you know? But those dudes accomplished a lot. Actually, this book here kind of spoofs a few black figures from the time. There's one that's based on W.E.B. Du Bois. In here he's called Shakespeare Agamemnon Beard. Heh, heh. But no, man, there were a *lot* of black writers active then. Take Rudolph Fisher. He trained as a doctor. Wrote novels on the side. Wrote this one, *The Walls —*"

"Gotta interrupt you, professor," Mr. Nye said from his desk, talking to Walter. "You're up. There's some documents at a firm on 19th and L. Here's the floor and phone number." He held out a slip of paper. "And hurry up, now. Mr. McGrady up on 14 needs those documents pronto."

Walter was silent. His eyes became like windows on which

someone had lowered the blinds halfway. As he stood, put on his pea coat, and went to take the slip of paper from Mr. Nye, Greg wondered what was going through his mind. But he almost didn't want to know.

One evening several months later, in early summer, Greg met Gina for dinner near where he worked. Afterward they rode the bus to his place, on the corner of a quiet, tree-shaded block of narrow, tall houses. Greg unlocked the high wooden door with its gleaming finish and led them into the foyer, from which they could see into the living room on the left. On the floor in there was a Persian-style rug. Two china cabinets, and the tops of several very small wooden tables, held numerous knickknacks made of porcelain and other fragile materials. The sofa and matching chairs, which seemed to have been built in a time when people were smaller, had dark wooden frames and legs and faded pink cushions with buttons. You had the feeling that pounding the cushions would raise a considerable cloud of dust, that no one had used this room for a hundred years — except that sitting in one of the chairs, wearing a long dress, her gray hair in a bun, was Greg's landlady. When he and Gina walked in, the landlady peered at them over her glasses, gave a curt nod, and went back to reading. Greg knew that she didn't approve when he went to his room with young ladies he wasn't married to, but as long as he didn't keep her awake at night, she didn't say anything. That wasn't a problem, since she couldn't half hear. ("Every time she looks at me, I feel like I just broke all ten commandments," Gina once said. "Just ignore her," Greg told her.)

They went up the staircase, with its polished banister, passed the second floor, where the landlady slept, and came to the third floor. There, a bathroom was at one end of the hall and Greg's room at the other. On one side of his room, a small refrigerator and a hotplate were near the window. His mattress was on the floor on the other side. That evening, as orange light from the setting sun poured in the window, Greg and Gina made love on the mattress.

Afterward they lay still, looking at the ceiling. Gina broke a couple of minutes' silence to say, "So … when do you think you'll go back to school?"

Greg didn't answer for several seconds. Then: "Did I say I was going back?"

"Well, you said a couple of things that made it sound that way."

"I did, huh." They were quiet again, until Greg said, "Be right back." He pulled on his undershirt and pants and went down the hall to the bathroom. When he was halfway there he heard his phone rang. He continued down the hall. When he went back to his room, Gina was putting her clothes on, as if she were late for an appointment.

"Hey, what's up? Where you going?"

She didn't answer. She just looked at him, angrier than he'd ever seen her.

"Did you answer my phone? Who was it?"

"I should be asking you that!"

Thus began Greg and Gina's last, and worst, fight. It wasn't bad enough, she told him, that she had to put up with how hurtful he was during his bad moods, which were just about every other day; it wasn't bad enough that she was trying to make something out of herself while he was twenty-three years old and didn't seem to have any kind of plan to do anything; now she had to put up with being two-timed. Well, she wasn't going to. Her problem, Greg told her, was that she just didn't know how to accept a nigger for what he was, instead of trying to make him into one of those hoity-toity folks like the ones in her grad program. If one of those folks saw her wasting her time with him, Gina said, they'd think she was a fool, and they'd be right. With that, she left.

Greg didn't see her the rest of the long summer of 1981. During those humid D.C. days in June, July, August, he went to work and came home; in the evenings he watched TV, or he and Melvin went to a video arcade and then caught a movie; some weekends the two of them went to a party with Carlton, and a few times he got some pussy. Once in a while he dropped by his parents' house and stayed for an uncomfortable half-hour or forty-five minutes, everyone steering the conversation away from anything of importance. He hardly ever saw Sherrie. He thought about her, though. He thought about Lester, too, as much as he tried not to. And he thought about Gina. He hadn't really thought he'd miss her much; so much of their conversation toward the end had been tiresome talk about the direction of his life. But he did miss her.

And then, one day in early September, she called. They exchanged pleasantries; Gina's voice had an oddly formal sound to it. Then she got to why she had called. After thinking about it, she said, she realized they couldn't be together anymore. The summer apart hadn't changed her views on that. But she did have something to tell him. She was three months pregnant, and the child was his. And she was going to keep it.

"She *say* it's yours. Don't mean it's true," Carlton said in his car one Friday night on the way to a house party.

Melvin said, "I heard about this white lady that had sex with a black dude and then the same night she had sex with a white dude. Then she had twins, and one was black, and one was white."

"How the fuck *that* happen?" Carlton said.

"'Cause she got pregnant by both of 'em!"

Why, Greg thought, do I tell these motherfuckers anything?

He called Gina on the telephone periodically to check on her, but he didn't see her again until she was nearly eight months along. She was as big as a house — a short house. That was when they began going to childbirth classes together at D.C. General Hospital, which was a two-block walk from him and a few minutes by car from Gina, who had moved back in with her father and sisters. Greg met her at the hospital every Tuesday for the class, and he dreaded those evenings as if he were facing execution once a week. He didn't mind the class itself as much as everything that surrounded it. First, there was waiting in the lobby to meet Gina and whoever had driven her that week, one of her younger sisters or her father; her father was the worst, but they all avoided eye contact with Greg as if it might give them whatever disease had turned him into the subhuman creature he clearly was. Then there was waiting for the teacher in the classroom with the other pregnant women and their companions. There was one young woman attending the class with her mother, but the others were actual couples, you could tell. Two of the couples had a definite upper-middle-class air (Why, Greg wondered, are they doing this *here?*); most were plain old black D.C. stock; but all were preparing to raise a child as a team. Even the two seventeen-year-olds, who would no doubt break up when they confronted the stress of having a real live child, were together for the time being. Then there was Greg and Gina. "This your first child?" one of the other women asked them. "Yeah," Greg said, adding in his mind, *Now shut up.*

Early, early one freezing morning in March of 1982, he was awakened when his telephone rang. It was Gina's father; she was in labor; they would meet him at the hospital. Greg would remember that day as one in which time went a little crazy, standing still for long stretches and then jerking forward, like a teenager learning to use a stick shift. There were the endless walks up and down the hall with Gina, as they waited for the baby to drop into position; the fruitless bouts of pushing, followed by more walking; the tension made worse by boredom, tension that made Greg forget food for hours at a time, until he suddenly realized his stomach hurt from hunger; more walking; more fruitless pushing; and then, all at once, the real thing, happening so fast that all he would retain were images in no special order: the nurse holding one of Gina's legs, Greg holding the other, while Gina screamed as if being stabbed to death; the first sight of the head coming out, the hair looking as if it had been shampooed; the moment when the baby slipped out, slick and a deep shade of purple. When Greg left the hospital and walked the two blocks home to get some sleep, it was as dark and cold out as when he got up that morning; nothing seemed to have changed, which was partly why he thought, *Did that just happen?*

But *something* had. He lay on his bed, too tired to sleep, and looked around his little room as if with different eyes. The small cube of a refrigerator, the hot plate, the mattress on the floor, the copies of *Playboy* and *Penthouse* next to it … what kind of father lived like this?

That, in his mind, was where his twenties ended. At twenty-four he entered his thirties, a long decade of getting himself together. He took out loans and re-enrolled at Howard. He spent his days being a messenger, his nights attending classes and then studying, his weekends helping with Karina. (The first part of her name came from Karen, Gina's dead mother; the second part rhymed with "Gina.") Greg and Gina were tender with each other during that period, and later, once in a while, Greg would wonder if they might have ended up together — if Gina had been in any shape for romance at the time, if Greg had had a free minute in his life. But his life had become a classical composition, planned in advance down to the last note and rest, leaving minimal room for stray moves or thoughts. He realized he preferred it that way, then asked himself why.

That was when he began going to her. It was pure chance that he found her — or chance and finance: the clinic where she worked while she completed her Ph.D. in psychology was about all he could afford. Her name was Theresa Wilkerson, and he saw her on Wednesdays between work and class, gobbling a slice of pizza on his way to the small office that she and several others took turns using. Then, later, he began getting the pizza *after* he saw her, so his breath would be better during the sessions, and, idiot that he was, he didn't even fully realize why he made the change. This willowy Theresa, who was nearly as tall as he was and couldn't have been any older, seemed only half a step ahead of him as they walked together through the thicket of his life — but it was a crucial half-step. "So you still resent your mother for showering all that attention on Lester, and yelling at you when you did something to show your displeasure. But you also resent your father for not intervening," she said, as if they had stumbled on treasure together, and she just happened to be the one to acknowledge it. "As different as you and Sherrie are, you identify with her, because the two of you were in the same position," she said another time, just as he was about to say the same thing — or was he? "And if you've always felt anger toward her, maybe it's because you feel it toward yourself. Why did you feel that? If people weren't paying attention to you, you thought it was because you didn't deserve it. Isn't that maybe what you felt?" Another time: "Maybe you have to give yourself the attention you always wanted. Find out about yourself. Who are you? What do you like?" Still another time: "You have to forgive your family. But that means you have to forgive yourself. Suppose you *did* contribute in some small way to Lester's coma. Face that. Look straight at it. And forgive yourself for it. You didn't mean to do it." At the end of their last session, when Greg told Theresa that he loved her, she said, "What you're feeling is probably gratitude — although you did most of the work yourself. See how you feel in six months." He took that to be the standard psychologist's brush-off, but he still called her six months later. Theresa's advice *had* been a brush-off, he discovered — one that had taken all of her strength to say.

Ninety-eighty-four was a big year for Greg: he finished his degree, began teaching, and got engaged to Theresa. One Sunday that autumn, after he had taken the two-year-old Karina for the weekend, he drove her back to the apartment where Gina was living then. Karina kissed him goodbye and went back to her bedroom to play. "So," Gina said as Greg stood near the doorway, about to leave. "You're doing all right for yourself."

Gina, like him, was teaching high school now. With Karina to support, her career in international relations was on hold, if not over; Greg told himself that that was her decision, just as having Karina had been her decision, though he had a hard time convincing himself. "Yeah, things are going all right," he said.

"You finally get yourself together," Gina said, smiling ruefully, "and you're gonna marry somebody else." He didn't have a thing to say in response. He just looked in her eyes. Then, suddenly, they were kissing. It didn't last long, but it lasted long enough; then Greg pulled away, mumbled something, and left, feeling that if he didn't, his life would become complicated in a way he wasn't built to handle.

Because life was certainly complicated enough, he thought, on that Wednesday in 1999, the night before Thanksgiving. He and his wife and daughter and son had finished watching *The Magnificent Seven* and were half an hour into *The Great Escape*; Greg was, anyway. He looked around and saw that everyone but him was asleep. Ha — calling *me* old, he thought about Karina, happy that he would have something to tease her about the next day.

\*      \*      \*      \*

Sitting in the leather chair in the room where his children once slept, wearing a checked flannel shirt, thick green corduroys on his thin, sixty-eight-year-old legs, Pat listens to his recording of "What Is This Thing Called Love?" on his turntable. It is the fifteen-minute 1952 version with Charlie Parker, Johnny Hodges and Benny Carter on alto saxophone, Ben Webster and Flip Phillips on tenor, and Charlie Shavers on trumpet. The rhythm section has a rapid tempo going, a sound like time itself ticking away; the horn solos are fast, too, as if the horn players are working against the clock, trying to get somewhere, trying to figure something out, before it's too late. They are beautiful. Transcendent. Each man gives his all, then turns it over to the next, as if to say, *Here, see what you can do with this.* They are in it together, working on a problem bigger than any one of them, but each works alone. Pat pictures each man moving quickly across the landscape, becoming visible over the horizon, but with the Earth rotating against him, threatening to carry him backward, out of sight. Near the end the men trade fours, now Webster, now Hodges, now Phillips, now Shavers, now Parker, now Carter; and at the end, do they make it? Do they figure it out? Who knows? The point was the journey, the attempt. Pat is lifted by their efforts, their artistry. Maybe a person who can appreciate this is not all bad, he thinks. Or maybe, he thinks, I am just losing my mind.

Downstairs, Maddie says to the room at large, "Why don't we put the leaf in the table and get the chairs together. Maybe if we have somewhere for him to sit, he'll come down. There's some folding chairs in the basement."

Sherrie and Greg head down there together, Greg in front. This room, where he used to sleep, looks very different now. Where his bed used to be is the old sofa, the one with the stain where his mother spilled the tea that time. On the walls, where his music posters once hung, are his mother's paintings, mostly landscapes — including the one that everybody likes but that she won't exhibit for some reason, the one of the house across the street with that pretty blue for the sky. The rest of the room looks like — is, in fact — the Hobbs family junkyard, an accumulation of things that are not used on a daily, or even yearly, basis, but that have avoided the trash for a variety of reasons, from sentimental attachment to laziness. There are boxes of old clothes, stacks of Greg's and Sherrie's school notebooks and term papers, thirty-five-year-old board games, and much more. Greg and Sherrie pass through here to the laundry room, where the folding chairs are kept.

Sherrie says, "How many of us are there?"

"Let's see ... nine, I guess. Yeah."

"There's five up there already. So these will do it." She takes two of the white metal folding chairs leaning against the cinderblock wall, next to the washing machine.

Greg takes the other two and says, "The leaf's down here too, right?"

"Yeah. It's next to the dryer, under that plastic. I guess we'll need a second trip."

"Or we can send one of our lazy kids down here."

Sherrie in front, they walk single-file, a chair under each arm, out of the laundry room and back through the Hobbs junkyard. Sherrie pauses at the bottom of the narrow staircase, looking up doubtfully. "I don't know if I can squeeze up there with two chairs."

"Put the chairs together and carry 'em that way, then."

"They're heavy together."

"Yeah, but you'll be using two arms to carry 'em."

"How will I *hold* them?"

"Jesus, Mary and Joseph. Like *this*." With a soft clang, Greg puts the chairs he is holding back-to-back, then holds them together on either side. "See?"

"Yeah, but when I get to the top I'll have to turn them sideways to get through the door. It's awkward. I might fall."

"I'll be behind you. You can land on top of me. I'll fracture my skull, but you'll be fine. How's that?"

"I'm going to take one at a time."

"Do what you want. I'm taking two."

"Show-off."

"Show —? Boy. You're lucky it's Thanksgiving."

"I love you too."

Two floors above, Pat thinks, not for the first time, or even the tenth, about something he once said to his children. It was during a drive down to Virginia to visit Maddie's mother, the last time they saw her alive. Sherrie and Greg were protesting from the back seat, saying they didn't want to go and that their grandmother never knew who they were, anyway. It's not important, he told them, that she doesn't know who you are; you know who she is. She's your grandmother. It doesn't matter what she can do. You have to accept her for what she is.

But I didn't apply that thinking where Lester was concerned, he thinks. Didn't appreciate that he was never in a bad mood, that he showed us love, in his limited way. Didn't even appreciate when he started rapping, which was a miracle in itself. No, I wanted more, convinced Maddie that we should seek more. A conversing Lester. A normal Lester. For whose sake? Pat knew there was a risk. For whom did he take it? It is not a rhetorical question; it may have been for Lester's sake that Pat wanted his son to speak like everyone else. Or it may have been to satisfy something in himself. Is any motive pure? Maybe not. Does this mean his was acceptable? Not necessarily. For Pat, these are not new thoughts; they are beginning to seem as old as he is.

In the living room, Greg says to Karina, Justin, and Quentin, "Hey, you lazy bums. Help your crazy Aunt Sherrie carry some stuff up from the basement."

From the dining room, Sherrie says, "I heard that."

"Good."

"If I'm lazy, it's genetic," Karina says.

"Come on, Your Laziness," Quentin tells Karina, standing up.

"Oh, all right."

The two of them head to the basement. Justin follows, with neither cheer nor complaint, but quietly. Maddie, watching him from the dining room, thinks — not for the first time — about what an enigma her youngest grandchild is.

Upstairs, Pat thinks, And what was I trying to satisfy in myself? As usual, this question puts him in front of two doors, neither leading anywhere good. What was he trying to satisfy by trying to make Lester "normal"? There was the old feeling of gratitude for having been spared during the war, along with its nagging companion, the feeling that he had been spared *for* something. Part of him thought back in 1979 that he had found the something: helping Lester to talk. But clearly that wasn't it. Maybe the something was to father Lester and appreciate him for what he was. If so, he failed. He told himself he was fulfilling Lester, when he was really trying to fulfill his conceited idea about his own purpose. And he made Lester pay the price for his mistake. He thinks, Were those my crimes? Monstrous conceit? A wrong idea about why I was still on Earth? And a willingness to sacrifice my son on the altar of that idea? (He thinks in his own defense: But didn't I *think* I was doing it for Lester?)

And then there is the other door, leading to the thought that he was spared in the war for the sake of ... nothing. Maybe it meant nothing. Maybe he didn't fail to identify his purpose. Maybe there was no purpose. Maybe it wouldn't have mattered if he had died. Maybe it doesn't matter that he is alive. Maybe it doesn't matter what he did to Lester. Maybe it doesn't matter that he acted as if Lester, the way he was, didn't matter. Did Lester matter? Do I matter? Maybe the answer is No. This is one way to avoid feeling that he is to blame. But what a way. The way into *nada*, like in the Hemingway story he read in college. *Nada y nada*. Like Moby-Dick, the great, terrifying expanse of white — the idea of nothingness — that must be fought and killed or, failing that, escaped.

Downstairs, the leaf has been put in the table. The chairs have been brought from the basement. Maddie says to the room at large, "In a minute I'm going to bring him down, whether he wants to come or not."

"He'll be down," Greg says.

Upstairs, once again, Pat backs away from this idea, for the reason — irrational though he knows it is — that this idea is too much. This leaves him back with his guilt. At least the guilt is something.

Back in 1979 Dr. Greer said that Lester had the words of bygone conversations still echoing in his head, words that he meant to speak — a cacophony of words. It was no wonder, Greer said back then, that when Lester looked at you, he seemed to be thinking of something else. He had a complex inner life, Lester did. A symphony of things he was thinking about, all at the same time. Haven't I done that my whole life, Pat thinks, only in a less complicated way? How many times have I looked someone in the eye and seemed to listen to his words while really trying to identify the saxophonist on the record playing in the next room? How many times, at the office, did I fantasize about getting on one of those planes taking off from

National Airport, while I was supposed to be thinking about the paperwork on my desk? Lester did the same thing, only more of it. And I took it away. Oh, Lester, I'm sorry. And I loved you. Please believe that. Pat sniffs, wiping the tears from his eyes. I don't know which of the other things I believe myself. But please know that, son.

A few nights after Lester was buried, Pat dreamed about him. In the dream Lester was forty years old, his hair a little gray at the temples. He was talking — not shouting rhymes, but speaking normally, in pleasant, conversational tones. And he smiled a lot. A smile of reassurance. He and Pat were walking. They started near the house where they lived, but as they walked, the surroundings became less and less familiar, and the sky got darker. But still they walked, and Lester talked, still smiling, because he seemed to know the way. And the darker it became, the more reassuring was Lester's voice. Even when there was nothing around them but darkness and stars, and Pat could just barely see his son, Lester kept smiling, talking in a soothing voice. Pat started to say that they should turn back, head home, but then it became clear that Lester had brought him to this place, had led him along like Virgil leading Dante, for a reason. And as they looked up at the stars together, Lester explained everything. It all came together — the explanation of this, the significance of that, the connectedness of both and of everything else, the reason why no one, ever, needed to be afraid. In his new knowledge, Pat felt wonderful, better than he had in years, better, maybe, than he had ever felt. He wept tears of gratitude, and he went to embrace Lester. But in the darkness he couldn't find him; his arms closed around dark, empty air.

And then he woke up, crying, unable to recall a single word Lester had said.

Pat remembers the dream now. Maybe the important part of it, he thinks, is not what Lester said. Maybe it is the feeling he got from Lester, the feeling that it was all okay, that Pat was forgiven. Isn't that what he wants, in place of having done right? The ability to forgive himself, the feeling that God will forgive him? Maybe the reasons are not important. Forgiveness is not about reasons. It is about the need for a bad time to end. It need not be overthought. It need only be set in place, like one sets a lid on a garbage can, putting an end to the stench, giving the air a chance to clear.

He thinks: It is time to go downstairs. He stands with a groan and makes his way with his old man's gait to the record player to turn off the power. And now he starts down the steps. At the bottom, in the living room, in the dining room, he sees his family looking at him, and they are smiling. They are happy that he has come. His wife, his children, his son- and daughter-in-law, his grandchildren, all seem to forgive him. Maybe God will. And maybe, he thinks, Lester would forgive him, too — if he were here, and if he could speak.

THE END